Wrong Daughter

Night of the Blood Moon

Amanishakhete

Wrong Daughter: Night of the Blood Moon

This book is a fiction. The characters, incidents, and dialogue are drawn from the author's imagination and are not to be construed as real. Although businesses, locations, and organizations may be real, they are used in a purely fictional way. Resemblance to actual events or persons, living or dead, is entirely coincidental unless it is true.

CREDITS
Copy reviewer: Pumla Manana
Cover Design: Beetiful Book Covers
Semperian Graphic: John Edgar Designer
Interior Book Design: Jera Publishing
Photo (pg. vi): Creative Commons
Printing and Distribution: IngramSpark
First Edition: December 21, 2023
Second Edition: December 21, 2024

BOOKS BY AMANISHAKHETE

Wrong Daughter Night of the Blood Moon
LaTonya 1 Mama's Daughter
LaTonya 2 Fathers Maybe

CDs BY BOSS AMANISHAKHETE

(LadyBoss)

Exposed Murder 2012 Becoming Boss Still Sexy Right Here
Right Here (extended) Cruizin
Mandingo Love Epiphany
Ignorance Will Not Be Televised

Author's Notes

Fact vs. Fiction

Wrong Daughter, Night of the Blood Moon readers will find an imaginative reconstruction of historical events. Remnants of true African and European history in the early 1600s are woven into this story, but the characters are fictional, including references to Emperors and Kings.

Aside from this novel, there is an enormous amount of factual information on Africa, its history, royalty, and hierarchical structures. Readers can do their own research if they are interested in African history, not rewritten by white supremacists and fascist governments. Africa has a sacred history. Tampering with it is blasphemy, and those doing it will reap karmic justice from our African ancestors and the Creator of all things.

Other factual accounts include slavery and its impact on Africa, like the Dutch, who were influential in the Transatlantic Slave Trade but have since apologized to Africans and their descendants.

References to a Hiding Tree and Hanging Tree are actual trees and are named as such in the city of Blakeley, Alabama, a ghost town. Residents died of a yellow fever outbreak in the 1800s. Throughout Alabama, there were countless lynchings of Africans, including in Baldwin County, where the town of Blakeley is. The city is also where the Confederates lost the war against the freedom fighters. Blakeley is listed on the national registry of ghost towns in America and is a historic state park.

Some graves are still there, and the park hosts re-enactments of the 1865 Civil War.

Wrong Daughter alludes to the greatness of Africa and its favor in the universe. Thus, the reference to Semperian created As a person of African descent, I am proud. We hold the key to the greatest spiritual truth revealed to humans, and it is more than what our ancestors were taught in slavery and Western religions.

Life is eternal and continuous and doesn't end in heaven or hell. Those temporary realms are merely passageways.

Moving forward, I encourage anyone open to spiritualism over religion to break free from invisible chains that limit your ability to think beyond the stars. Break free from a beginner's existence. Earth is not the only planet, and humans are not the only living beings in this billions-of-years-old universe with millions of galaxies and planets.

The Creator I'm in touch with is genderless and concerns itself with more than this young planet of ignorance.
Enjoy your journey with us, heeding the words of Semperian.

Standing in my truth,
Boss Amanishakhete

Personal Note:

To all the beta readers and reader reviews. Thank you for helping me to see through your eyes.

A special thank you to Pumla Manana in South Africa for her thoughtful feedback.

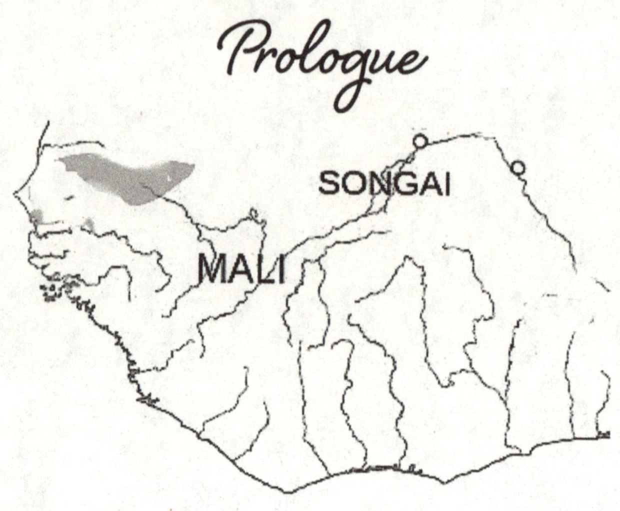

Blood Moon of 1630

In the mountains of West Africa, we were training one hundred recruits ages thirteen to sixteen for military service, finishing up twelve months of intense physical exercises and battle drills. Once completed, they would join forty thousand warriors serving the Songhai-Mali Dynasty, the most powerful partnership in West Africa.

Coming from the leaders' tent, I shared with my good friend, whom I called brother, hiding my feelings, I could not. Senegal, in full body armor, noticed the big grin on my face as he jogged up to me.

"Ah huh, my brother, what is the good news?"

"Ahhh," I lowered my eyes, looking like a schoolboy with my first crush.

"Come on," Senegal pushed. "What did the messenger bring you?"

"Okay, okay, a note from Father. In the coming weeks, I will marry Kalinga Njinga from Mali. She turned sixteen, and her father gave us his blessing."

"The brother of the late emperor gave his blessing." Senegal clapped. "Miss Kalinga is good to look at, and fresh as the day is young."

"Stop," I scolded, friendly.

"As you wish, my prince." Senegal bowed.

My friend knew that I disliked formality, especially from him, because of our close friendship. But Senegal often adhered to tradition. I was the prince of a powerful family and the future heir to the Songhai-Mali throne.

I returned the formality playfully, "What say you, General Nirobi? How are the boys shaping up?"

The general responded, "My prince, they will be ready in a week. Don't worry. We will be home before your big day."

"Good. We've been here for nearly four seasons. I am longing for my bed."

"Soon to be accompanied by the future Mrs. Ndanga-Njinga," Senegal grinned.

"My beautiful wife-to-be who will bring me much warmth and beautiful children," I winked.

Prince Shaman Ndanga III
Second son of King Hyson Shaman Ndanga

Located on seven hills in western Portugal, the sun shone often in Lisbon, a city along the coastline at the river's mouth, where the Portuguese Conquistador received confirmation from an ally planning to betray the Songhai-Mali Empire.

The Conquistador relayed the information to the security chief, "Commander, prepare our troops for war. Show no mercy and leave no stone unturned. Those who have claimed allegiance must turn from African paganism and accept our way of life through the Catholic church if they are to remain under our protection," he warned.

After hearing from the Conquistador, I spoke privately with my mother about the plan. A plan I set in motion after my father's betrayal.

I am Prince Ndanga III, the second son of the late King Hyson Shaman Ndanga of Songhai. My father betrayed me by choosing my half-sister, his firstborn daughter, Shandake Aminata, as his successor and not me. I hated him for it, and I would have my revenge.

Shortly after my father's death, Lord Chancellor, the King's Hand, called a meeting of its members and the royal family and read aloud the late King's orders. The Chancellor opened the elongated scroll from the skin of a mystical sea urchin, signed in melted gold and a symbol that swore allegiance to Semperian, a six-pointed star with a half-moon underneath.

"I read to you the final words of King Ndanga of Songhai," said Lord Chancellor. "I, Hereto Shaman Ndanga, King of Songhai, West Africa, swear allegiance to Semperian. Upon my death, my daughter, Princess Shandake Aminata Ndanga of Songhai, will be my successor. She will honor my wishes for the health, wealth, and protection of the good people of this land of Africans."

Lord Chancellor explained, "King Ndanga wrote and sealed his final words in my presence. He wrote them after his first wife, Queen Shandake Aminatusa, died while giving birth to their daughter. In honor of the queen, the King promised that his second-born, Princess Shandake, would be his successor in the event of both of their deaths—he and his first son. Despite King Ndanga's second marriage and the birth of a second son, he chose not to change his final words."

I stood abruptly with Mother by my side.

"How could he?" I shouted. "I'm the rightful heir."

My half-sister lowered her eyes, not allowing me to see the contempt she held for me. She also refused to acknowledge my mother as her stepmother. Nandak, her mother's housemaid, took on that role after the Queen died. Aminata preferred to keep it that way, and so did the King, dishonoring my mother.

My mother, referred to as the Royal Mother, was my father's second wife. She wanted to ensure my succession by secretly ordering the assassination of the King and his first son, my half-brother, Prince Ndanga II. Calling for their heads did not work in our favor because Mother did not know of the King's final wishes. The King was a wise man. He suspected foul play in his eldest son's death and envisioned his death forthcoming.

My sister's husband and bulldog, Prince Abiola Hysan Njinga II, stood and faced me. Before he could speak, I turned my back on him and stormed out of the palace hall.

My sister and her prince soon had a son who would one day serve in a powerful role within his parents' court, reigning over the Songhai-Mali Partnership. Again, I would not inherit the throne, which years later would become a dual role under Prince Ndanga-Njinga. The young prince, once of age, would be Emperor and King, succeeding his parents.

Hearing that, I suffered in anguish despite my sister giving me a meager role on the leadership council. To me, it meant nothing, for I had no power.

The court ignored me and any of my suggestions, like opening our ports to trade. "I spoke with a boyhood friend from Ghana who said his countrymen are thinking of working with the Portuguese on trade. You know my friend," I said pointedly to Amanita. "He and I attended the education consortium for children of African royals."

Prince Njinga was recently installed as emperor after the death of his father. He spoke, "Yes, we have heard of movement from Portugal, Spain, and the Netherlands wanting to trade with Africans because of our resources, primarily our precious stones. Songhai-Mali will not entertain dealings with outsiders coming from across the seas. Those of skin kin to the moon cannot be trusted."

In defiance, I set in motion a plan to overtake the throne, which unfolded years later.

The Ghanaians made a trade deal with the Portuguese but needed passage through the Songhai and Mali ports. Through my Ghanaian friend, I connected with the Portuguese and made a secret deal. Our agreement, unknowingly to me, led to the destruction of the Songhai-Mali empires but allowed me to take back what was rightfully mine.

"Tonight, Mother, Portuguese soldiers will descend upon the prince's training camp. Shandake and her husband will be at our mercy."

Mother lightly kissed my lips, "Soon, she will be forced to abdicate the throne for you, the rightful heir."

The Prince nodded, "My undeserving sister will feel the pain my father caused me."

"Then we will deal with Emperor Njinga," said Mother.

Senegal kicked off the nighttime celebration, honoring each recruit. He raised his cup, "Each of you has worked hard, and I proudly salute all of you."

"Whoop, whoop, yip, yip, kuru, kuru, kuru," they all cheered.

"Now we will have words from our future Emperor and King,"

General Nirobi stepped back, and I stood before the boys.

"Whoop, whoop, yip, yip, kurukuru, kurukuru."

"I am also honored and pleased to see such strength. You are no longer boys; you are warriors. In the memory of my grandfather, the late King Ndanga, may each of you live a long life, honoring Semperian with your lives. And, of course, may you marry a beautiful woman, have plenty of babies, and build more soldiers."

"Whoop, whoop, yip, yip, kurukuru, kurukuru."

The general spoke, "Okay, okay. Before we carry on, it is time to take the ultimate step as Songhai-Mali soldiers."

Although it was a serious matter, the general laughing said, "Bring your ugly heads over to our quarters. You will receive the symbol of a red X atop your shaven heads, honoring your entry into the military partnership."

The invaders came from nowhere. They crept into our camp while we slept, exhausted from celebrating into the night.

"Boli, Boli, run, run," the general ordered as spears flew around us. Then I heard a sound like thunder, never heard before.

"Get your weapons, Aw ka marifaw sɔrɔ."

I watched as young soldiers jumped up from cots and ran for weapons. I joined them along with Senegal, both of us wearing warrior skins.

"Boli, boli, Aw ka marifaw sɔrɔ."

The invaders with skin the color of the white moon had spears of thundering fire, blowing holes into our soldiers, leaving them to drown in their blood.

I killed moon-faced men with arrows, dropped others to the ground with a machete, stabbed them, slashed their throats.

"Senegal," I yelled as the fire spear crashed through his chest, blood shooting out his back. I ran to him, held his head in my lap, tears in my eyes, "Senegal."

His eyes pierced mine with love for me as his good friend and brother, "Boli, my prince." His eyes closed.

I cannot. Run. They killed my brother, so I made him a promise, "We will have our revenge, kill them all with the power of Semperian."

The invaders captured sixty of my trainees, and forty lay dead. They pulled my brother from me, forced my hands behind my back, roped them to my ankles, covered my mouth, as if I had strength to shout, and wrapped heavy chains around me.

A strong wind upheaved from the night dirt; the granules of dead souls pulling from still African bodies. Their souls turned into golden spirits and ascended beyond the moon, defaced by drunken blood. I heard their whispers spread like wildfire across the seas through centuries to come.

"Semperian, I accept my fate. Seperian, n bɛ sɔn n ka siniɲɛsigi ma."

The Songhai-Mali Commander hid Aminata while the Emperor went in search of their son in the Americas.

Before leaving, he ordered the Commander to arrest me and the Royal Mother and interrogate us, but the Portuguese Conquistador arranged swift and safe passage for us out of West Africa.

After the Portuguese killed the Emperor and forced King Shandake to abdicate the throne, Mother and I returned to West Africa. I installed myself as King and Emperor, the dual role meant for the captured Ndanga-Njinga heir.

As Emperor King, I used the Songhai-Mali military to help the Portuguese and Dutch invade the rest of Africa. We slaughtered elephants for ivory tusks and leopards for pelts, and stole diamonds, rubies, and emeralds.

Under my rule, I would be blamed for destroying Africa. However, it was the Portuguese, Dutch, and Spaniards who demolished thousands of Villages, and enslaved hundreds of thousands more Black-skinned natives to serve Spain, Portugal, the Netherlands, and the Americas. It started under Queen Shandake who was forced to cooperate but once her son and husband were killed, she refused to help them any further. Her defiance had made it easier for me to move in and take the throne.

With our help, we created the Transatlantic Slave Trade, which would be cemented in history as the most horrific, capturing, and brutalizing millions of Africans for profit.

1630 - Thonis Baldwin

Proudly, I stood as ship crews forcibly unloaded African men, women, and children, made to travel the thousands of miles I once traveled. During the treacherous journey, human cargo was shackled side-by-side, face-up, face-down on rows of unfinished wooden slats—the dead fed to sea creatures.

The cargo I paid handsomely for paraded past me, chained foot-to-foot, wrist-to-wrist, neck-to-neck, reeking of dried shit and vomit. The cargo was malnourished and dehydrated, their skin torn from shackles and whips.

The crew shoved the Africans into the caged homes we prepared for them, anticipating their arrival.

One African male dressed in full-body attire and lambskin boots walked up to the front, grabbed the cage bars, and shook them fiercely. The captives behind him bowed their heads in reverence and backed away.

I walked up to the cage and stood before the angry caged African, whose wide nostrils flared, strong jaws clenched. His daring eyes bore into my soul, growling like the leopard skin he wore. His head was shaven except for two thick reddish-brown braids entwined with brass coil. They lay side-by-side, attached from the tip of his forehead over the top of his head, down past the base of his skull, stopping mid-back. His body had managed to escape the filth. The African appeared regal with unspoken power over the others.

I kept my eyes glued to his, watching me like prey, "Prince Hereto Abiola Ndanga-Njinga, I am Thonis Baldwin, master of Baldwin Town. I am your new King."

The African couldn't speak English, but he understood my authority and would regard me as the enemy.

Prince Njinga responded in his father's Malian language, Bambara, "Ni fanga ye ka bɔ Semperian fɛ, ne bɛ i n' i ka mɔgɔw danga ka taa jahanama banbali la ani saya banbali la. With the power of Semperian, curse you and your people to endless hell and continual death."

I laughed loudly as I moved closer to the caged prince. Showing him no fear, I promised, "May your numbered days here prepare you for your rightful place in the endless hell."

Kate Baldwin

Prince Abiola Hereto Ndanga-Njinga was the only child and son of Emperor Abiola Hysan Njinga II and King Shandake Ndanga of the Songhai-Mali Dynasties, the largest and most powerful tribes in West Africa. His presence endangered Baldwin, so Thonis planned to put fear into the enslaved by ridding them of their prince.

Africans were my people, and I often walked with my sister through the fields. I wanted her to see the hardships experienced by the enslaved. Juelle would do her best to intervene when she saw something as heartless as pregnant women tilling in the hot sun.

"Isn't that what God would want from us?" Juelle challenged Thonis. "For us to treat these poor souls with care."

"Woman, mind your business and keep Kate in line, or she will join the others," threatened Thonis.

Sometimes, Juelle could get through to her husband, but she noted a different man that day. He hardened in his new authority to secure his legacy and wealth in his town.

Out walking the plantation with Juelle, I caught the prince's eye. He worked alone, tilling the soil in one of the untamed fields, preparing it for a new crop. Three of Thonis's men on horseback held a whip in one hand and a rifle in the saddle's holster.

Recognizing the prince from my grandmother's stories, I hurried over to him.

"Wait," Juelle called and ran after me.

The prince stopped shoveling, faced Juelle and me, and bowed his head. He still wore the leopard skin he arrived in, now torn and battered, along with his muscular body. His handsome brown face was weathered, and his eyes reddened from sleepless nights.

Thonis ordered the guards to keep the prince away from the other Africans. But despite those orders, I saw a proud man.

One of the men shouted, hauled back the whip in his hand, preparing to thrash the prince. His skin was already blemished with marks.

"Stop!" Juelle shouted.

The man stopped and scowled at us.

The prince smiled and bowed.

I did the same and said in Bambara, "Prince Njinga, ne bɛ yan ka i dɛmɛ ani ne bɛna na i sɔrɔ. Prince Njinga, I am here to help you and will come find you."

Juelle grabbed my hand, "Come, my sister. The longer we stay, the worse it will be for him and you."

Into the night, I walked quietly, keeping a promise. I found him hidden deep in the forest, away from the other enslaved, with one guard on duty and a rifle, looking for any excuse to murder the prince before his time.

Thonis kept him in horrific conditions, worse than the cages holding the other Africans who suffered almost as much. Inside a wooden box like that of a coffin, the prince lay on his side, feet and hands shackled to chains attached to metal stakes driven into the ground. He barely slept, shivering from the cold and rain seeping through the few holes meant for breathing, and thinking of another day without food.

Prince Ndanga

I used my circumstance as a test of humility, starting with the rodents who eyed me curiously.

"I kɛra ka wuluwulu i n'a fɔ danfɛn min tɛ hadamaden ye. I n'a fɔ ne ye fanga sanfɛla ye cogo min na, i bɛ sɔn yan, i b' i yɔrɔ dɔn. You were made to crawl as a creature, not as a human. As I am of higher authority, I will allow you to stay; you know your place."

Hidden among the mice was a fat grey rat better fed than me, which came out from the corner. There was little space between us, but the rat kept its distance.

"We are aware of you, royal one. We scavenge for food left by the drunken guards as they sleep."

The rat pushed a biscuit, landing near my mouth.

"Thank you, my friends. May Semperian bless you, releasing you from this existence."

I leaned my head forward and grabbed the biscuit between my teeth, pulled it into my mouth, and chewed.

Kate

I hid behind the tree. Swiping my hand across the air meant for the sleeping guard, I chanted, "Umaya, umaya, umaya, eyes do not see, ears do not hear, will not awaken until I tell thee."

When I saw the prince, he called me Kalinga and questioned his sanity.

I answered, "I will be your Kalinga during your time here. Rest, my prince."

As permitted, I came each night and indulged the prince. Erasing his pain from the day gave him rest and energy to endure another day. His rodent friends continued bringing food.

We struck up a secret friendship. He communicated to the enslaved Africans through me and gave them hope with a promise of freedom, although in a vision, I was told the prince, and I wouldn't be long for this world.

Prince Ndanga remained in good spirits, and it angered Thonis and his men.

Thonis provided care to Africans who would spy on other Africans. One renamed African, Tilly, learned of our plan and shared it with his headmaster. He also told me about my relationship with the prince.

Thonis hatched a plan to kill the prince in 1634 and put me to death after the birth of our son.

Death of a Prince and a Wiccan

That night, my sister warned me of it. But I didn't have time to alert the prince. Thonis's men had come for me.

As they dragged me away, I heard Juelle screaming, "Thonis, I will never forgive you."

My hands bound and mouth gagged, they threw me in the back of a wagon. As we rode away from the Baldwin plantation, I saw the ghostly distant hills and mountains that shadowed the hundreds of twisted oak trees crowned in Spanish Moss. Leading into the town square, where Towners would hang thousands of Black bodies in the coming years, leaving their restless souls lingering in the wind.

Reaching the square, the wagon slowed to a halt.

Two Towner men pulled me by my ankles from the wagon, and the back of my head smacked the ground. They forcibly stood me up and dragged me to the front of the crowd in front of what they later named the Hanging Tree. Men, women, and children were pumping their fists and shouting, preparing to celebrate the first African to be hanged in early Alabama—Prince Abiola Hereto Ndanga-Njinga.

The prince stared at me and smiled as the noose tightened around his neck. His mind connected with mine and I heard him say, "Semperian tɔgɔ la, fɛn bɛɛ bɛ i n'a fɔ a ka kan ka kɛ cogo min na. Ne bɛna aw ye sɔɔni u ka jate la. [On behalf of Semperian, all is as it should be. I will see you soon at their reckoning]."

My eyes acknowledged the Semperian within him, and his eyes closed as did mine, ignoring Thonis, who stepped from the crowd.

His face scrunched tight and glaring eyes, he said, "You are but a mortal creature whose misguided people think of him as a God. There is only room for one God here, and I stand before you. By my hand, I sentence you to death by hanging. May your soul drop to hell where ye belong, and burn."

The hangman pulled the rope holding the mortal man Prince Ndanga Njinga up to the tip of the tree's tallest branch. He was no longer of the flesh, for he had ascended before the final pull.

The air surrounding the Towners fumed of stank sweat and putrid breath, "Hooray, hurrah, hooray, hurrah," ignorant of what awaited them. For they would suffer despite their future call to immortality.

As for my fate, Thonis imprisoned me inside a cave on an abandoned mountainside rather than burn me alive at the stake meant for witches and pagans—a promise he made to his wife, Juelle, who hated him. His men stacked branches into a tepee and set it afire using the live body of a light-skinned African woman of my height and build. Whose screams were heard long after her death.

The story of the Wiccan and a prince soon faded, leaving only Jewell and Thonis knowing of our unborn child.

I gave birth to a beautiful baby boy inside that cave. It hurt me to my core when I had to hand him over to Thonis. Glad my sister Juelle was there to say goodbye. She would ensure the young prince's safety.

Juelle named the prince Emanuel, meaning God with us. Thonis gave him the surname of his parents, Janssen, as a reckoning for giving up what he saw as a pauper's name.

Because of his dark skin, one of the African women cared for him as her own but under Jewell's watch. Despite Thonis wanting to get rid of him like he did his father.

The Curse of 1634

Not long after I rid Baldwin of the African and a witch, a deadly plague came. Our Dr. Wolstein knew not how to treat an illness that had no name.

Towners died after a bout with a prolonged fever, drenched in sweat, coughing up bloody mucus, and their skin turned yellow.

"Today's count, sir, is two hundred," Dr. Wolstein reported. "Adults and children are dead."

Baldwin Town of twelve hundred people, would become a ghost town by year's end.

Among the last to die were my wife and son. I found them in our cold home where the fire had long since died.

That was the only time I wept but then became outraged when I saw Kate's bastard child still alive, coddled in Juelle's other arm.

I grabbed the boy and held him with outstretched arms. Stared into his tiny brown face, and almond-shaped brown eyes, his mouth wide open as if pleading for his life.

I planned to finally kill him until I saw the apparition of a black-skinned woman with long white hair, tapping her buttocks. I recognized her. The woman from the cave.

"You must not kill the boy yet," she warned me. "Follow my instructions, and Prince Njinga's son will give you renewed life and unimaginable wealth."

The woman I met in the Mountain cave in the Netherlands. She was a powerful Wiccan named Luna. In that cave, she foretold my future.

"You want to be wealthy, eh?" she chuckled. "I'm afraid you cannot."

"What do you mean, I cannot?" I said angrily. "And who are you to tell me that?"

"The hand you've been dealt comes from the ignorance of your parents. They've chosen to come into this new life as indigents to learn humility. You, my boy, will continue that fate unless you allow me to rid you of those circumstances."

I did not know what she meant. We may not have been a religious family, but Far and Mor believed in one God and his son, named Jesus, who was a pauper. I hated the stories they told and wanted nothing to do with a belief that allowed some to be rich and others to be poor.

The Wiccan Luna said she would ensure my wealth in the Americas if I followed her instructions. But first, it required sacrifice. It began with drinking the blood of the Clondike.

1651 First Blood Covenant

I carried to the Americas the knowledge about a Semperian, the universal designer and protector of Source. It granted Africans the key to riches and immortality.

A West African prince who was set to ascend to a dual role as King and Emperor of the Songhai and Mali Partnership was the purest connection to the Semperian.

I often thought of how unfair that was and questioned why Africans were given that kind of power. I was determined to cheat them of it and take away their God. I would be their

God, because I would own them and the Semperian power.

With Luna's help, I arranged for the capture of Prince Ndanga-Njinga. Once he arrived on our shores, I swore to him I would be his God. Later, I hanged Africans who carried on a practice related to their Semperian and sentenced their prince to death.

Luna intervened after his death and sent his soul to Apollyon Diabolus's hell.

Luna, with Apollyon's energy, created the blood covenant, which required killing the newborn prince. We used his blood and that of my sons to begin the ritual of sacrifice every seventeen years. The covenant immediately resurrected both boys who had turned seventeen and would be the first to receive "the gift" during the Rites of Passage ceremony. The gift was the magical power we pulled from Semperian through Prince Ndanga-Njinga, so we kept him hostage in the third hell. The covenant sealed the fate of mortal Africans brought to Baldwin, for it was their blood that sustained our wealth and immortal life.

The number seventeen represented the Apollyon energy, the most diabolical of the three dark lords. Handsome Luciferno (Lucifer), Fallen One, ruled the first lower realm, and Satana (Satan), Fallen 2, ruled the second. Apollyon Diabolus Fallen 17 ruled the third realm and operated outside of the universal laws.

The covenant only allowed me limited use of Semperian power, but Luna promised me that it would one day change.

"We will own it all," she promised.

I was grateful for my newfound wealth, but I didn't trust Luna. She was keeping something from me, and I wanted to be prepared for what that might be.

So, I secretly created a special elixir for myself that gave me additional powers. It was mixed with the blood of the prince and the clondike. Luna advised against it when I teased her with the idea.

"For a human to use Semperian power with dark magic would be deadly," she said. "You know not how to combine the two. Only those of us from the higher realm could attempt such a fate."

Despite her warning, I will use it if necessary.

Over several decades, incarnations of Thonis Baldwin and Emanuel Janssen resurrected and rebuilt Baldwin.

Thonis Baldwins had pure Dutch blood, and Emanuel Janssens descended from the Ndanga-Njinga clan. We bound our blood under the blood moon on the Solstice every seventeen years. As legacy holders, we carried out the legacy of the original Thonis and Emanuel. A legacy committee comprised of unnamed men of Baldwin managed the existence of the covenant and the sacrifices it took to keep it alive.

I was the elite legacy holder influenced and protected by the Dark Lord Apollyon Diabolus. Emanuel Janssen, whose original soul we kept enslaved to maintain the blood covenant, was the secondary legacy holder. It is through his incarnations and bloodline that Towners lived life immortal.

We, as legacy holders, pass on the magic to our sons in that seventeenth year to maintain our immortal circumstances. That included Towners continuing to receive immortality through a transitioning procedure once their bodies aged. Transitioning began as early as age sixty, depending on the Towner's desire.

Mine and Emanuel's were exempt from transitioning because of our direct connection to the prince.

Over the next several years, the Thonis Baldwins and Emanuel Janssens built Baldwin into the wealthiest port city and a prominent entry into the south.

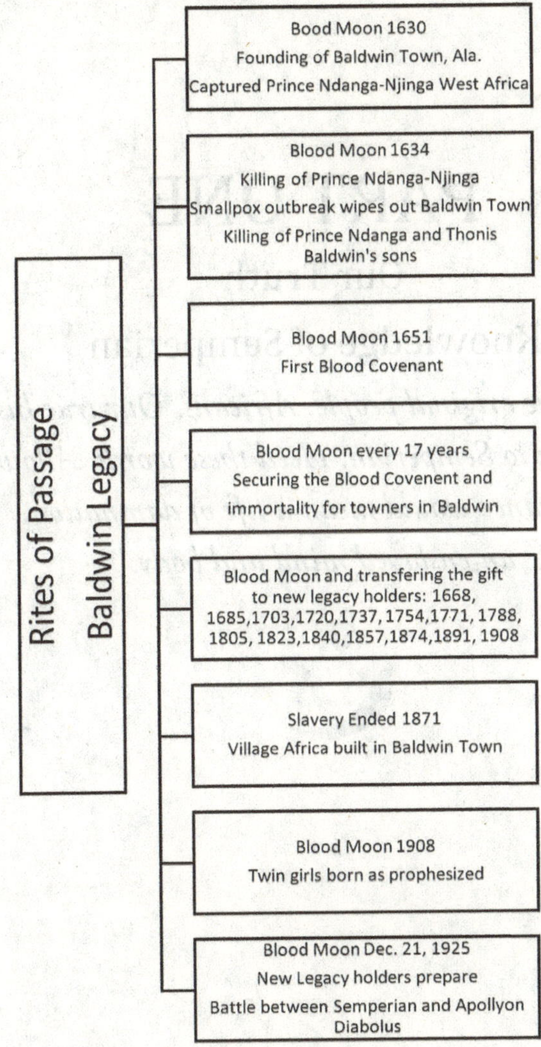

PART ONE

Our Truth

Knowledge of Semperian

"We are the original people. Africans. Our true history leads back to Semperian. Heed these words. Allowing ignorance would mean a life of damnation, an enslaved mind and body."

Chapter 1

Blood Moon of 1908
Before and After Birth

6278 days to solstice

17 years, 2 months, 8 days to Solstice

The Semperian gave its Daughter to this world to die, to free the enslaved Africans whose spirits are damned to the hell of lake fire because of the Blood covenant that brought about the rebirth of Baldwin Town. Semperian disapproves of this, for it is unnatural, not of the spiritual laws protecting Source Consciousness and its universe. As permitted, the Semperian used its energy to create a design for life, perfected and protected by the Guards above and below. If Semperian Daughter fails her task, the heavens will fall, and the darkest realm will rise to live life immortal for eternity.

—Knowledge of Semperian: Origin 1-17

Day 13 October 1908
Baldwin Town, Alabama

Tears bubbled up deep inside when I remembered my birth. Papa transferred a universal power to me at age seventeen with the vision to see the before, the now, and the future. Vision to remember being born, inside a room where the crackling of the heated wood stove spewed sweaty mist into the air. Sunlamps hung overhead, warming the midwife's delicate hands as she

1

carefully cut the cord. The final connection to my birth Mother, who hated me.

Before I was born, Mama conspired with the Village witch to murder me. Worked with a demon to create another daughter. She would attempt to steal my life and legacy promised to me. As the firstborn Daughter, I was sent to Earth from the highest spiritual authority in the universe. Semperian.

Like Mama, the other version was Dutch with a hint of African blood. She was also part demon, created to secure the blood covenant for eternity, made from the blood of Africans centuries ago. The final covenant would allow the rise of the most diabolical evil trapped in the third hell, Apollyon Diabolus Fallen 17. With help from his minions, Apollyon planned to take over Earth and rule the Universe for eternity.

Mama hated me for my Blackness and my mission. The witch warned her that I was sent to destroy the blood covenant and free the Africans and the prince who was next in line to inherit the throne of the most powerful partnership in West Africa: Songhai and Mali. The pure souls of Africans were what fed the blood covenant. Through me, Semperian would end their enslavement, and before Apollyon secured full power on the Solstice of 1925, the night of the blood moon.

Inside Mama's womb, I prepared for my destiny. The demon daughter mysteriously appeared, and I fought to live. She blinded me with purple mist made of lilac rot; I would guard against the foul odor in the coming years.

The demon daughter wrapped her umbilical cord around my neck, pulled, and pulled, leaving me almost lifeless. Yanking free, I slid down the narrow passage and pushed through headfirst, landing outside Mama's womb.

With the other cord loosely around my neck, I dripped with remnants of warm water, chilly air against my body, and minted steam tickling my nose.

"It's a girl," the midwife announced.

She picked up my tiny body, removed the cord, turned me over, and swatted my butt until I wailed and wailed. Laid me atop a thin blanket. My little body shivered, arms and legs flailed as if to beat heat into the room.

"Lord, she's got strong lungs," the midwife noticed. She cleaned me before wrapping the blanket tightly around my belly, little legs, and feet. Placed me in his arms—not hers—my Papa, who I will never forget, his thick, tightly curled black hair and dark golden skin of pure African blood. He would spare my life despite Mama wanting him to dispose of me in an unmarked grave prepared before my birth.

"Welcome, my firstborn," his soft voice quivered.

"Umaya, umaya, umaya."

His almond eyes, shaped like mine, filled with water, falling warm to my chest. For he felt Mama's silent anger, pulling away from me, their firstborn, who was different from the one who came after. Papa's pain was felt throughout the universe.

I had skin of Blackwood and hair like sheep's wool. Large almond eyes and full lips bejeweled my small, round face. A sacred mark hidden beneath my chin, a six-pointed star and half-moon. Symbolizing the sacred power of Songhai and Mali off the African coast near the Niger River.

Where the Dutch and Portuguese enslaved millions of my people, and sold them into a brutal life in a new land called America, where they would become Afrikaans.

As Papa wept, the outer elements responded, standing in honor of the Daughter who came before, angered by the coming presence of the one who came after.

The wind whirled through the Spanish Moss Trees, pushing up to the ranch doors, knocking, knocking. Trembling shutters flew open, backhanding the brick. Horses heard in the distance braved the night, whilst others hid.

The sunlamps flickered as her evil crying took all of Mama's attention.

I howled, wanting Mama to cuddle me too. Let me lie on your chest and suck your other breast.

She shunned me and praised the one who came after, "Ripe as cream and sweet as goat's milk, your heritage is yours alone, my only daughter."

She named her Mirabella. Favored her white chocolate skin and soft brownish-blonde curls despite her dark soul linked to the lilac cream Mama rubbed on her naked body.

Mama. You created her and made a pact with the devil.

You ignored the name Papa gave me, your firstborn. Named after him, my soul was kin to the Semperian universe.

Papa wrapped me snugly inside a blanket. My ears and face, loosely covered, would not shut off the midwife's tears and Mama's voice that sang to Mirabella.

As it was my destiny, Papa took me into the warm night and set me inside a makeshift basket on the buggy floor. Grunted as he lifted himself into his rawhide seat. Grabbed the whips—snap, snap. "Geddup Black Bo."

The wagon jerk-wobbled, wobbled down the broken dirt road into the fall's blackened night, we rode. Overhead, a blood moon against a jet-black sky backlit the path, warning off anyone wanting to pass our way.

Wobbled, jerk-wobbled, snap, snap, "Geddup Black Bo."

We passed through Baldwin-Janssen Square, set off by ghostly distant hills and mountains across the bay. They shadowed the hundreds of twisted Oak trees wearing crowns of Spanish Moss.

About a mile from the road, trees carried painful stories whispering in the wind.

Listen.

The angry shouts of the town's spectators fumed with stank sweat and putrid breath. They crowded there in the not-so-distant past, in front of the Hanging Tree. Pumping their fists into the sky as they celebrated the first enslaved African hanged in early Alabama. More enslaved soon followed whilst African children stood a few feet away, watching from behind the Hiding Tree. Confederate soldiers lost the battle against freedom fighters there.

Before then, African children lost their fight before it began, were sold to new masters, or were hanged to keep enslaved in line. The murdered Africans cannot rest until the prophecy unfolds, breaking the blood covenant and releasing their souls.

The broken mud smoothed, quieting the buggy's wobbling wheels and mare's clop, clop. Calm awakened the ancestral spirits that surrounded me as my light of protection.

They whispered in the Bambara language of Mali:

"An ye Afirikikaw ye. A bangeli bɛ fanga di an ma ni yeelen ye walasa ka boli dibi la u y'an bila kaso la. An bɛna bonya da a kan, den fɔlɔ min ka bangeko ye an ka ciyɛn ye. Semperian b'an lakana, ka mɔgɔ minnu ja gelɛya k'a ka kojugu kɛ, a bɛ olu tiɲɛ. [We are Original Africans. Your birth empowers us with light to flee from the darkness they have imprisoned us. We will pay homage to you, the firstborn Daughter whose birthright is our legacy. Semperian keeps us safe, destroying those who dare cause you harm]."

Chapter 2

The One Who Came After
107 days to solstice
3 months, 16 days

Day 5 September 1925
Baldwin Town, Alabama
Thonis Baldwin

Baldwin Town awakened at the earliest sunrise until after the moon dropped behind the Mobile, Alabama mountains. Founded by me, a Dutchman named Thonis Baldwin, immigrants from New Amsterdam lived there, in the vibrant waterfront town.

The original Thonis Baldwin, with the help of the first Emanuel Janssen, built the exclusive town beginning in 1651. Emanuel, an African, married a Dutch woman, creating the Janssen family Dutch-African bloodline. Emanuel's ancestors were of the Malian tribe in West Africa.

Those who immigrated from New Amsterdam were known as Towners. I promised them a long life and extreme wealth. Hiding a secret no one outside the town knew about. Not even the African Villagers living on the hill above the town.

By 1925, Baldwin had become the wealthiest small town in Alabama. The busy main street made of cobblestone was usually filled with horse-drawn carriages alongside the growl of gas-powered vehicles.

Saturdays, the busiest for shopping and recreation, began as early as 6:00 in the morning, during the summer months, to beat the heat. The weather forecasted a continuing summer drought with temperatures reaching a record of one hundred twelve degrees by early afternoon.

Our town's three clothing stores, two barber shops, three cafes, one grocer, and a theater would be open until after sundown so families could stay cool. The theatre and businesses installed air conditioning machines, making their way across the United States. The town church opened with workers from the Village, serving up iced water, tea, and freshly squeezed lemonade.

Strolling through town, stopping in here and there, women came dressed in loose cotton and linen dresses to the knee with modest necklines and short sleeves. Some came with little girls wearing playful short A-line cotton dresses. Men wore simple short-sleeved shirts and brown knickers; boys wore the same.

Dr. Wolstein

One elderly Towner couple stopped in to see me, the one town doctor. The room was empty, so they didn't wait long.

"Hello, Dr. Wolstein," the elderly woman greeted, who was sitting beside her husband, who also greeted me. It was almost past time for their transition, especially for the wife. She had deep wrinkles, her dull blonde hair as thin as her physique.

"Hello, Mr. and Mrs. Hawesville, I have everything set."

I led the couple down the hall to a large room bustling with chatter and laughter. Ten recently transitioned couples were in patient gowns, sipping on red beverages.

One fellow said to a couple sitting next to him, "Is it me, or does this drink become tastier each time we come?"

The man answered, "You are right, my boy. I feel more alive than before."

I nodded toward the group, "We've been busy today. Many elders are transitioning."

I motioned for the Hawesvilles to enter an empty room near there. The windowless room had two beds with fresh sheets and a doctor's chair. On the side of each bed was a silver pole for hanging liquids.

"Please undress and put on these gowns. Nurse Wolstein will bring you your fluids." I chuckled. "She is feeling mighty chipper today, having come back through earlier than me this time. I've always wanted to experience being the older man married to the younger wife half my age. Have the two of you decided on your next roles, or will you stay as you are?"

Mrs. Hawesville spoke, "We enjoy our façade but want children this time."

"Ahh, yes. Being a parent is special. Kitty and I had children during a few lifetimes. I'll have Mrs. Wolstein bring you the information."

Two hours later, I released the other patients, and Nurse Wolstein escorted the newly transitioned Mr. and Mrs. Hawesville to post-op.

"The two of you look ravishing," said my perky wife, wearing a pink nurse's uniform, and her bouncy blonde hair flipped.

"Thank you," said Patty. "It's the fluids. I feel better this time around, right, Jim?"

"Much stronger," he said. "Appears we are having no problems getting what we need."

"No, we are not," said Kitty. "We thought it would be a problem post-civil war, but Mr. Baldwin predicts urban communities across the country will lose a lot of lives in the future. That will be our new supply."

"Quite good, then," said Jim.

"Yes, indeed. Please stay here in recovery for at least two hours. We want to make sure everything is all right. We have a special treat from a dear friend of Mr. Baldwin's: a tray of white lilacs."

"Oh, goody," said Mrs. Hawesville.

On her way out, Kitty said, "Patty, you being a redhead this time suits you. I can see Jim already salivating."

Jim laughed, "These Mandigo muscles can't wait to show her some new tricks."

Later that evening, we uploaded the last of the bodies into the covered wagon. I told the African driver, "You may take your people home now."

Mirabella Janssen

As the daughter of one of the wealthiest families in Baldwin, I had significant advantages.

My daddy, Emanuel Janssen, brought Mummy and me to town in our black, gas-powered vehicle to visit the town's exclusive fashion boutique owned by Suanne Baldwin. She was the wife of Thonis Baldwin. Towners and Villagers referred to her as Lady Baldwin.

The Baldwin and Janssen names came with considerable history and prestige. The Baldwin-Janssen Square was named in honor of both families. It was built on thirty-eight hundred acres and extended west to the Janssen ranch and the Baldwin estate, east of the square.

Our town hosted the Rites-of-Passage there every seventeen years on December 21, the first day of solstice, since 1651. The patriarch of each family transferred their power, called the gift, to their firstborn at seventeen. Then they would protect the blood covenant until their heirs turned seventeen.

This year, I will receive the gift from Daddy, and Trevor Baldwin will receive his from Thonis Baldwin.

I will be the first and only firstborn girl to receive the gift since Baldwin was resurrected. As prophesized, the birth of a firstborn girl will end with having to make a sacrifice every seventeen years.

Trevor and I will be married in a special ceremony on our birthday, October 13. The special union will prepare us to accept all power on December 21, the night of the blood moon.

Daddy gave Mum, Delilah Janssen, money to pay for my custom gown made for the Rites-of-Passage event.

"You ladies do your business. I'm due for a cut and shave. Check on you in about an hour."

"All right, dear. Mirabella and I will wait for you on the inside. This hot weather is ruining my mood."

Despite Mum and me wearing short-sleeved linen dresses and sandals, it didn't ward off the extreme heat.

Inside 'Beautiful Things Ladies Fashion' was nice and cool. Lady Baldwin sat near the front in a blonde wingback chair behind a four-legged white marble oval desk. She served customers by appointment only and greeted us cheerfully.

Lady Baldwin's style outshone Mummy's. At age forty-six, she was an esteemed businesswoman. She wore her silk brown hair pulled back into a French bun and a one-of-a-kind garment designed for her slender and shapely physique. The daring above-the-knee, short-sleeved, canary yellow chiffon dress hugged her thighs and hips.

Suanne staged the front of the boutique for customers with workers and sewing rooms in the back of the building. The customer area had purple velvet walls, a large crystal chandelier, and purple roses painted across the ceiling. Four headless mannequins were clothed in the latest styles out of Europe: a Black-Flapper style sequined dress, a beaded, beige chiffon gown, a two-piece light blue suit, and day wear in a silk blouse, pants, and matching sweater.

Suanne led Mum and me to the back and opened a door leading to an area with a private room for changing on the left. On the right, a restroom stocked with expensive toiletries.

"I put your dress in here, Mirabella. Call if you need help."

Suanne pointed to a table with coffee, tea, fresh crumpets, a Victorian couch, and two matching chairs in gold velvet and asked Delilah, "Care for refreshments?"

Instead, Mum bypassed the refreshments and browsed along the wall, admiring the assortment of hats on hooks, jewelry, gloves, and shoes lined on open shelves.

"A delivery came this week," Suanne said enticingly.

Delilah marveled at the wide-brimmed peach-colored linen sun hat with a large linen rose appliqué attached.

"You have great taste. Would you like to try it on? You would stand out at any tea party."

"Don't tempt me. Bringing home another hat? Not sure how Emanuel would feel. I hardly wear the ones I have."

Outside the front of the store, a gentleman passing by tapped on the window. He tipped his hat, "Howdy do."

"Mayor Shipley," Lady Baldwin waved.

Delilah bowed her head, thinking she didn't like the man much. Something about him made her nervous when in his presence.

Mayor Lazarus Shipley rarely showed himself publicly. Always busy at the office doing town business.

Shipley was kin to the Baldwins but had grey catlike eyes, unlike the family's traditional blue. He came to town years ago, staking his claim as next in line to uphold the legacy, if the covenant faltered under Thonis. Towners accepted him, no question asked, as if hypnotized. As the town's chief spokesperson, he remained a mystery.

I came out of the fitting room and stood in front of the three-paneled mirror. My eyes widened, "All for me, Mummy?"

Suanne adjusted the panels.

I twirled right then left, back to front, the silk chiffon dark red A-line gown swaying from side to side, "This dress makes me look like a movie star." Batting my large almond eyes, I smiled while ignoring the full lips I hated.

Elegant with style and grace, Mum smiled warmly, her pastel-colored lips pushing up her lollipop cheeks. She pulled out a small compact of powder from her small yellow purse and dabbed away beads of sweat from her oval face and slender neck. "I certainly agree with how you look. The hand-beading and sequins around the corset are exquisite."

Suanne nodded, her soft peach lips turned into a half-smile about all she could muster when it came to Delilah Janssen and her Mirabella. *To think my son will marry and serve with her over the next seventeen years.*

"Well worth the money your father paid for this dress."

"Hmph, we can afford it, Mummy." I lifted my chin, puckered my lips, "I must look my best for my wedding day."

Lady Baldwin's Scandinavian face, parched pink from sun rays, tightened as she held her tongue.

Eyeing her, I smirked as I thought about her son, my future husband Trevor Baldwin's handsome grin. I loved his crystal blue eyes and strong jaws, a family trait except for his name.

Suanne named him Trevor rather than Thonis, a name carried down through centuries. Master Baldwin didn't argue as long as he got what he wanted come solstice.

Lady Baldwin pinched her brows, tilting her nose while side-glancing at Mummy, and it irritated me.

Unlike Suanne, Mum depended on Daddy for her financial needs and to keep up her appearance as one of the affluent women in the South.

Suanne did not allow her husband's wealth to define her. Southern women either envied or admired her for her business savvy and independence.

"I love the feel."

Lady Baldwin moved closer, "We purchased this silk from France on our last visit. As for the future, my husband's physical illness…" Suanne laid both hands over her heart. "He can only travel during spring and summer. His damaged leg is allergic to cold." Suanne giggled to cover her perceived sadness.

"I'm so sorry for…," I cut Mummy off, not wanting to show Suanne empathy. The woman was heartless.

I hadn't forgotten how Suanne treated Mummy, nearing Easter. It was around the time Mayor Lazarus came to Baldwin. Papa disappeared for weeks, leaving Mummy without extra spending money.

That woman would not wait for Mum to pay the balance on my frilly pink Easter dress when Daddy returned. She told Mummy, "No!"

"I will never forget her ugly smirk. Mummy pleaded embarrassingly like a Villager."

Daddy spoke to Thonis, who scolded Suanne for her ill will and reminded her that the Janssens and Baldwins built the town with strict, unspoken rules. Breaking them would mean the town's destruction.

"Eh bien, nous devons le prendre mum," I said in French.

"We must take it. Suanne may need the extra change."

Mum's eyes burned with disappointment, wishing I would show a little compassion.

But I will not. I refused to be treated like a Villager whom God looked down on with hatred. My birthright comes with having the best, so no one better get in my way, not even you,

Mum. You know what I am capable of, and she does too—the one who came before.

I learned my power at age five from an apparition, a thin elderly woman with white hair down to her buttocks. She visited me regularly and told me stories.

"My daughter." The woman called me. She had darker skin than mine. Didn't annoy me like the Villagers with the same skin. I felt close to her and listened intently to the stories that prepared me for my role in the coming new world.

"My dear, you will find use for this lilac potion when you get a little older. Feel free to wear it as protection against bullies that come your way. We will not have our daughter be touched by such nastiness."

The special potion came from purple lilac juices, animal blood, and human flesh. I could use it against my enemies and control anyone, including Trevor, mind, body, and soul.

Purple lilacs grew plentiful in an invisible field outside our ranch. I played there as my source of pleasure and strength.

When I turned ten, I began to experiment. The Towner children made fun of my features, accusing me of being one of the Villagers contaminated with African blood. After I used it to stop them, Mummy hid what I did from Daddy.

A mix of African and Dutch blood on the Janssen side helped resurrect Baldwin. Despite the significance of our family history, those ignorant children learned cruelty from their parents.

In the school playground, I confronted the bullies, cousins Kathy, Jonathan, and Damon.

My hair was freshly curled that day, and I wore a lacy, blue dress. I had a small bottle of Lilac, one of many that would mysteriously appear in my room.

"Get away from us, you awful Villager." Kathy twirled her

blonde pigtail with her finger.

She, too, had on a freshly starched yellow dress, ready for singing in that afternoon's gathering of families in front of the Hanging Tree. An event I refused to participate in. I hated those Towner children as much as I hated the Villagers.

"Go away," Damon pointed. "You're not one of us."

Jonathan started to speak, but gagged and couldn't move his lips. He fell to the ground. "Umm," he squirmed, grabbing at his cheeks and mouth.

I was amused.

Kathy and Damon backed away, ran to help Jonathan, tripped, and fell beside him.

I followed them as they screamed, my eyes black, my face a hideous grey.

Kneeling in front of those scared brats I threatened, "May my father Apollyon kill you whilst you slither away like vermin."

The three children crawled like slithering snakes. They hissed, flicking their tongues at the other children who ran.

The incident caused panic in Baldwin after the three snakes disappeared from the schoolyard, and parents found one in each of the children's beds.

Daddy supported and respected the Villagers because of his African roots. But I stood by Mummy when denying that part of our heritage. I was glad they lived in their community uphill from Baldwin proper, in Village Africa. The Village looked down on Baldwin and could be seen from the docks.

Despite our hatred for Villagers, Towners needed the blood of Africans to survive. The covenant required help from Villagers who maintained the stage for Baldwin as a bustling city in Alabama for the earlier arrivals from New Amsterdam.

Chapter 3

The One Who Came Before
69 days to solstice
2 months, 8 days

Day 13 October 1925
Event Day at Baldwin Janssen Square

Tuesday morning in Baldwin Town and Village Africa opened with warmer weather, three weeks into autumn. Residents anticipated the weather reaching upwards of 80 degrees by afternoon at 3:00, cooling to sixty-five early evening.

The timing of the weather was right for the big event happening in Baldwin Janssen Square tonight at 7:00. The day was for Towners. Domestics and dock workers from the Village enjoyed a day off, except for Janssen and Baldwin's in-home staff. House butlers and house ladies prepared the future legacy holders for the event.

Emanuella Crumley

The added rest day gave time for personal business, chores, or time with families.

My parents, John, and Josephine Crumley, also had the day off. Mama J spent today making a special family dinner for my seventeenth birthday while Papa John tilled in his backyard garden.

My siblings, paternal twin brothers Ezekial and Gabriel, ages ten, and my sister Cecelia, who turned sixteen last month, looked forward to the gathering and giving me gifts.

We lived in Village Africa, located up the hill from Baldwin Town. With the help of freemen, Mr. Emanuel built Village Africa for African mortals who lived there. Families who remained in Baldwin after the Civil War worked for the twelve hundred Towners.

The five-hundred-acre land had hundreds of green trees and large fields fed by spring water running from the mountains into the creek between the Village and Baldwin.

Cottages similar in size and shape lay side-by-side, stacked up the hillside in rows with sufficient green space. The homes were constructed using concrete or rubble stones in greys, browns, and whites with rectangular windows on all sides, front and back wooden doors, and shingled roofs.

We kept to ourselves, protected by Semperian, a truth only a few of us Africans accepted. Other Africans practiced the European religion of Christianity, passed down through their enslaved ancestors.

Mr. Emanuel, a Guardian I would come to know one day, watched over the Village where I lived on Jonah Road. As one of a handful of Village cottages made of faded brick masonry, our home sat at the Village's end, uphill from the main street leading to the town center.

Reaching downtown Baldwin was a twenty-minute buggy ride or five-mile walk.

That morning, I slept in late, snuggled under a summer blanket in a large enough bed shared with my sister Cecilia. Family and friends called her Cece, and our brothers called her

Sissy. She slept soundly while I lay awake, wondering about plans for my special day. My siblings called me E, rather than Emanuella.

"Ummm, Mama Josephine is baking biscuits." The aroma seeping in from the kitchen teased my nostrils.

Mama rarely baked because she worked full-time at the Janssens except for today. When she did bake, she got up early and prepared the dough with yeast that needed to rise before baking.

I sat up and stretched, enjoying the cooled air, stopping the heat from the sun, and bouncing off the window.

One of the benefits of living in the Village was cool air, magically piping into homes and businesses during extreme heat. No cooling machines pumped cool air into homes anywhere in the United States except for the Janssen and Baldwin homes.

Village Africa provided families with an abundance of food from one grocery store and gardens like Papa John's, producing bountiful fruits and vegetables year-round.

I looked over at the snoring Sissy. Her twisted locs of hair and mahogany brown face were half covered under the blanket. I giggled and pushed her teasingly, and she stopped but started up again, quieter.

I rolled out from under the blanket, stuffed my feet into my pink furry bedside slippers, and pulled on the matching robe hanging on the headboard corner. My slippers and robe were birthday presents from Mr. Emanuel. Mama J brought them home yesterday, along with a fancy floor-length evening gown. The gown was bronze chiffon, and hand-laced down the front and back bodice, stopping at the waist with a modest neckline, and lace sleeves.

Yesterday, Cece saw the dress laid out across the bed, curtsied and teased, "Queen Emanuella."

But Mama J's mouth was scrunched, frowning, when she came in from work with the dress, slippers, and robe. She showed the same scrunched mouth and frowning forehead when Emanuel Janssen, who called me Ella, insisted we address him as Emanuel. And that included me, which Mama forbade.

I liked the sound of his name. It reminded me of mine. I called him Mr. Emanuel when I turned sixteen, and Mama didn't argue.

The twins came in right behind Mama, carrying packages wrapped in shiny gold paper. Carried the evening gown over her shoulder, locked in a black dress bag. Cece and I were in the front room with Papa John, listening to his favorite performer, Bessie Smith, singing Downhearted Blues on the radio.

Mr. Emanuel and Papa John saw the Empress of Blues at a Juke Joint in Mobile. A bonus for Papa for the work he'd done for their family. That's when Mama gave her opinion about Mr. Emanuel giving gifts to me.

My siblings loved Mr. Emanuel's generosity because sometimes he would give them gifts. He recently sent hazel green knit sweaters with caps for the boys and a dark yellow hooded shawl for Cece.

I tickled inside, looking at my beautiful gown hanging in the closet. The color was perfect and would complement my almond-colored eyes.

I took it out and laid it across the chair near the nightstand. Pulled off my night garments. Unclamped the right and left side of the bodice, stepped into the dress, and wiggled it up over my slender thighs and firm derriere. Rezipped the sides. It fit perfectly and matched the half-inch-heel shoes on the closet floor.

"Oh, my goodness. I looked like an African queen in the history books I got from Mr. Emanuel."

I bet the family planned a birthday surprise because why would Mr. Emanuel give me this fine dress, I thought.

Wearing my dress and shoes, I crept up on my parents in the kitchen, standing in front of the wood stove.

Mama, stirring the pot, looked shorter beside my six-foot-tall Papa. Wearing a leisurely plaid shirt and suspenders attached to the waist of his corduroy britches, he leaned down to listen to Mama Josephine.

"On days like this, visitors from bordering cities know not to come to Baldwin. The Crumleys will stay in, mind our business."

I started to interrupt until Papa John said, "Josephine, it is Ella's right."

"No more talk, John. It's too dangerous. The Solstice is less than two months away; our Daughter can wait until then."

Papa slammed his thick brown fist down atop the stove tray. The pot shook, "We do not have a say in the matter; it is already decided."

He walked away, the heels of his heavy boots clomping on the linoleum, out through the kitchen, passing through the back-covered porch.

Mama looked over her shoulder.

"What do you think, Mama J. Beautiful, huh? For my party?"

Mama turned around and faced me. With her black hair tied in a bonnet, she held onto the wooden spoon. Her scrunched mouth wrinkled her narrow face and thick brows.

"What party girl?"

I stared at Mama, who looked weary. Sometimes, she looked over her age of forty-seven, like now. Papa John would say, "Her ancient wisdom sometimes shows."

Mama shook the spoon at me, dropping bits of grits on the floor.

"It ain't for you, Emanuella Crumley. Not now." Her eyes watered as she punched her balled fists to her hips, the wooden spoon pointing backward.

"Take that dern dress off and put it away as I told you."

My face tightened. I pursed my lips, tempted to defy Mama, but they raised me to be respectful.

I turned and stomped out like Papa John, now standing in the front room. He winked, "You look pretty in your dress. Perfect for wearing to the big event tonight."

That helped me shrug off Mama being overbearing, which I did most times. I dreamt of my parents watching over me when I was a baby and while I slept. They wanted to shut off the cruelty around me, and how I came into the world, they said. I grew up knowing that they would do anything to protect me until time. To let go.

Papa John called the family together for an early dinner at 4:00, shortly after returning from taking Zeke and Gabe to the Village barber. They looked nice for the occasion.

The family gathered around the dinner table and feasted on the big dinner made especially for my birthday: fried chicken, biscuits, yams, collards, and a chocolate cake, one of Mama Josephine's special recipes.

We ate until our bellies hurt.

"Mama, everything was so good. Thank you for making me my favorite dishes." I kissed her cheek.

"I agree," said Papa J.

"Now, now, y'all always come first."

"Want you to know we all love and appreciate what you do. You did me justice on my birthday."

"We're coming up on a birthday, too," said Zeke.

"Right before Christmas," Gabe chimed in.

"How about we talk about y'all's birthdays later? Ella needs to open her gifts."

"Right, Papa." I grinned, mostly thinking about the event.

In the front room, the twins sat together, legs crossed, in the middle of the floor.

Cece, Mama, and I were on the sofa, Papa John in his favorite armchair.

Zeke, the oldest twin by five minutes, tallest by two inches, and most talkative, spoke first, "We caught you a frog jumping out back in that little creek. Thought it'd be nice for you to show when you teach bio.'

"But got away," Gabe confessed, rocking back and forth, watching Mama J out of the side of his eye.

It wouldn't be the first time the boys lost a pet indoors.

Like that past spring, the boys captured a mouse out back and kept it in one of Papa's old cigar boxes laid out for trashing.

Not knowing the mouse's sex, they named it Henry and hid it underneath the bunk. Each would take turns bringing in bits of cheese and crackers snuck in from the pantry cooler, hoping Mama wouldn't notice.

"Huh, Zeke, how do we know it ain't a girl?" "Because he ain't a girl, Gabe."

"But how come?"

"Because black mice are boys," Zeke fibbed. "Henry is black."

"Ahh, you making that up? We didn't learn that in bio."

"Who cares? We're going to make this mouse a boy."

"Fine by me. If Mama finds out, she won't care if it's a boy or a girl."

Coming in from school, the twins ran into Mama. Her face scrunched, mouth tight. Right thumb and finger, holding a dead mouse by its tail.

"Right when I come into your room, this thing comes from underneath your bed. John wasn't here, so I got it myself. It ran back under there. I took off my shoe and got on my knees. That's when I found this box with bits of crackers and cheese."

Mama J breathed, calming herself, "I finally got that dern thing. Now, your turn, where is my switch?"

"You killed Henry."

Round-faced Gabe, a tad heavier than Zeke, blinked back his tears, "I don't blame you, Mama. We should've asked."

Mama's soft spot for her youngins allowed them to bury Henry down by the creek with a promise to never bring pets into the house without asking.

Remembering what happened, Mama anxiously looked around the room. "Where?"

Gabe scooted back, "Outside. It ran away outside."

I giggled, "By the way, it's Biology, not bio."

"Speaking of biology, we need to work on lessons."

"Oh, yes. Thanks for the reminder, Cece. Can you help?

"Love too."

"Make it easy work," Zeke requested.

"No need for easy. Hard work keeps you and Gabriel out of devilment. Finding creatures to bring in."

I hugged my parents. Leaned down and hugged the twins.

"No mushy," they groaned.

Cece helped me prepare for the event while Zeke and Gabe played tag out back, and Mama and Papa sipped lemonade under the row of backyard trees. The small creek behind them, where the twins caught their small critters, was at peace.

Cece pinned my thick hair in a bun, added rouge to my cheeks, and polished my lips in dark red.

"Thank you." I hugged her.

"Have a good time," she whispered as I tiptoed out the front door.

I hurried off. Turned right at the corner, putting me on the main road, leading to Baldwin-Janssen Square.

The heat tapered off, and I was grateful for comfortable birthday shoes.

I looked down on the city of Baldwin as I passed Mrs. Lucille's home, the last cottage before walking through the tunnel. Coming out on the other side put me at the door of the SugaShack. Except for tonight, men frequented the brothel, a business most Villagers and Towners disapproved of, but it wasn't illegal.

In the field beside the SugaShack, buggies sat waiting to carry villagers to work the following day.

The grocer, Mr. Jeb, owned the farm up the hill. Harry and Sam, ages nine and ten, helped tend to chores. Mrs. Jeb sold homemade pastries.

I rested at the corner in front of the church, across from the road that led to the Janssen ranch.

Recently, we welcomed the Jeb boys to school, held at the church during the week. I was the head teacher, and Cece was my assistant. Because there were few children, we taught all grades, making lessons fit the age of the students.

I reflected on the benefits of having a public school for Village children. Before then, Mr. Emanuel paid tutors to homeschool the few children living in the Village. Cece and I were among the few children homeschooled along with Arthur Brown Jr., who was now a doctor, and Nyna Levin, the owner of the SugaShack. Towners like Mirabella Janssen attended school in Baldwin.

"Only a little way to go. Get moving, E."

I picked up my pace. The dusk overshadowed my walk downhill toward the square as the moon transitioned to red. Some Villagers called it the devil's moon and stayed inside until it changed.

My family didn't fear the red moon. Our parents explained that it was part of a greater plan.

"Owe. My feet." I stepped onto the grass to cushion them, tempted to kick off my shoes. But I thought it best to keep them on as protection against hard-to-see insects, late-night critters, and poo left by wild dogs.

Despite what people thought, I saw beauty in the night, especially with the cluster of stars. It brightened the sky, making the blood moon less eerie. The stars also made the river on the right of me glitter.

On the left of the road, streetlamps brightened as the remainder of the day turned in for the night. The lamps buffed the road and reflected across the forest, made up of Spanish Moss and Coffee trees. The forest covered the grasslands below the village down to the square.

Huffing, I was tiring, hoping I was nearing the Hiding Tree to meet Mr. Emanuel, when a horse's clop, clop came up from behind. I twitched at the sound, reminding me that being out alone at night was unsafe for a Village girl.

"Hello, young lady."

Hearing the familiar voice, I turned and grinned at the man in the buggy.

"Uh, hello, sir." My happy feet anticipated riding the rest of the way to the event.

He reached across the seat, held out his hand, and helped me up next to him, "Happy Birthday, Ella."

"Thank you, Mr. Emanuel, for my beautiful gown. I'm happy for a place to wear it, even if I can't sit with Towners. This is such a wonderful surprise. "

"It won't be like that always, Ella. The day will come when everyone will remember your name." He winked. "How are things at home?"

"Papa John was okay with me coming. Not Mama."

"He's a good man, and that is why I chose him. Your mother, too."

I was puzzled by Mr. Emanuel's comment and wanted to ask him to explain, but we had arrived. He came around to the passenger side to help me down. "Thank you, sir."

"My pleasure, Ella. You will be safe here as long as you stay hidden behind this tree. Understand."

"Yes, sir."

"I'll send someone to fetch you after the ceremony. Now move along, young lady."

I hurried over to the hundred-year-old Oak named the Hiding Tree as Mr. Emanuel hopped back up into the buggy seat. Under it was a white Victorian Wicker chair, an umbrella leaned against the left arm, in case of unexpected rain.

"My goodness, look at the size of this trunk." I could barely touch the edges as I stretched out my arms and marveled at the moss hanging from tree branches halfway to the ground.

"Oops," I giggled, forgetting Mr. Emanuel. I turned around and waved, letting him know I was all right.

He tipped his hat, snapped, snapped the horse's straps, "Geddup Baby Bo," jolted forward, pulling the buggy down the cobblestone road.

Neither Papa John nor Mr. Emanuel told me what to expect.

When he left, I sat in the chair and sneaked a peek, looking around the tree trunk. My eyes widened while quickly adjusting to the brightly lit arena. "Ahhh, the square."

The only other time I saw it was at night during the Christmas Tree lighting ceremonies.

Towner and Village churches joined together to celebrate the birth of a white Jesus. A picture of Jesus with long brown hair hangs in our church. It bothered me immensely. In my visions, the Jesus I remembered had Black skin. He walked among African priests and priestesses in ancient Africa.

Looking at the stage, I cringed, reminded of the wooden sign nailed to the large oak tree. The words Hanging Tree were written in large white letters. Slave owners in the 1600s hanged a West African prince and his followers there: men, women, and children. From what I had read, Baldwin's ugly history included hanging nearly fifty thousand Africans over the two-hundred-year history of slavery in this country.

Tearing up, I shut my eyes, pushed away the horrific memories, and refocused my attention.

The sparsely furnished stage included a wooden podium with a microphone. I assumed the speaker would be Thonis Baldwin. Stairs led down in front of it where twelve ushers, six on each side, wore black tuxedos; one held a loudhailer.

The usher with the loudhailer announced, "Ushers coming down the aisles will help you to your seats. The ceremony will begin shortly."

I was guessing there were enough chairs to accommodate the nearly two hundred thousand Towners. The left front row had chairs draped in red cloth, matching the carpet runner across the front of the stage.

"My, they all look stunning, but my gown tops them all."

I stood up and held out my arm, pretending to wait for an escort. Then stood on my tiptoes, twirled, and curtsied before sitting down again.

Girls and Mamas wore shiny, laced dresses, girls in short yellow ones, and Mamas in white gowns.

Boys and papas, in suits; boys in brown, Papas in white.

As the crowd flowed through, I spotted Mr. Emanuel and Mrs. Delilah. She was dressed in red, whilst Mr. Emanuel's suit, which I just noticed was bronze like my dress. How odd, I thought. They followed a young girl, whom I believed to be

Mirabella, whom I had never met but had heard stories about.

"Huh, her dress is red and resembles mine, but mine is much prettier." I smiled.

Mama mentioned that Mrs. Delilah paid Lady Baldwin for Mirabella's custom-made birthday dress. She also said that Mrs. Delilah did not approve of Mr. Emanuel giving us gifts.

"No talking about this to anyone," Mama warned.

"Oh my." My arms and legs tingled, responding to the fair-skinned boy with loose curly hair, wearing a red suit, and following the usher. Trevor Balwin, I'd seen at the tree lighting and thought of him as handsome.

Lady Baldwin was behind him, and behind her was Thonis Baldwin, the town founder who walked with a limp. They also wore red, as did Sarah Baldwin, who followed him.

The Janssens and Baldwins filled the red-draped chairs. Once seated, an usher leaned down and spoke to Mr. Baldwin.

He stood and limped over to the stage, paused, then climbed the five steps, using a swivel-shaped wooden cane.

Tall and lanky Mr. Baldwin stood behind the podium. Held his long face and chin up, staring into the crowd. His light brown hair was tied back into a tail. When he wore it untied, I told Cece he looked like the white Jesus in the picture. She snickered but agreed.

"Heller, my friends, and family. You know me as Thonis Baldwin," the microphone vibrated. "Grand manifestation of Thonis Baldwin of 1630. I am honored to be here to officiate the joining together of two members of our legacy families to honor the covenant."

Grand manifestation of the Thonis Baldwin of 1630? I quivered inside, remembering something I couldn't quite place.

"First, allow me to apologize on behalf of the Mayor, who has taken ill."

Thonis began to question why the mayor and Emanuel never appeared at the same time. One or the other was always missing from covenant meetings or events. It started a couple of years ago. He also wondered about Emanuel's suit. The color bronze represented his African heritage. Red, however, was the color worn by legacy families during the Rites-of-Passage ceremony.

"Ye Emanuel Janssen, please take your rightful place here, so we may proceed." He extended his hand.

Emanuel headed up the stairs and stood beside Thonis.

"This momentous event is the Rites-of-Passage for Baldwin and Janssen's firstborns, now turned seventeen. As was prophesized, the first girl was born, allowing us to end the ceremonial sacrifice every seventeen years, right, Emanuel?"

Emanuel Janssen smiled.

"Your firstborn daughter, Mirabella, will marry our firstborn son, Trevor. We will bestow upon them the power that gives them the ability to see the past, present, and future. A past before there was a beginning. A present we control. A future that belongs to him. What makes us who we are and why our God Apollyon sees fit to give us eternal life."

I began to feel dizzy. An Apollyon God? I hadn't heard God referenced as such. Perhaps it was how the Towners referenced their God. As in ancient Africa and according to us African descendants, the creator or God was Semperian, all-knowing, with no beginning or end. Those of us who were awakened practice in secret. Passed down through generations, it was the only African spiritualism not lost, stolen, or banned on Earth. Banning it forced Africans to succumb to organized European-based religions. Those of us awakened protected the Knowledge of Semperian as the ultimate source in the universe.

"Their union gives us life immortal for all eternity. No longer fearing the yellow death cursed upon us."

Thonis stepped around the podium, closer to the edge of the stage. Emanuel took two steps to the right.

"Will the two of you come to the stage?"

Mirabella jumped up, grinning. Turned to her proud Mummy, ignoring Suanne and Sara's annoyed glares.

With less enthusiasm, Trevor stood ready to go next when his mother laid her hand on his upper back and whispered, "All will be well, Timmy."

Trevor gave his mother a puzzling look as he stood next to giddy Mirabella, who was itching to touch him. The strong scent of lilac she wore nauseated him, and he quickly blocked its intent.

The two stood on the stage between Emanuel and Thonis. Thonis raised his cane, signaling to the Towners.

"Everyone, stand and lock hands with the person next to you. The person on each end of a row, please lock hands with the person across the aisle, keeping your hands locked during the ceremony."

Mirabella and Trevor locked hands, and so did their families in the front row.

Emanuel held up his two palms, and the town founder held up the palm of one hand and the crane.

"Complete silence and all eyes closed."

I held onto the chair, hoping not to faint. A familiar faint scent of lilac invaded the air around me. I forced my eyes to stay awake as my inner guard kicked in.

The crowd at the event remained quiet, with only the sound of whistling wind.

Thonis used the tip of his cane to draw a circle around the couple.

"Now for the covenant prayer."

I slid down the chair and fell to the ground. Above me, ghostly faces of African children watched. It took me back to a yesteryear, traveling through a darkened night with a blood moon and children whispering.

"My children. Rites-of-Passage is your legacy, the bond that binds us. This covenant we made to save our town, to stop the unfair curse of a plague that destroyed all of us. No new generations born, only ghosts of the past made to wander."

Trees swayed, the wind howled.

Thonis forced his words above the sound of the elements, "He is angry, cursing us again and again, wanting vengeance." We will know, no peace lest the blood of he and his followers stay imprisoned in darkness for eternity. Never allowing their light to heal the blood of their bastard-born heir, bonded to my firstborn, given as sacrifices in his name, Apollyon Diabolus. It's he who gives us immortality through the lives of two boys who grew up as protectors of Baldwin, as witnessed beneath the blood moon."

The wind whistled as Thonis's thundering voice softened, "We, the Baldwins and the Janssens, pledge our blood inside this covenant we pass on to our children. This power comes with privilege and honor. Empowering you to rule with dominion over all life here, walking among us as gods. The vision to see all and the choice to live immortally is yours and ours, reducing one to mortality if you must. You pledge to keep our town alive and prosperous, never dishonoring the sins of our fathers."

The ground trembled, the wind howled, and thunder erupted, lighting the sky. The powerful magic appeared as a gold and yellow ball of light swirling inside their palms.

Thonis released his magic, sending it toward Trevor, who jolted when feeling the magic enter his body.

Emanuel's power, meant for Mirabella, he redirected toward the Hiding Tree. The magic ball shot through the air…

I didn't see what tased me as my body spasmed. Suffocating, I gasped for air.

The children above me chanted umaya, umaya, umaya as my eyes, drowning in tears, closed, silencing my mind to only the light in my soul.

Thundering. Stopped. Wind. Stopped. Forced back into the elements as stars hid. The moon trembled.

Thonis opened his eyes abruptly. His face hardened, watching towners drop their hands, coming out of the trance. He looked as bewildered as they.

Emanuel Janssen was calm and appeared unaware of what was happening.

Trevor's red suit had changed to gold, signifying he had been granted the power. He looked at Mirabella in the red dress she came in. Frantic, she ran to Mummy.

Trevor returned to his seat beside Lady Baldwin, who grabbed his hand. Although smiling inside, she feared the inevitable. *Mortality may be better for us all, she thought.*

The Towners' angry eyes followed Mirabella, who was shivering and shaking, face pressed into her Mum's chest.

"It's you." Thonis pointed to the Janssen girl. "You have threatened the covenant. You are a lie, not the firstborn child of the Janssen family. December 21, we will perish unless this lie is made whole."

Delilah looked up at the stage. Avoiding Thonis's wrath, her eyes moved to her husband.

Emanuel stood stoically, locking his eyes with hers.

The storm in Delilah's eyes through angry tears asked, "What have you done?

My eyes blinked open to the quiet but peaceful darkness. The warm air blanketed my body, cushioned by soft grass. My chest bumped up and down, breathing in the sweetness of oak and cedar.

"Uh, hello." My voice echoed. "Where am I? I need to get home."

"Don't be afraid," a male voice whispered. "You haven't met me, but I'm a friend."

"Show yourself. Where am I?"

"Hello Emanuella, my name is Samuel. We're inside the Hiding Tree."

Chapter 4

The One Who Came After
68 days to solstice
2 months, 7 days

Day 14 October 1925
Janssen Ranch Event Day After

Mirabella

Early birds sang as they cruised the sky above our ranch. I hated the sound of them as much as I hated the rising sun.

My bedroom faced the front, overlooking five acres of plush green meadows. Although my curtains kept the sunlight out, I was awakened by the rooster's cock-a-doodle-doo, chickens clucking, pigs oinking, and cows mooing. Village ranch hands hollered at Village boys, "Go fetch dem eggs as I told you. Slop doze dern hogs."

As the largest in Baldwin County, our ranch grew and sold corn, lima beans, lettuce, tomatoes, cucumbers, and okra to Towners and the county's close-in southern cities. Fresh fruits came in peaches, plums, pears, an assortment of melons, and nuts of peanuts, walnuts, and pecans. Heifers and goats gave off good milk. Chickens laid plentiful eggs and were slaughtered and plucked along with butchered cows and hogs.

The best was saved for our cook, Mrs. Josephine. She would cook family favorites like beef stew and fried chicken for Sunday dinners with homemade desserts.

In the back of our estate, an additional thirty acres extended to the forest of Spanish Moss and Tobacco trees. We should be grateful for our prosperity and nature's pleasantries, Daddy always said. But a farm full of animals and Villagers running wild was not what I called a pleasure.

In the largest of the two stables, six of Daddy's premium horses stayed. He gifted me one when I turned sixteen. I didn't care much to give her a name, so Mama named her Mira. Short for Mirabella.

Hmpf. I didn't much like a horse having my name, but I tried to attend to the dumb animal. I rode her only twice within the first year because I couldn't stand going inside the barn. It stunk, and the hay made me sneeze.

The Hand told me, "That's the way a horse barn smells. Nothin' can be done even when we clean it."

I looked at the Hand, a Villager who spoke improper English. Ignorance made me angry.

"Happy to bring her to ya, Miss Mirabella."

It didn't help. Mira's coat took on the rotten stench of the outdoors, like the Hand. That was the last time I visited the stalls.

That Hand cared for and rode Mira to give her exercise. Probably set up the whole thing so he could have her.

I told Mummy, and she admonished him. Daddy scolded her for doing it, calling me spoiled and unappreciative. I didn't care much for Daddy after that.

After what happened at the Rites of Passage, I reveled in my darkness and waited for my furry friend. I named it Pet. It attached itself to my window ledge on my thirteenth birthday.

I was curious about the black furry ball the size of my fist and thought, "Probably one of those silly animals that run up and down the trees."

I banged on the window to scare it away, but it sat motionless. Ignoring it made the thing eventually disappear, but it reemerged two days later. As if showing off, it sprouted tiny claw-like teeth around its body, rolled over, and exposed its flesh underbelly. Quite grotesque, but I was unafraid.

I opened the window, "Come on in, little one."

We had an instant connection, unlike with Mira. The ball attached to my arm. What felt like sucking tickled, sending a sensual sensation throughout my body. It calmed me and made me happy.

Pet remained invisible in my room. It showed when I needed it like yester-night. I refused Mum's efforts to console me and pulled the pink bedspread over me after getting into bed fully dressed. Releasing angry tears, I hissed and growled, wanting to hurt Daddy for what he'd done and Mummy for her failure.

So, I did what the lady taught me. The one who came to tell me stories when I was a little girl. I called Pet and imagined us falling into a field of purple lilacs. Moments later, we vanished.

We dropped into a field of thousands of lilacs. They covered my nakedness as I walked, inhaled, and tasted them.

Up near a hill, seven-foot-tall lilac knight trees awaited my arrival.

Time I calmed my guests, I said aloud, "My goodness, all that noise. Must be hungry."

I walked through the lilac archway. On the other side, three thirty-foot pythons thrashed around inside a twenty-five-foot-wide, six-foot-tall glass cage. I laughed at two of the snakes fighting. The brown-spotted one smacked the lime-green one against the cage. The yellow python stayed curled up in the corner.

"If only you two had enough gumption to kill my Daddy."

The thirty-foot pythons had grown considerably in the past ten years. From slithering human children, frightening Towner children in the schoolyard, to grieving parents finding them in their children's beds.

Cousins Damon, Kathy, and Jonathan could be useful, so I kept them as pets. Wanted them to torture and kill, but only the yellow serpent, Kathy, complied. She practiced on unsuspecting Towner children. Village children were untouchable at the time, but the lady told me she knew how to get to them and would teach me how one day.

"I had one of the Hands catch some fish from the lake for you, Kathy, since you've been most willing. Your cowardly cousins only scare people; that's not enough. What do you have to say for yourselves? I am not in the mood for simpletons." I hollered at Damon, the brown snake, and Jonathan, the lime green one, who flickered their tongues while fleeing and curling up in a corner.

Kathy moved forward, "I promised I would do what you asked, there is no need to bother with them. Please let them go."

"Well, aren't you ungrateful. I brought you fish, and all you do is beg for mercy." Stomping my feet in irritation, I hollered, "No fish for you. You can eat the handful of crickets I brought for the other two."

I pulled a jar of live crickets from underneath the cage and dumped them inside. Hardly enough for the three, but they sucked up what they could before the crickets got away.

Kathy allowed her cousins to share the small meal. While she watched, tears formed but never fell. She was no longer human.

"I'll give you another chance to make good, Kathy. I will let you know what that is and when."

I had to move cautiously, otherwise, the elderly woman with white hair would admonish me.

"Your powers are to remain inconspicuous. Use lilac when necessary. No one but you should understand the depth of its magic."

On my way back through the archway, I promised, "One day, Daddy, one day."

When I returned to my room, I heard Mummy shouting at Daddy about Baldwin Town being in danger of losing its rebirth. The Legacy Council demanded the whereabouts of the firstborn Daughter before the solstice.

I began to realize there was more than what Mummy told me about my birthright. My memories of not being alone in her womb were real.

"The only one I can trust is the elder woman. I called to her, hoping she'd come soon."

Mummy revealed to me that important men of Baldwin made up the Legacy Council: Thonis Baldwin, Daddy, Mayor Lazarus Shipley, and eight additional unnamed men elected to serve in secret every seventeen years.

The unidentified members of the council managed the sacrifices for the Blood Covenant. The Covenant guaranteed immortality for Towners from the blood of slain and deceased Africans.

"The Council must rectify what happened, or we will return to ashes. You and Thonis will be sent to the lake of fire."

Emanuel Janssen

As prophesized, I transferred the power to my firstborn Daughter, the rightful heir.

From her beginning, my duty was to guard her until the final ceremony on solstice. Through the power of Semperian, I wrapped her in a protective shield at birth. Semperian assigned Guardian Samuel, not of that world, to protect her from the dark forces, including Apollyon Diabolos, its demon daughter, witch Luna, and Delilah, who protected Mirabella.

As I stood before the new moon, I declared allegiance to the Semperian people. In the Bambara language of Mali, West Africa, "Umaya, umaya, umaya. An ye Afirikikaw ye. A bangeli bɛ fanga di an ma ni yeelen ye walasa ka boli dibi la u y'an bila kaso la. An bɛna bonya da a kan, den fɔlɔ min ka bangeko ye an ka ciyɛn ye. Semperian b'an lakana, ka mɔgɔ minnu ja gelɛya k'a ka kojugu kɛ, a bɛ olu tiɲɛ. Umaya, umaya, umaya. [We are Original Africans. Her birth empowers us with light to flee from the darkness they have imprisoned us. We will pay homage to her, the firstborn whose birthright is our legacy. Semperian keeps us safe, destroying those who. dare cause her harm]."

Chapter 5

The One Who Came Before
68 days to solstice
2 months, 7 days

Day 14 October 1925
Crumley House Day After Event

Papa John dropped Mama J at the Janssen ranch. The mess inside, she was prepared for.

"I am nearing my time and rest. I will speak with our eldest. See you soon, Josephine."

Emanuella
School was to begin in three hours, but I woke up early after our parents left.

I grabbed hold of the bed's edges to get my bearings. My mind was foggy about how and when I returned home.

A warm chill settled inside me as I thought about yesternight. Remembering bits and pieces: the Victorian setting made for me beneath the Hiding Tree. The staging area with Towners dressed in white gowns and suits. Reminded me of how people dressed at a baptism or christening.

"Samuel? Who's Samuel?" I threw back the covers. I was wearing my pajamas, and my dress hung in the closet. "Thank you sissy."

6:30 a.m.

A knock at the door.

I cracked it open, guessing who'd be on the other side.

"Morning, Papa."

He smiled impishly, "Good morning, Daughter. A beautiful, warm morning for a meeting in the garden. See if we got any new buds."

I kissed his cheek and nodded, "See you soon."

I wondered about Papa wanting to meet with me in the garden before school. If it were a serious matter, talking was best outside in the garden he created many years ago. Over the years, he tamed it to regularly produce bountiful fruits, vegetables, and flowers.

Not long ago, we spoke about how my life would change. I would be given a special gift and would understand more about that power when the time was ripe. He laughed heartily when using gardening as a metaphor to talk about what was to come.

"Don't tell Mama about our conversation. She worries."

I didn't want Mama to worry or be upset by Mr. Emanuel's gift-giving. But we agreed it would be disrespectful to say no to his generosity.

Before meeting in the garden, I bathed and dressed in a hazel-colored, mid-length linen skirt, blouse, and brown loafers.

Papa John faced the garden, talking to the cabbage and lettuce, "Yes, ladies, y'all are looking mighty fine for more picking."

"Don't let Mama hear you," I teased.

He greeted me, his eyes staring into mine, "There's my beautiful Daughter."

I looked into his eyes, which reminded me of Mr. Emanuel.

Papa grabbed my hand and placed it inside his arm. We walked down the edge of the garden.

"Little ladies are sprouting," he pointed at the vegetables. "We'll have tasty vegetables for a garden salad."

"And Mama's boiled cabbage and okra with ripe tomatoes for stewing."

"Flavored with salt pork."

We gleefully shared about Mama's cooking. Loved her for making wonderful fresh dishes for the family, despite her busy schedule at the Janssen ranch.

Mirabella and Delilah took up a lot of their workers' time, despite Mirabella hating the Villagers. Mama and Lucille were the only two cooks they appreciated. Mama J especially.

Papa's garden gave up vegetables all year, and he shared them with the Villagers. Always with a twinkle and curious smile, he'd say he learned his gardening tricks from the Janssens' gardener, Mosiah.

Mosiah worked for the Janssens's for going on twenty years and nearing eighty in true age, but looked no day over forty. He sprang into action each day, except for Sundays, spewing his love into the flower patches and garden that peaked brightly all year round. Like Papa's, quite magical.

We walked to the end of the garden, admiring the watermelon and cantaloupe waiting to blossom shortly.

Papa raised his brows, a playfulness in his smile, "How was your evening? Emanuel Janssen drove you?"

I nodded, "I can't remember much of anything, but what I felt was exhilarating. And a name I'd since forgotten. We met, but I can't recall what he looked like."

Papa held both my hands as he moved close enough to speak slightly above a whisper, "Emanuella Crumley, I enjoyed being your father. For seventeen years, you have given me joy. It's time to spread your wings." He let go and wiggled his fingers upward, "Regardless of where I am with you."

I lowered my eyes to hide the sadness I felt and hugged him.

Papa John lowered his lips to my ear and whispered. Briefly disturbing a memory long since passed. "Umaya. Umaya. Umaya. We are the original Africans. U geboorte bemagtig ons met die lig, bevry ons van die duisternis wat ons gevange geneem het. Ons groet u, die eersgeborene wie se geboortereg ons erfenis is. Mag die gees jou goed hou, almal wat waag, vernietig veroorsaak dat jy skade het. [Umaya. Umaya. Umaya. Your birth empowers us with the light, freeing us from the darkness that imprisoned us. We pay homage to you, the firstborn whose birthright is our legacy. May the spirit keep you well, destroying all those who dare cause you harm.]"

15th day of October 1925

A high-pitched wail awakened Cece and me.

"Mama," Cece said nervously.

I knew what had happened and grabbed Cece's hand.

We rushed into our parents' bedroom. The boys were beside Mama, weeping softly, Gabe's right hand on her shoulder. Papa's eyes closed as he rested peacefully beneath the bed quilt. Mama's hand atop his.

Smoke invaded the air, smelling like the fancy cigars Mr. Emanuel gave Papa for smoking on the back porch after the workday.

The aroma slowly faded as Papa's spirit ascended.

Chapter 6

Papa John Crumley Day
65 days to solstice
2 months, 4 days

Day 17 October 1925
Saturday in Village Africa

Emanuella

Towners and Villagers came to honor Papa John Crumley.

Guests packed the inside of the church with visitors overflowing outside, sitting in chairs along the side and in the back churchyard.

A loud megaphone, built up near the steeple, and the church bell were used, making John Crumley's sendoff that of a king. And he was to the Villagers and highly regarded among the Towners.

On rare occasions, Towners and Villagers gathered together. Like at the Square for the annual Founders' Day picnic in July, and the Christmas Tree Lighting. At those segregated events, the Baldwins, Janssens, and Mayor Shipley ingratiated themselves among the attendees.

Today, Mayor Shipley couldn't attend but sent his regards through Mr. Emanuel, and his house butler, Hiram, assisted.

The church elders and Papa's friends organized the funeral. They picked a variety of flowers from the Janssen and Baldwin gardens: Hydrangeas, Magnolias, and Camellias, adding in Pine and Dogwood shrubbery. The flowers covered the inside front and side walls down the outer walkway and the arch behind Papa's open casket. Laid around it, branches from the weeping willow tree. The botanical energy of sweet, citrus, and floral helped turn saddened hearts into joy.

Jeremiah, the Village pastor, arrived in his long black robe, a red bible tucked under his armpit. He'd carried it with him for the twenty years he'd been pastor. At a height of only five feet two, Pastor Jeremiah's towering voice during Sunday sermons preached the word he claimed came directly from God. The pastor's soft, round, white hair and smooth skin showed no signs of aging, although he was in his seventies.

As he made his way through the crowd, Pastor Jeremiah greeted the visitors, "Thank you for coming."

Inside the church, the Pastor stopped and inhaled the cool air. With his hanky, he dabbed away the dribbles of sweat from his forehead, then walked down the aisle to the front of the church, acknowledging seated guests along the way.

At the front row, he greeted my family, starting with Mama Josephine in a black two-piece suit and a Fascinator Hat with netting covering her eyes. Zeke, Gabe, Cece, and me sitting beside Mr. Emanuel. Mrs. Delilah, but no Mirabella; Lady Baldwin and Thonis Baldwin; he wore his hair down like Jesus in the picture. Sara and Trevor.

Lucille sat in the second pew behind Mama. Tapped her shoulder and whispered words of sympathy for her ears only.

The Village choir sang after a brief welcome. Elder Ms. Claudette, who taught Sunday school, directed the choir. They sang Swing Low, Sweet Chariot, Going Up Yonder, and Gunna Lay Down My Burden.

Cece pinched me as Pastor Jeremiah strolled to the podium. On Sundays, he preached, keeping most folks in church for two hours. Our family usually sat in the back and left after the first.

"Enough praising the Lord for one day," Papa John would whisper.

On occasion, Mama stayed behind with Lucille to be polite.

"Thank you, sister Claudette, and the Village choir, for the beautiful medley. I heard John Crumley tapping his feet along with the Lord right from heaven."

The crowd chuckled.

"Please keep his family in your prayers. Church, say Amen."

"Amen," said the church.

Pastor Jeremiah began the sermon, "Who was this man we knew as John Crumley? He was a devoted husband, father, and friend. A man whom God sent with his loving wife, Josephine, all the way from Chicago and before their first child.

In Chicago, John learned woodworking from an African Woodsmith. At twenty-five, he became smitten with a young lady named Josephine Jones."

The audience chuckled.

"Josephine worked in a colored café in South Chicago. John visited regularly to enjoy her company and fried chicken."

The crowd laughed warmly. Mr. Emanuel served Mama J's chicken at Founders' Day picnics. She helped fry it up and provided the ingredients to trusted cooks.

"Emanuel Janssen invited John and his new wife, Josephine to Baldwin to help with his family. Once here, John used his skills to help build Village Africa."

The church applauded.

"With God's hands, John created masterful wood pieces. Our admiration for him will live on. May he rest in peace with God and his angels."

Mr. Emanuel squeezed my hand, his eyes smiled.

"Thank you." I mouthed.

Mr. Emanuel paid for Papa John's funeral, his pine casket, and his headstone. Made sure Papa's body was untouched by Dr. Wolstein's embalming ritual.

After the Funeral.

Delilah Janssen left, but Mr. Emanuel stepped in line with us in front, followed by Towners and Villagers. The ten-minute walk to the burial site uphill from the church drummed with the pattering of thousands of feet.

We buried Papa underneath a thick oak tree. The diggers threw the last dirt on top of the casket and padded it tight. Four men lifted the large headstone from the wagon and placed it at the head of the grave. Secured it with rope and poured cement around the bottom.

Memories overwhelmed me. Before I became a teacher, I traveled with Papa in our six-seat horse and covered buggy, which Mr. Emanuel gifted us after my birth. He got up early in the morning to transport workers to Baldwin town and home, saving them the ten-mile journey. Getting ready to ride, Papa would grab the whips—snap snapped ordering Midnight the Black horse to, "Geddup."

I whispered, "Midnight and I will miss riding with you, Papa. Cece and I will drive Mama around. The boys told me you already taught them to drive while out in the woods. Mama doesn't know." I grinned.

Pastor Jeremiah spoke, "We have children passing out flowers, retrieved from our hall. We thank the Janssens and Baldwins for providing them for John's send-off. The Crumley family,

Ms. Lucille, the Baldwin, and the Janssen families will start us off. Say your final words or prayer before dropping the follow atop John Crumley's grave."

We stepped forward.

Pastor Jeremiah said, "Please bow your heads for the Lord's prayer.

Heads bowed.

"Our Father, in heaven, hallowed be thy name…"

Then, one by one, we said our goodbyes.

"John, the good lord got you in his hands now."

"Bye, papa, I will be the man around the house."

"Wish you didn't have to go. Zeke is already trying to boss me."

"Papa, I will stay strong and help Mama. I know you are nearby. Your youngest daughter loves you."

"Bye, Papa, see you soon. I will remember our talks."

"John, you're gone for a short while, but I will be expecting you for supper before the solstice. I plan to make a chocolate cake, especially for you."

"My friend, you've done your part. Rest for now because we have much more to do. Let me know if you need more cigars."

The final flower was placed, and the attendees proceeded down the hill.

Peace filled the air with a final *puff, puff* of sweet smoke. Umaya. See you soon.

Mirabella

Mummy asked me to go to the funeral. She angered me when she came in unannounced, entering through the door used by maids, who cleaned and ran my bath. "Mum coming through the maids' entry is beneath you. You are supposed to be Lady of the Manor. It's bad enough you visit the farmhands and house domestics on holidays, giving gifts. So, the answer is no. I prefer not sulking over a family I care little about."

Mum left. So annoyed, she almost slammed my door. I didn't like that and hollered, "Watch it, Mummy."

John Crumley didn't like me. He barely spoke, squinting his eyes when he did. I tolerated Josephine for her cooking and had no desire to meet their eldest daughter. But I was curious about her birthday and age being the same as mine.

I did enjoy looking at Lucille's son, a nice-looking African man. Made me feel gooey inside like after a feeding with Pet. Dr. Arthur Brown didn't live in the Village but had a medical practice in Mobile. Quite sophisticated compared to his Village Mum, who spoke ignorantly. Can't fathom him being raised by her.

The doctor came to check on Mummy and me when we got sick with a cold. A couple of times, I faked being ill, and Mummy summoned him.

He'd do a thorough check-up. Laid his hand on my head, checked my heartbeat above my breast, and my pulse. Pressed my tummy if I claimed to have stomach pain, and my legs, calves, and feet. It tickled, so faking numbness no longer worked.

Daddy wised up and told Mummy, "Do not call Dr. Brown before checking with me."

"Ugh." Daddy spoiled my fun, and I never understood why he cared. Flirting with Dr. Brown was all I would do because I was promised to Trevor Baldwin.

Mummy spoke to me through the door, which I now kept locked, "Josephine won't be in for a few days, so Lucille will bring in temporary help from the Village."

I figured Josephine would play the grieving widow to get out of doing work.

"Thought you should know. I know how you prefer Josephine's cooking, but we will make do."

Mum told me Daddy paid for the funeral. He probably checked in on them, too, giving them what they needed. Villagers' meager wages were no fault of the Towners. That was the way things were in Baldwin.

Daddy did not share my and Mum's sentiments. He even suggested packaging and selling Josephine's chicken to generate additional income for the family. Josephine refused the offer. He increased her wages instead and against Mummy's wishes.

I lit the lamp on my nightstand, lighting the room a bit. I didn't want to chase away the shadow figures across my walls and ceiling. Among them, Pet waited patiently, hoping to have a feeding soon.

I sat on the wool rug spread across the floor's middle. Steepled my legs, wrapped my arms around, and held them tight to my chest. Rocked and hummed a tune I remembered while inside Mummy's womb. Agitated and confused because of having to share space with a light being, shocking my inner darkness.

To her, I sang, "Ticktock, ticktock, the countdown has begun, ticktock, ticktock, find the one who came before, ticktock, ticktock, before the final tock, and dead before the solstice moon."

Tap, tap, tap at the door.

"Not again!"

My bathroom door opened. I forgot to lock it!

Mummy holding a lit candle, ruining my mood, chasing away the shadows.

"My darling. Are you all right? You haven't touched any of your favorite foods, Lucille has been cooking, especially for you. Breakfast, lunch, and supper with crumpets and warm milk in between. Dear?"

My body quivered as my veins pumped, pulsating up and down my skin. Stupid Mummy. I wanted to snap her neck.

Holding the candle to see me closely, Mummy's voice trembled, "You do not look well."

I growled, and Mum stumbled back through the entrance and shut the door.

My body calmed as I breathed in, and my shadow friends returned.

I got up to stretch and saw my reflection in the mirror. My fair skin and face had turned smoky gray, brows thickened. My golden hair lost its luster, was ratted, and knotted.

I grinned, showing teeth tainted red, dropping spits of red ooze. I liked what I saw and expounded, "My strength comes from my true father. Together, we will spill her blood and his."

The Lake of Fire sent up a thick cloud of smoke, suffocating my spirit as it reminded me of my true home with him. In the Third Hell.

Chapter 7

Before and After Births
57 days until solstice
1 month, 26 days

Day 25 October 1925
Because She Insisted

Emanuella

Returning to work after a week, Mama walked the four miles, wanting the exercise. I accompanied her.

We took the back road. No walking down the main street, crossing over to the private road from the church. It led to the Janssen ranch and would have saved a mile. But Mama wanted to avoid the SugaShack.

"I stay clear of Luciferno's playground unless I have to," Mama said, crinkling her face.

Luciferno? Her comment made me curious, but I didn't ask for clarification.

The back road took us near Lake Baldwin, located on the other side of the hill and dark forest. The river, running through Baldwin and the village, ended up at the mouth of that Lake. The lake was the only large body of water close enough for children to play. But dangerous for African children.

According to myth, Lake Baldwin lured African children there, promising them a treasure of pearls hidden at the bottom of its cave. Villagers called it the Lake of Sacrifice and warned children to stay clear because of what happened there decades ago.

Most disturbing was the tale about a witch.

Witch Luna wandered the grounds, hiding inside the cave until children came to play. Described as an elderly African woman who practiced dark magic straight from hell, God threw Luna out of heaven because of her devil's work.

Occasionally, children visited accompanied by an older sibling. If true, the lake only preferred younger children, so they returned with their siblings unharmed.

Cece and I took Gabe and Zeke once. While there, I warned sissy about the potential danger and to be on guard. The appearance of beauty couldn't hide the dark energy I sensed.

Mama agreed and asked that we keep Zeke and Gabe away from the Lake. Then commented, "Witch or not, Luna, don't scare me."

This was my first visit to the Janssen ranch. Out front, the staff offered us lemonade when we arrived. None for Mama, but I graciously accepted.

Drinking it, cooled me down.

"Well now, how was the walk over? Quite warm for October." Mr. Emanuel raised his brow at me.

"Long. Drummed up a sweat." I said.

Mama shrugged, "Four miles of walking ain't long, good for the heart."

Mirabella

"Voices? Josephine and…" I jumped from bed, stomped, stomped barefoot over to the window. Cracked the curtain, and looked down, but a flash of light blinded me. Sharp shards attacked, pricking my body, causing droplets of blood on my arms, but they quickly disappeared.

"Owe, where did that come from?"

I stepped back from the window and rubbed my eyes.

No longer blinded, I went back to the window.

A girl with Josephine reached over and touched Black Bo Baby. The male offspring of Daddy's now-dead mare, Black Bo. Named after the Indian who sold Bo to him. Daddy favored and protected that horse and was the only one who rode him like his offspring.

The girl petted the mare as the sunlight picked up her skin color as black as his.

"Huh, that damn horse kicks up a scream if I go near it."

Papa's deep concern for the Crumley family annoyed me more than it did Mummy. The gathering below made me angry, and Daddy's wicked smile made my body tense as I struggled to hold onto my anger.

"I must speak to Mummy."

Emanuella

"Thank you again for helping with John's funeral and burial arrangements."

"John Crumley was a good man and dear friend. He built fine cabinetry in my house and elsewhere. His work is in every home in Baldwin, and he helped me build Village Africa. I couldn't have done any of that without him."

Mr. Emanuel whistled loudly. Waved at a brown-skin boy by the stalls, a few gallops from us.

The boy placed the bucket and mop against the barn. Straightened his cap, suspenders up over his shoulders—snap. Brown khakis tucked inside thick black boots.

He *plunk, plunked* across the field.

Up close, I admired his golden face, long brown locs, and dimpled smile.

"Yes, sir, Mr. Janssen."

"Samuel, say hello to Mrs. Crumley and her daughter Ella." Mr. Emanuel handed him the mare's straps.

"Hello, Mrs. Crumley. Miss Ella."

He locked his walnut-shaped, hazel eyes on mine, his energy familiar, even his name.

Bashful, I lowered my head.

"Samuel, I need you as transport for the Crumley family. Josephine, I'll hold Midnight and the buggy for now until things settle."

"Happy to do so, sir."

Mama wanted to refuse but accepted the generosity.

"If you ladies will excuse me, Bo needs a feeding." Samuel tipped his hat and then led the horse back to the stalls.

Mr. Emanuel gestured to Mama and me to join him inside.

The house butler greeted us, "Welcome back, Josephine."

My eyes went directly to the silver chandelier. It was massive, like the foyer with marbled floors.

"Thank you, Jim, for helping out at the church."

"My pleasure. John was one of my closest friends."

"And how are you, Miss Emanuella? First time here at the ranch?"

I was staring at the grand oak staircase with wide steps. "I'm well, thank you."

"Ella, if you look up at the top of the landing, that painting is a rendition of the Songhai-Mali fortress in 1600s

West Africa. Our history documents a robust partnership that outshines today's world."

"Beautiful. By the way, the students love learning from the pictorial books of West Africa, you gave us. I recognized the symbols on the walls. They are carved into some of the pyramids and fortresses."

I thought of how those symbols replicated the one barely visible beneath my chin. A half-moon with a tiny star in its center.

"Good to hear the children are in good hands." He winked.

Mr. Emanuel also gave me a copy of the: Knowledge of Semperian. A book of Origins dating back centuries. The cover was wrapped in Gold lambskin with the words Our Truth written in bronze lettering across the front. The inside pages, made from papyrus paper, had introductory text on the first page that said, "We are the original people. Africans. Our true history leads back to Semperian. Heed these words. Allowing ignorance would mean a life of damnation and an enslaved mind."

Suddenly, my heart tightened in an unfriendly way.

Mama J acknowledged the incoming visitor, "Good midmorning, Mrs. Janssen."

Delilah Janssen and Mirabella were hugged arm and arm, coming down the stairs step, step, step. Stop.

Mirabella looked over at me.

I inhaled and exhaled.

Mr. Emanuel stepped between us and turned to me. His energy calmed me.

Turned back around and greeted them.

Mrs. Janssen wore her hair pulled back in a bun and dressed in a long-sleeved, ankle-length brown chiffon dress. Mirabella was in a gray dress with white lace around the neckline and puffed sleeves to the elbow. Her curly blonde-brown hair locs, made fresh, draped over her shoulders.

"I see you feeling better," Mama empathized.

"Yes, much stronger."

Mr. Emanuel kissed Delilah's cheek and Mirabella's forehead, "Alas, back among the living."

Mrs. Delilah looked at Mr. Emanuel sternly, but he ignored her.

"I guess." She answered, puckering out her lips.

"Josephine, again, accept our condolences. It was a lovely service."

"Thank you for your kindness."

Thanking Mrs. Delilah for what Mr. Emanuel did for Papa John annoyed me. I blamed her for Mama coming back so soon to please Mirabella. She preferred Mama's cooking, although she didn't mind Lucille's.

"I thought it would cheer up our daughter if you came back to cook for us." Delilah gently squeezed her daughter's arm.

"Mrs. Josephine, did Mummy mention we would like Buttermilk Fried Chicken and cornbread for dinner?"

"What Josephine decides will be fine with this family," said Mr. Emanuel.

"I'd best move on to the kitchen and get started. Come along, Emanuella."

"No, wait. I could use her help with picking up my room."

Mirabella stepped around Mama. Her smell like rotten lilacs, made me nauseous.

"In case you didn't know, Mirabella, I am a schoolteacher. Not a domestic unless Mama needs my help."

"Emanuella Crumley, please apologize and help Miss Mirabella."

"That won't be necessary. The handmaids are tidying up for Mirabella since she's seen fit to leave her room."

Mirabella growled and slammed her fists to her waist. Her lips quivering, she turned and stomped up the steps.

Mrs. Delilah glared at me, "You need to mind your place."

I shrugged. I was in no mood for their lack of empathy and pettiness.

She pivoted, lifted the sides of her dress, stomped stomped up the steps behind Mirabella.

Mama opened her mouth to scold, but Mr. Emanuel touched her shoulder.

"Ella is not at fault here, and you will not punish her, Josephine."

"Yes, sir, Mr. Janssen."

"Very good, then. Ella, please go find Samuel. Have him show you around the meadows. Enjoy the sun and fresh air. Josephine will have plenty of help."

"Thank you, Mr. Emanuel."

Avoiding Mama's frown, I hurried past her and out the front door.

Emanuella

I used my hand to shield against the bright sun. It softened to a hum around Samuel, who was standing beside Mr. Emanuel's buggy pulled by Baby Bo.

Mr. Emanuel must've arranged the outing. The thought of riding with Samuel tickled me inside.

Samuel extended his hand and helped me up into the buggy seat before taking the reins.

"I thought we'd take a ride down to the lake and enjoy the remainder of this lovely day. Between the two of us, we can banish an old witch." He grinned.

I nodded, "I'm up for it. Nothing to fear."

"Geddup Bo." The buggy jolted forward.

Riding with Samuel felt different than being around other boys in the Village like York. He was a year older than me. York once helped at the school and assisted Papa John while learning cabinetry. York now worked in a woodshop in Mobile. Mr. Emanuel put in a good word on Papa's behalf.

Polite and a gentleman like Samuel, York didn't make me giddy. A handsome and muscular fellow with dark skin, he boasted about his tough-to-comb kinky hair.

"Mama says God gave me these thick naps, so I should love on them and not worry about what folks say." York laughed. "And that means you, too, Miss Emanuella." He teased.

Twice, he and I strolled along the creek between home and Baldwin. On one occasion, York tried to kiss me, but I quickly offered him my hand.

I fell out of favor with him, and he chose another Village girl who was more amenable to his advances. They ended up marrying, and she moved with him to Mobile.

The buggy jumped into a jerk-wobble as Bo picked up speed. The wind swooshed by, cooling the suffocating heat as we rode through the field, over the hill, and down toward the lake.

It was exhilarating, bumping along the dirt road, winding through the dense forest. I imagined children laughing, the patter of their feet, running alongside the carriage and Bo's hoofs, hastening through to the forest end.

Samuel beamed, and his eyeballs glistened each time the sun peeked through the tall trees.

"Hold on," he alerted before Bo sped up.

I held onto the seat.

Samuel snapped the straps, "Geddup Bo."

Inside the lake's mouth, he halted the buggy near the sand and stroked the horse, "Good boy."

Jumped down and ran over to me. I scooted to the buggy floor, feet over the edge, and Samuel helped me down. I was glad I dressed for the outing in a pair of ankle-length brown baggies and loafers. I kicked them off and carried them as we walked beyond the grass onto the warm sand.

We stopped near the log used for sitting, but decided to stand.

It was eerily quiet, except for nature's offerings within the bows of the mystical lake. Like gawking geese flying high above, and colorful wood ducks wading through the gurgling water sprinkled with sunbeams.

Samuel was quiet, no longer chatting like on the ride over. Somber even.

I followed his gaze as he looked up toward the crown of the lake, the cave. Children once dared to search for pearls at the cave's bottom. I swear I heard their screams echoing from inside, "Help us. Please, help us."

I strained my ear to listen.

"Help us. Please, help us."

I grabbed Samuel's arm. "Children are inside the cave, don't you hear them screaming?"

Samuel's eyes moistened.

"Help us. Please help us."

Samuel didn't respond. I was frantic while pondering his mood and hearing the trapped children. I started to run toward them, but he grabbed my hand.

"Sush."

The ground trembled, water rolled up from the lake, and covered our feet up to our knees.

"Samuel!"

His eyes stayed closed as he squeezed my hand.

The water rose quickly, passing our knees up to our chests. White pearls spit up from the lake's bottom, crowding at the lake's top.

"Samuel!"

The trembling forced me to lose balance. I fell into his chest.

He wrapped his arms around my back and held me close. I shut my eyes.

In the darkness, I envisioned two children—one African, one Dutch—struggling to stay afloat, water jumping inside their open mouths—spit, phew, spit.

Samuel's heart bumped, bumped, remembering. The white-skinned boy was pulled beneath the water while the black-skinned boy watched in shock.

"Timmy."

The raging water meant for the African boy came for him. He dived in after Timmy, the tan soles of his black feet kicking, kicking, pulled under, too.

Standing on the side, she witnessed it. Jealousy drove her there, and she didn't get what was promised.

She trembled. Broke down into blistering tears, covering her face. At an early age, she shouldn't be carrying such a burden. So, she prayed to the God her mama prayed to, "Lord, help me. I have seen the devil. I've done wrong, and one day it's gonna come for me.

Silent at the lake as before. Satisfied that the one soul was sucked into her hell, the other was given back to repeat existences. Unaware that the one spared would return to the highest calling. Reborn anew to help during the final reckoning.

When my eyes opened, I couldn't remember what had happened like the night of the Event.

Samuel was standing beside me, his face calm, "Miss Ella, it's time I get you home. I'm glad we have become friends."

Chapter 8

The One Who Came Before
57 days to solstice
1 month 26 days

Remembering

Pact with a Wiccan

At the Janssen ranch, Mama J and Lucille cooked up a feast for the family and workers. The menu included: fried chicken, collard greens with turkey necks, macaroni and cheese, fresh biscuits, potato salad, and another with iceberg lettuce, cucumbers, shredded carrots, cauliflower, and tomatoes, and homemade gravy.

The aroma from three lemon pound cakes escaped from the electric oven, reminding Mama that dinner for the family was almost ready.

Unlike the woodstove at home, turning on the electric stove didn't require feeding it chopped logs.

"Ain't got to keep putting in wood. Makes things easy and gets done quicker."

"Hmpf. Maybe you could use one of d'ese fancy stoves, Josephine. But my wood stove does double duty, warms the house well, and cooks good in the kitchen."

"Mine too. John chopped and stacked plenty. They should last through the winter. Then I'd have to ask for help until the boys are strong enough to wield an axe. We'll worry about that then."

"Lord will provide. Yes, he will. My neighbor across the way chops his and mine."

"I'll say, Lucille. Abram is sweet on you."

"Now you hush, we ain't but friends."

"Okay, ain't but friends."

While waiting for dinner to finish and cool, the two ladies prepped meal ingredients for the following week. They chopped vegetables and potatoes, rinsed them, and put lima and red beans on the soak. Prepped a fresh turkey, the farm hand had rung the neck and plucked. Mixed the flour, yeast, butter, eggs, and lard for rising before kneading and storing.

The oven timer rang, and the pound cake was fully baked. In time for Mr. Emanuel to come poking. Came through the double doors, stepping into the nest of the kitchen where cherry-stained cabinets John had hung across the back wall. The only Jannsen who ventured inside the working part of the kitchen. Walked across the tile right up to the counter, pulled in by the citrus teasing his nostrils.

"Mighty fine cooking going on in here. May I sample?" Mr. Emanuel pointed to the cake.

Lucille looked up from scrubbing pans, "Hello, sir."

Nearest to the counter, Mama J scrunched her forehead, oven mitt in her hand, "Now, Mr. Janssen, you'll ruin your dinner. You know Mrs. Janssen would frown on that."

"We don't want that." He shrugged. "Speaking of Delilah, she is out. Hold supper until after 6:00. But feed the Hands, and help yourselves. Make sure you feed Ella once she returns. Looks like her bones are thinning." He chuckled.

"One last thing. I promised John an electric stove for you, Josephine. It will be delivered by the end of the week. Let me know how it works."

He strolled out whistling. Called back, "I would get one for you, Lucille, but your wood stove works just fine, warming in and outside the kitchen."

Mama J smiled at Lucille, "Thank you, Mr. Janssen. I will remember to thank John in my talks with him."

"Oo-we, he got long ears." Lucille snickered. "Gotta watch my mouth."

Mama spoke under her breath, "Thin? She eats fine."

"Yessum, her bones are no smaller than Mirabella's," Lucille whispered. "But a brand-new electric stove. Oh, lordy, that man sure is good to y'all."

Mama J nodded, ending the conversation about the generous Mr. Janssen.

In the woods again

The sun faded when I reached the forest. I came to commune with the witch whose power extended beyond past and future, strengthened by sacrificed African children. Time would end for me if the one who came before lived until the solstice.

I steered my one-seater horse and buggy, its fan-shaped red top designed for all types of weather.

I stopped near the Oak trees outside the entry to the dark forest. Wrapped the horse's straps around the footrest, covered her head with a red tweed scarf, and waited.

Thinking back seventeen years ago in 1908, I ended up lost in this barren area where no one ventured but I enjoyed the quiet and hoped it would calm my little one.

I pulled the reins, preparing to turn the buggy around, when a black-skinned woman came from the woods. Aged by only her long white woolen hair and walking cane.

I thought how odd that an elder would roam the woods alone. Perhaps a Village worker, heading to the Baldwin estate, but she had no intention of offering her a ride.

Boldly, the Black-skin woman walked up to the buggy, "Ahh, you are having a little one, Black as the night she will be."

"Excuse me. Do I know you? Are you a domestic from the Village?"

"No ma'am. I am one who knows."

She eyed the smiling lady. "I need to get going if you don't mind."

"The child you are carrying is of pure African blood. Connected to the Ndanga-Njinga empire. She is the one the prophecy speaks of, sent to release the enslaved spirits, ending the blood covenant. Baldwin will die and live no more. You understand what I am saying."

"Now look, I don't know what prophecy you speak of. My child comes from an authority greater than you or any African. The matter is of no concern of yours."

The elder woman touched my stomach, "Creating one with her likeness, kin to your soul, the first Daughter once born must live no more. Her soul will belong to our lord. Yes?"

Looking into the elder African woman's black eyes, made me shiver. At that time, I did not understand that the woman's power could ensure the heritage of the child I so desired.

"I must go."

"Already done, we have our wish. Remember, I must collect by the solstice, or we will all perish." The woman warned.

Thinking back to that night when I made him take her away to the grave made for her before her death, when he returned his mood had shifted. Now I wonder why.

"Emanuel, you will not have defied me," I said aloud.

A familiar voice interrupted my rant.

"Oh, but he has."

I looked down at Luna, who had mysteriously appeared like she did all those years ago, her fiery eyes baring into mine.

"The One Who Came Before still lives.," she said. "You promised me you'd deliver her soul to me, but I was told the grave is barren. Because she lives, her power is getting stronger and soon I will not be able to control her and give my lord what he demands." Luna's voice boomed as her face seemingly aged, boning and wrinkling beyond any elder living today.

"She no longer lives. I made sure of it," I insisted.

"Your husband, Emanuel, would not let her die. The power within him must have been approved by Semperian. He cloaked her in light where none of us could see her. But I sensed her earlier when she came to the lake with her earthly Guardian."

"Who is she? Who is this Guardian?" I demanded.

"I do not know but whoever it is, has the power of shapeshifting. Who among you is a lie?"

Squirming, I looked away feeling the burning reaching my soul. I knew what my fate would be and for all of us in Baldwin. Ashes to ashes. I held my head high, looking above her, "I will find out who."

"Very good. It must be done before the solstice. If not, your precious one who came after will be no more. The Africans will be free to rule the Earth, and you will perish along with the rest of Baldwin, " Luna warned, vanishing into the woods as before, leaving me to contemplate my fate.

I am Luna Diabolus

Back at my place beyond the cave, I fell, pounding the wooden floor with brittle fists. My body was slowly catching the years I had managed to leave behind centuries ago.

Delilah's end of the bargain should have been completed in 1908. I have worked for centuries to stop the Semperian prophecy and she must not fail me. The birth of an African girl of pure blood born to the Janssens will end the blood covenant if we do not find her. She will free the African Prince and his loyalists, whose souls and Semperian power were enslaved in the third hell.

I cringe, thinking that may happen. My power had its limits unlike before.

I was once a powerful Wiccan from the light realm but turned to dark magic on one of my journeys to Earth. Unaware that I was being influenced by the third hell, I explored the allure and one day submitted.

It required drinking the blood of a clondike. Found in the caves of Europe, the species broached humans dabbling in dark magic. Part animal and humanoid, it walked on all fours with the head of a gator. It also had twelve-inch claws and shark teeth. Its fleshy pink body stunk like dead carcasses, for it feasted on mountain climbers, campers, and hunters.

I encountered it in a secluded mountain cave in the Netherlands. Because I carried powers from the light realm, I was unafraid when it sauntered out from the dark of the cavern. The beast stopped about three feet from me.

"Ah, so you've heard the call, eh?" Its large, thick black tongue hung down from its mouth, drooling red spit when it spoke.

I remained silent.

"I am called a clondike, the only one of its kind," it explained. "I am created from a human, an alligator, and a shark. A human played with the darkness and was forced to mate with these two sea creatures. You now have touched the dark one's soul and must follow through."

"I am of the light realm. I walked in light with Semperian and am allowed to have a human form. I do not wish to mate with sea creatures."

The clondike laughed, "We know all this, but you are no longer pure, for soon your kind will dispose of you."

"How do you speak of that you know not?"

"But I do. The powerful dark one speaks through me. He also does not want you to mate with sea creatures. You would be his and continue to experience the lustful joy you've come to appreciate."

"He?"

"Apollyon Diabolus, the lord of the third darkest realm. It is his fire with which you have played. Now, you must submit or risk removal from the life cycle by your Semperian. Apollyon is set for that same destruction. Together, the two of you can stop it from happening and overtake Semperian.

"You speak foolishly, Semperian cannot be touched."

"Oh, but it can. And you can be by its side, ruling the universe as you desire. Your sister will no longer be of use."

I was intrigued by the clondike and all it knew. Her communion with the energy, Apollyon Diabolus intrigued her.

"What must I do?"

"You drink from my blood. It will give you the power of his powerful magic. You will bestow that power upon your future minions. Chanting his name in triplets each time you call forth a spell, will finalize the outcome you wish."

The clondike walked up to Luna and stood beside her. Its horrific odor clogged her nostrils. She vanquished it from her energy field.

"Ahh. You have the use of light magic. Do not let them take it from you. It will be useful."

The clondike held up its paw, "Humans who use this dark magic must be careful and use it sparingly. Their arrogance in wanting power could kill or severely maim them. You will be

Apollyon's most loyal soldier and the source of beauty it so misses. It is through you that others will be able to experience his darkness and will. The light magic you use can only be used in love, for good, and to help others. It requires humility. Greed and the power to rule others against their will come from extreme darkness. We will make a way for both to become one."

The clondike opened its paw. Blood flowed, "Drink until you are full."

I opened my mouth and allowed the blood to fill me down through my throat, into my stomach. It seeped throughout my body, overtaking my soul. Full, it spilled down my body, soaking me in blood. It warmed me.

"You are ready," said the clondike. "You are his."

The dark energy, aligned with mine and filled me with joy, satisfying urges I wanted to explore in Lucifer's realm, but my sister forbade it.

The demon Apollyon Diabolus found his first soldier in me, Luna. I promised to help it rise on its final birthday, December 21, 1925. The day Semperian set for me and Apollyon's permanent removal from the universal life cycle.

Chapter 9

Before and After Births
57 days to solstice
1 month, 26 days

Where the Heart Is and Not

Ms. Josephine and Lucille set the table in the smaller dining room, using the blue and white porcelain China that sparkled like a lady in waiting. The table China passed down through Delilah's Dutch ancestors started with the Dutch Queen, who received the gift from the Emperor of the Qing dynasty during the 1400s.

"Can you handle things from here? Mirabella may be in an ugly mood."

"Don't you worry none Josephine, I will be fine. Learned to swallow my pride around their youngin' long ago."

Lucille remembered occasions when the Janssen daughter created tension at the dinner table. Rude to staff until Mr. Emanuel put her in her place.

Emanuella

The oak-stained grandfather clock bonged at 6:30 supper time, reminding us that Mama would be home soon. The clock stood tall against the wall outside the kitchen entry, one of Papa John's finest pieces.

I moved the red beans and rice off to the side, shut the cooktop, and smothered the fire coming from the stove drawer.

"I'll set the table." Cece offered. "Mama said to start without her if she's not home."

"I'll call the boys in."

Cece took out a large white porcelain bowl from the storage cabinet for the red beans and an elongated white plate for the freshly baked cornbread. Placed it on top of the counter between the stove and cabinet.

Papa worked on upgrading Mama's kitchen with teal-colored tile floors and yellow walls. The three storage units stacked dishes and food. Glassdoor cabinets along the far wall with glassware and porcelain dishware inside came from Mrs. Delilah. Mama rarely used those dishes, calling them scraps from rich folks. Despite her disdain, the porcelain plates, tumblers, and sterling silverware made a grand statement like the electric stove Mr. Emanuel was sending. The stove will match the refrigerator and freezer, a Towner gifted to Papa for building his wife a cabinet.

I looked out the kitchen window at Zeke and Gabe, playing catch with the baseball. They attended Negro Southern League Baseball games with Papa and met Satchel Paige, a famous Negro pitcher from Mobile. Paige was the best and good enough to play for the major leagues. The all-white leagues wouldn't allow Black players, regardless of how talented they were.

"EEK. Is that Papa?" A man dressed like a lumberjack with broad, wide shoulders sauntered out from the woodshed. Holding a hatchet down by his right side, he stood not far from the boys. He looked up at me, his wide face shining from beneath a brown hat.

I waved, letting the tears drop freely from my eyes. He pinched the tip of his hat, nodded, took one last look at the boys, and stepped back into the shed.

Sissy came into the kitchen. I had dropped the ladle, falling to the floor with a clamor.

"E, you all right? E."

Sis ran to me and picked up the utensil.

"E, why are you crying? Did something happen to the boys?" She looked out the window.

Zeke and Gabe were still tossing the baseball. Their laughter spilled through the open window, letting out residual steam from cooking.

"I'm gonna be the next Satchel Paige," Zeke bragged to Gabe, who dropped the ball for the third time. "I let you be my warm-up man. By then, you will have skill."

"Huh-uh. I'm gonna be Satchel before you."

"Ha. Ha. You can't be Satchel, cuz there is already a Satchel, doh-doh."

"No, you a doh-doh, Zeke."

Cece hollered out the window, "Both of you doh-dohs come in and wash up for supper."

The twins packed up their gear and dropped it in the shed before coming inside.

I was wearing Mama J's red apron. Wiped my tears with the bottom corner, stained with bits of flour.

"E, you have flour above your eye." Cece giggled.

She grabbed a clean towel, wiped it away, and hugged me.

Given what happened at the lake and seeing the ghost of Papa John, I questioned whether or not I could hold it together. All I wanted was to sleep, sleep, sleep.

Samuel told me he would be there for me anytime. Mr. Emanuel and Papa told me they would be there for me, too. I reminded them both that I wasn't the one needing the extra care. It was Mama who rarely showed her feelings, even when she hurt the most.

"Thank you, sis. I'm going to freshen up."

"Okay, mademoiselle."

I removed my apron and tossed it into the basket inside the laundry room.

As I left the kitchen, Zeke and Gabe busted through the back door. Sissy hollered at them to take off their dirty shoes, "Leave them on the back porch."

I kicked off my shoes, pulled back the bed cover, and laid down.

I'd fallen asleep and gagged when lilac invaded my nostrils, paralyzing me. I struggled to wake up.

An unfamiliar voice spoke to me while a fresh mist cleansed away the lilac. The apparition of a white male with crystal blue eyes came out of the mist. It said, "I am Trevor Baldwin. I do not know you, but I sense you. You are the one who came before. The one I must find before the solstice."

Mirabella

At the dinner table, Mummy and Daddy sat across from each other. He wasn't talking to me or Mum, and frankly, I didn't care. I couldn't take the silliness anymore. We were not family.

I stood abruptly and shouted, "No!" Threw my knife and fork down, slammed my fists on the table. It shook.

Lucille had served us, and Daddy permitted her to leave.

Mum, sitting on my left, extended her trembling hand, thinking she could calm my tantrum. I was angry with her for showing weakness and not standing up to Daddy, who was staring at me. I hear his thoughts, calling me spoiled and unappreciative. He'd better not say it out loud, I dared.

My rising anger turned the whites of my eyeballs black, and they burned. My trembling arms stiffened by my side.

"It's your fault, Mum, and his."

Daddy scrunched his face, "Enough. Speak no more. Do I make myself clear?"

Mummy stepped in to defend me, but Daddy shut her down too.

"Stop coddling her. She is no longer a baby." *If she ever was, he thought.*

"Mum, I would like to be excused."

"But darling."

"Let her go! She may return once she's settled."

I pushed my chair back and stepped away from the table. Held my head up, grabbed the sides of my dress, and stomped out. Ran down the hall, upstairs, and back to my room. Slam, click, locked the door.

Mummy set her handkerchief on the table, scooted her chair back, and stood up.

"Sit," Daddy ordered.

"I must see about our daughter."

"Your daughter is a young woman who needs no further coddling, yes?"

Mum glared at Daddy for referring to me as her daughter. As usual, she said nothing.

"Right, Delilah?"

Mum sat back down, scooted her chair up to the table, and returned the napkin to her lap. "Tell me, Emanuel, is our firstborn dead or alive?"

Daddy pulled his left lip up into a half smile, "I did what you asked, took our firstborn away." Dropping his smile, he grabbed a biscuit from the platter, bit into it, and chewed. "It's nice to have Josephine back." He said, meeting her glare. "Finish eating. Your food is getting cold."

Chapter 10

The One Who Came Before
56 days to solstice
1 month, 25 days

Day 26 October 1925
Power to Walk Alone

"E, are you okay? Are you hungry? Mama cooked a pot of stew with lots of potatoes, fresh garden tomatoes, and thick chunks of beef."

I couldn't respond, making me wonder if I was awake or dreaming. Like when I dreamt of the white-skinned boy with the bluest eyes, coming from out of the mist. He vanquished the presence of a powerful enemy.

I pondered what he wanted and why he needed to find me. Papa J said all would become clear as my mission unfolded. I didn't know yet what that was.

My condition worried Mama. I had been asleep for a few days, so she sent for help. He came today to check on me.

"Josephine, you know Dr. Arthur Brown Jr., a friend from Mobile and one of the best doctors we have near Baldwin."

"Of course, Mr. Janssen." Mama hugged the young African man in a gray suit. "I haven't seen you since you were a little boy; now you are all grown up. Graduating at the top of your class from the Howard School of Medicine in Washington, D.C., made us proud."

The caramel-skinned Dr. Brown lowered his head modestly. He reminded Mama J of his father, Arthur Brown Senior. Dr. Brown had his father's L-shaped nose, sullen brown eyes, tamed brows, and wavy black hair. He had little of Lucille, only his thin lips.

"Good to see you again, Mrs. Crumley. I remember you and Mother baking cakes, and me eating so much, it made me sick."

"Good thing you're a doctor." Mama laughed.

"My belated condolences regarding Mr. Crumley. I wanted to attend his going away but couldn't catch a break."

"You were there in spirit, Dr. Brown. I'm sure John felt it." Mama held her tears.

"And who are these fine young men?" He said extending his hand.

"I'm Zeke, the man now." He shook the doctor's hand.

"Yeah, he thinks he is. Bossy is all," Gabe wined while shaking hands.

"Your father would be proud of you both." They grinned.

Dr. Brown extended his hand to Cece, "And you are?"

She stepped in front, leaving little room to shake hands, "I'm Cecilia."

"We don't call you Cecilia. Stop acting, Sissy." Gabe said.

"Cecilia and Cece are both nice names. In some cultures, it means shining light."

Cece blushed.

"She shines when she wears too much grease on her ashy arms." Zeke laughed. His brother joined in.

"Oh, be quiet."

"Y'all hush." Mama pinched Zeke. "Owe." He yipped.

"Ya'll move out the way, so the doctor can do what he came here for."

"Art, come with me." Mr. Emanuel motioned for him to follow. "Be here if you need me, Dr. Brown, Mr. Janssen."

Mr. Emanuel winked at Art, "Do not expect Josephine to call you Arthur. We've been acquaintances for years, and she still calls me, mister."

"Just how I was raised."

Voices seeped into my brain. One familiar, the other not. He was male and cultured like Mr. Emanuel.

He sat beside me and touched my forehead. Used his forefinger to lift my left eyelid, then the right. Pulled back the blanket from my chest and laid a cold object atop my heart.

"Normal." Picked up my right wrist, pressed two fingers against the underside, "Pulse and vitals good."

He stood up and looked at Mr. Emanuel, "The young lady appears comatose. Can't give you any reason for it unless I take her up to the hospital in Mobile. Run more tests."

"That won't be necessary, Art. We expect Ella back soon."

"If she doesn't awaken, could be serious." Art cautioned.

"We will keep that in mind. Meanwhile, I need your help keeping her nourished."

"Absolutely. I'll run an IV that will keep her hydrated and nourished. I'll leave a couple of bags that need to be refrigerated. I will show Josephine and Cecilia how to change them. Meanwhile, if you change your mind, Emanuel, I can arrange for transport."

"Thank you, Art, I will call you if we need to. And Art, please come to me with any updates about Ella's condition. It is my role to protect her, agreed?"

"Yes, agreed." The doctor suspected his friend knew more about what was happening with Ella. He contemplated that thought and planned to watch his patient closely.

Dr. Brown prepared the solution and demonstrated to Cece and Mama J how to hook up a new bag once emptied.

Mr. Emanuel moved beside me, leaned down, and whispered, "Hello, my firstborn. You were born on the night of the blood moon, giving you the strength to move the heavens. Rest well, my child. Semperian will protect you until you take your rightful place under the solstice moon."

Am I in the hell the Village preacher spoke of?

Barefoot walking alone, fenced in by thick fog, stepping into cold, gushy silkweed. Scorching heat biting at my skin, threatening to steal my breath. Except for no flames, no red man with horns, no people in agony, burning for their worldly sins.

I waited and listened.

Breathing came from inside the lurking shadow, "Turn so I can see you. Show yourself."

I waited and listened.

"Show yourself," the shadow came slithering forward, drenched in lilac rot. Spitting its scent into the air, her hand reached for me. Shards attacked her, "Ugh." It rubbed its hands. "You will not win. My heritage is my birthright, for I am the daughter of Apollyon, ruler since the beginning of time. We are stronger than any light, and soon your Semperian. We shall not be silenced."

I pushed out my arms, my hands in a temple. A spinning ball of gold formed between my palms, "I am Semperian Daughter. Your permanent hell will be with the one who holds no power over me."

"Eh," a feeble voice echoed from one with ancient powers.

The shadow fled, leaving behind a scared girl. Her head down, rocking and trembling, hugging her knees to her chest.

The echo, "Your cloak of protection will not hold for long, for there is weakness around you. We will find it, and you."

Flames rose from the ground and ran toward the demon girl. Stopped before devouring her. Taunted, surrounded her inside its enflamed circle.

"I am the firstborn. The Daughter of Emanuel Janssen was born from the womb of a Dutch woman who swore allegiance to our captors. My heritage seed comes from the first African hung in Baldwin Janssen Square. His soul is held hostage, and the blood covenant is forced upon his offspring, who took the name Janssen. Indebted to the founders of Baldwin Town, the covenant binds all African souls to those promised immortality."

Thunder unleashed. Flames roared as I expounded, "Prince Abiola Hereto Ndanga Njinga. Our strength comes from your rage and the rage of our ancestors. Reaching back to the most powerful, we will vanquish the darkness and release the true heirs. Darkness shall weep, removed from life eternal."

Semperian light workers in the universe and on Earth bellowed across the dreamscape. They exploded, raining buckets of boulders and sea salt. Enraged.

The wrong daughter, the one who came after, cowered as the echo defended their stance, "We will not lose, my daughter, for we have his darkness. You will take your rightful place."

Semperian lightworkers showered warnings with bolts of hail.

Evil ran and no longer stood before me, the right Daughter, the one who came before.

As I stood in silence, the golden light crowned my body as I held my hands to the sky, sucked in a whiff of rose milk, "On our day, we become one."

Chapter 11

The One Who Came Before
51 days to solstice 1
month, 21 days

Day 31 October 1925
Rising with Memories of Cece

Sunny days would soon end in Baldwin with rain coming the following week.

With the first signs of winter a month away, darker mornings and earlier sunsets would see fewer Jaybirds outside the Crumley home, pulling up the last of the worms. Good morning squirrels would scavenge for fewer crumbs once the twins played inside, preferring log fires over burr.

Papa John felt my spirit despite others in the physical world seeing a face with closed eyes. He was there when I walked barefoot alone and fought evil.

Semperian strength protected me against the one I shared a womb with, who was created by a witch and a demon.

Cece stayed in Mama's room, giving me space to heal, but she, Mama, and the boys visited me daily.

Mama came earlier to bathe me and left oil beside the bed

for Cece to rub me down. Sissy also brought a tube of lipstick, hidden in her pocket. Like the Village women, Mama forbids wearing makeup, saying it reminded her of the made-up ladies at SugaShack. Even though the Towner women wore it.

"Guess what, E? I have a small tube of our favorite cherry. I'm going to visit Lizi and get more."

Sissy gently spread it across my upper lip, tap, tap, did the same to the bottom, spread, tap, tap. My lips moistened.

"Aren't you pretty. Now all you need is to wake up. Put on one of your pretty dresses. Go out with Samuel." Cece snickered. "He comes here every day, helping out. Mr. Emanuel's orders, even though Mama believes she can do it all."

She leaned her ear to my mouth, hoping I'd respond. No words from me, she sat upright.

"You were a blessing to Mama and Papa. They thought Mama couldn't bear children, but a year goes by and here I come, then the twins down the way."

Sis used the palms of her hands to massage me with rose oil. Starting with my hands, rubbing up my arm to my shoulder, and then back down. She did that a few times and then did the other side, my legs and front.

"Come on, E. Open those almond eyes. Remember how your eyes smiled on your birthdays? When you got a new dress from Mr. Emanuel. Not that girl's hand-me-downs like Mama tried to make us believe."

Cece paused.

"We all love you. Come home soon, okay? We'd all like that, even Samuel. He is smitten." Cece chuckled.

Samuel was assigned to me as a Guardian before I came through an angry womb.

At the lake, he exposed a past incarnation. He drowned in imaginary pearls with his friend. Timmy.

Chapter 12

The One Who Came Before

1908 Unmarked Grave
Papa Janssen Will Never Forget

Tears bubbled up deep inside when I remembered my birth. Papa transferred a universal power to me at age seventeen with the vision to see the before, the now, and the future. Vision to remember being born, inside a room where the crackling of the heated wood stove spewed sweaty mist into the air. Sunlamps hung overhead, warming the midwife's delicate hands as she carefully cut the cord. The final connection to my birth Mother, who hated me.

He took me, his firstborn, out into the cold, to the open carriage, and set me inside a makeshift basket. Grunted as he lifted himself into his rawhide seat, grabbed the whips—snap, snap. He ordered the mare, "Geddup Black Bo."

The wagon jumped into a jerk-*wobble wobble* down the broken dirt road into the fall's blackened night with Papa's hand on my tummy snuggled inside the wool blanket.

"Little one, your Papas will keep you safe until this moon comes back 17 years from now, welcoming your return."

The buggy slowed when the broken mud smoothed, quieting its wobbling wheels and mare's crunch, crunch.

Bo pulled the buggy uphill, the basket shifted, and the wind moved in behind the carriage, giving it an extra push. Papa and I rode into the naked arms of ancestral spirits, awaiting there to cloak my body in protective light.

"Whoa, Black Bo," Papa Janssen pulled Bo's straps.

Bo stopped.

"Good boy," Papa leaned up and ran a hand down the mare's mane.

Papa jumped down from the wagon as the ground rustled from up ahead, moving toward us a sweet-smelling, colorless smoke. It reached out and playfully tickled my nose. The smell belonged to a kind soul who would be my protector, during his life and his after.

50 days to solstice
1 month, 20 days
1st day of November 1925

At the Janssen ranch, no ranch Hands were roaming, no one preparing for the workday. Mr. Emanuel gave the Ranch Hands and caretakers the day off because Sunday was a church-going day for us, Villagers and Towners.

I insisted on preparing Sunday meals with the help of Lucille. We came in extra early to prepare, serve up breakfast, and store lunch and dinner in the cooler before heading to church ourselves.

Our Sunday dresses hung upstairs in the guest quarters. Mr. Janssen had the house built with rooms upstairs in the back for domestic staff. The butler and his wife, a middle-aged couple, lived onsite, and Lucille stayed on occasion. She'd been with the family since the birth of their firstborns.

Towners worshiped at the Baldwin Christian Temple in the center of town, and Villagers at the Village Church.

In common with Towners, we worshiped God and a white-skinned Jesus. A reminder nailed to our Village church's wooden walls, painted yellow.

We didn't always have a place to worship.

Led by John, we built our church ten years prior at my urging. Before that, the outdoor church in summer started after sunrise, and attendees sat for an hour. When the rains came, we stayed home and prayed for better days.

As summers grew hotter, high humidity suffocated the thin air, and worrisome mosquitoes stung through our sweaty clothes. Church barely made it through the first choir song, and the preacher hollering, "God shall provide in heaven."

One Sunday, the heat was so bad I complained to John and said enough. "Folks getting too old to sit in this weeded grass. Sun smothering the tree shade, can't fan fast enough to cool."

My wonderful husband, with the help of the Village men, built our double-entry church, which took about six months. Then another week to paint the inside, install the brown wooden benches, and a podium up front for the preacher. Behind him, a row of seats for the choir and a grand piano donated by Mr. Janssen.

A tight fit sometimes, but we managed to squeeze inside with children attending Sunday school in the kitchen in the back. They sat on the floor in a circle with a stool at the head for the teacher. A door off to the right led outside to a fenced-in yard with benches and tables used for a playground and church events.

Baldwin residents and Villagers prayed to the same God, but Sundays remained segregated like school.

The Janssen family were the only colored members of the Baldwin church. On occasion, Mr. Janssen came to our church and brought African missionaries and dignitaries visiting from Montgomery. He also took them to the Baldwin church. Towners allowed them in as their way of saying God loved everybody up to a certain point.

Lucille and me were almost finished, and I was looking forward to putting on my Sunday best. John bought me a nice new purple dress and a wide hat to match from the clothing store in Baldwin, which the Villagers were welcome to buy from. We didn't shop at Mrs. Baldwin's store. Paying all that money for fancy clothes didn't sit well with us humble folks.

"So sorry to hear your daughter is not awake." Lucille stopped stirring the grits to face me.

"No need to feel sorry. She's sleeping deeply for now, is all. John watches her."

"You say that like he's still here." Lucille went back to stirring.

"Always watching. I'm grateful for your son checking in on her."

"Umph." Lucille scrunched her lip. "Prayer is the most medicine you need."

"That may be true, but you should be mighty proud of him. He's helped a lot of the sick in our Village."

Lucille didn't like talking about her estranged son. She told me that in his presence, there was sadness around him, and that troubled her.

Lucille started humming, something she did when she was done talking. Especially when it was about Dr. Brown and memories from her childhood. It still haunted her about what they did to her mother. I pray often that the greatness of Semperian will ease her spirit. She didn't believe in the Knowledge of Semperian, and it was not a subject I discussed during this existence.

"You have a beautiful voice, Lucille. The choir is still waiting for you to join."

Lucille smiled, then sang a hymn:

Lord knows I've seen trouble
Lord knows my sorrow
Lord knows I've seen trouble
Glory, Glory, Hallelujah
Please Lord, end my troubles
Please Lord, end my suffering
Thank you, Lord, for I am your child
Glory, Glory Hallelujah
I'm up now, and I will stay
Oh, yes, my Jesus. Oh, yes, my God.

The song I sung reminded me of good and troubled times. I was born before slavery ended, and the Baldwins sold my father, leaving me with my mother. I was named after her but wanted no part of her powerful visions passed down through generations. She predicted that they would sell him and urged him to run. She told him where to go. An underground railroad he could pass through with help from Northerners. But he refused to leave us behind.

As a little girl, I was allowed to run free as long as I minded my place. Amongst the Africans.

That day, Mama kept me with her in the kitchen, sitting on a stool. She scolded me for disobeying, running off to the lake with Master Baldwin's nephew, Timmy, and Ezra, an African.

"If you get caught with Timmy, Master Baldwin will have African parents whipped to prove a point."

Mr. Baldwin strolled into the kitchen to get more coffee.

"Sir, I would've brought it to ya, if you'd rung for me." Mama poured him a cup of fresh brew.

"Thank you, Lucille."

He never acknowledged me.

"Sir, I have something to say most concerning."

"What would that be, Lucille?"

Mama paused, staring down at me. I knew what was coming. Towners disallowed Africans to use their ancient spiritualism, which included visions. But Mama often told others she had grown fond of the family despite them selling my Papa.

"Sir, I smell trouble comin', best you protect yo' family. A war will be fought here."

Thonis Baldwin walked up to Mama and stood right in her face. "What you say, woman, about a war comin' here? Protect my family. You hush that talk, old woman. I'm gonna overlook your crazy talk this time, but no more, hear."

"Yes, sir."

The war came as Mama predicted. The Confederates fought the Freedom Fighters near the Hiding Tree, and the Confederates lost. Slavery would end with southern states refusing to acknowledge freedom for Africans.

Master Baldwin accused Mama of cursing the Confederates, causing them to lose the war.

He made me stand beside him as his men hanged Mama. Watching her swing from that tree hurt me deeply.

He looked down at me with his angry, crystal blue eyes, "Having visions is a curse and witchery. God is the one who can see the future, best you remember that or follow your mama."

I remained there as an in-house domestic, having to take over Mama's kitchen duties as punishment for her visions. I also became a devout Christian, obeying the Baldwin master, who put the fear of God in me. Prayer brought Art Brown Sr. to me, and took me from that hell, living with the man who murdered Mama.

Lucille finished the song with:
I'm almost to the ground, oh, yes, God.
For I've seen plenty of trouble and sorrow
But Lord, I've been plenty sorrowful
Glory be your name, I am healed.
"Hallelujah. Come on, Lucille, that's get dressed for church, and change those troubles into glorious blessings."

Unmarked Grave Remembered

I demanded that Emanuel prove he disposed of our firstborn.

I rode with him out to the Village graveyard. His silence was irritating, but I shrugged it off, caring only about our Mirabella.

"Geddup, Baby Bo." He steered the buggy through Baldwin Janssen Square.

If I could only read his thoughts.

On the night he returned from supposedly ridding us of her, he refused to acknowledge me or celebrate our true firstborn.

I could sense Emanuel's angst as he smacked the buggy straps, moving the buggy uphill. He stopped at the entrance to the burial site. This was the first time for me, I had no reason to come, not even to pay respect to John Crumley. I must admit it was beautiful, surrounded by elder oaks and October's fallen leaves turned yellow and brown.

Emanuel laid the buggy straps atop the footboard and pointed his forefinger into the distance.

My eyes followed, stopping at the largest tree hovering above John Crumley's majestic headstone, which my husband purchased on our behalf. Peaking from behind it was a smaller headstone. I couldn't make out the name.

I must know for sure.

I hoped Emanuel would come around to help me down, but his silence said otherwise.

"Hmpf, so be it."

I turned my body, set a hand on the seat arm, and lowered myself down. Not easy, but thankful for my ankle boots. My feet landed on the cushioned ground as a powerful force of wind circled me. I was astounded when a memory surfaced and whispered, "Why not let me lay on your chest, suck your other breast, Mama."

I fell against the buggy, steadying myself with the palms of my hands, and said aloud, "I will not fear you. I must know."

Clenching my scarf, I stepped through the entrance and onto the walkway, courageously entering the sacred place where African spirits slept. Or not.

Inside was an eclectic mix of wooden crosses with name plaques and headstones the height of a large bowler pot, carved with initials and year of death.

I walked up to John Crumley's grave and lowered my eyes on the small one behind it. Perhaps I should've felt remorse but felt nothing for the child supposedly buried beneath the dirt of the tiny headstone that bore no name. I only felt disdain and turned up my nose, "You were not meant to be."

As I turned and walked away, I saw Emanuel, standing at the burial entrance, arms reaching to the sky.

"Hmpf, maybe I can count on his help this time."

Before I could reach the carriage, wind flurries and thunder erupted. Lightning struck the ground where I walked, and the voice returned, not of a child, but a force.

I shut my eyes, slammed my hands to my ears, and reaffirmed, "I will not fear you. You are not my God."

The booming voice intensified, grinding its will through my body. Reminded me of the cursed infection, rancid and vulgar, the black death turning bodies to ashes. Threatened as solstice neared on December 21, 1925.

It said, "You made a pact with the devil. Shunned me, and praised the one who came after. You will not escape your fate. The one you honor will be your demise."

Chapter 13

The One Who Came Before
50 days to solstice
1 month, 20 days

Day 1 November 1925
Lakeside Warning On Time

Cece

It didn't matter what the weather was like outside, church indoors was warm; stuffy if full. Villagers didn't complain.

Together, they praised the Lord, sang, and clapped while cooling themselves with handheld fans. The fans kept them seated during the African preacher's hour-long sermons, with help from the choir and band.

After church, my brothers came looking for me. I was with Mama and Lucille, talking to the minister.

"Pastor, Jeremiah." Mama shook his hand. "Thank you for your kind words and prayer for Emanuella."

"My honor, Mrs. Crumley. Your daughter is a fine young lady who is much needed to continue teaching our children. She's in God's capable hands. He will send her back to us soon. Her work is not done yet."

"I agree. She has much to do among the living."

"Your help from this Samuel fellow has been a godsend. Wouldn't mind meeting him one day."

"We are grateful to Samuel for staying with Emanuella. Gave us a chance to come out."

Ms. Lucille stepped up to say hello, "Yes, sir, mighty fine words. Your sermon inspired me to make amends for sins I've made in the past."

"I will pray for you, sista, Lucille. God forgives all wrong. He is a good God."

Both twins came running up.

Zeke pulled at my hand, "Sissy."

"Shush. You know not to interrupt grown folks."

"Me and Zeke gotta ask you something."

"Ezekiel and Gabriel. You've forgotten your manners." Mama scolded.

"No need for apologies." Pastor Jeremiah chuckled. "It's hard for our kids to sit so long. We are blessed to have the fenced yard."

The pastor spoke to the twins, "Ezekiel and Gabriel, your names are in the bible. Has Ms. Clarice given that bible lesson?

They shook their heads.

"I'll make sure she does that soon." Then he returned his attention to Mama. "Yes, Josephine, they are mighty fine young men." Then back to the twins. "Y'all keep a watch out for your Mama and sisters."

"Yes, sir. I'm the man, now."

"Zeke is bossy."

"Come on," I grabbed both their hands. "Excuse me, pastor, Mama, Ms. Lucille."

The pastor spoke, "Y'all run along. I'll send your mother along here shortly."

Away from Mama, Zeke pleaded, "Can you take us to the lake, please?"

"Lake? Y'all are to stay away from there."

"If we go with older kids, we're fine," Gabe assured her. "Bessie is taking her brother, Frankie, and four of his friends."

Bessie was my age. She and her brother lived with their grandmother after losing both parents.

"Okay, maybe later. But Mama can't know."

While in town picking up groceries for Mama, I planned to stop by SugaShack to say hey to my good friend Lizi.

During the day, Lizi helped her Mama, the owner, who protected her from the entertainment side of the business. Those nights she spent locked in her room with plugs in her ears, listening to the radio.

I enjoyed being around Lizi. She was the only girl in the Village my age, I called friend. E and I agreed she had a loving nature. She was different from her mother, Nyna Levin, nicknamed Cheeky because of her beefy cheeks.

Mama said Cheeky's past made her stern and mentally tough. Voluptuous with full lips, Cheeky had thick black silky hair, and dark eyes that held many secrets.

Village Christians, not Mama, thumbed their noses at her for the type of work she did. Mama J didn't like the energy from that place, saying it had nothing to do with Cheeky but Luciferno. A name I didn't know, a name she never explained.

Despite their judgment, Cheeky didn't tolerate anyone treating her daughter with disdain because of it.

Out of earshot, though, those same people questioned the identity of Lizi's father because of her fair skin and straight brown hair. They had heard rumors that he was a rich white man from Mobile, but Nyna insisted he was from the Village and ran off and left them.

Lizi was out front picking up trash and sweeping the walkway. She stopped mid-sweep when she saw me, coming out of the grocery store, carrying two brown bags.

"Cece." Lizi broke into a smile. "You in town for how long?"

I crossed the street and joined my friend.

"Just long enough to pick up groceries for Mama. I promised the boys I'd take them to the lake."

"It's a little chilly for laken but a beautiful sunny day, probably our last for a while. We're heading into rainy season. How's E?"

"I used the last bit of red lipstick on her, making her sleep pretty. Mama hasn't said anything."

Lizi pulled out a tube from her pants pocket, "Here. I got this from Sweet Tea. Payment for styling her hair for last night's masquerade ball. She also gives me lipstick and other makeup. Mom doesn't like me to wear it. But I play with it in my room."

"Our Mama's the same way. Ahhh, hey, how did it go last night? I forgot SugaShack celebrates Halloween, a holiday that Towners and Villagers don't celebrate. Were you able to sneak a peek?"

"Despite them calling it a pagan holiday, girl, you should've seen the costumes. People were dressed like animals, vampires, queens, and kings. One came like a red devil with horns. Sweet Tea dressed up as a witch. She looked pretty, though."

"Ooo Lizi. I'd love to see it regardless of what people say. Next year, maybe I'll come dressed up, like a princess wearing a mask. No one will know it's me."

"Let's make it a date. We'll figure out how to get you out of the house."

"E owes me a favor. I helped her out." My mood sullied when thinking of E in a coma.

"I can get more rouge if you need it."

"No, this will do." I put the lipstick tube in my pants pocket and hugged Lizi, "See you soon."

"Please tell E, I love her and miss all that good teaching."

"Will do, but keep studying. I'm teaching in her place for now."

"Hope the lake shows up for y'all." Lizi hollered as I passed under the tunnel.

Zeke and Gabe were bundled up and ready to go, waiting on the front porch.

"Yay," Gabe hopped up.

"Bout time," Zeke whined. "I was getting sleepy."

"How about you go take a nap? Or y'all can help with these bags so we can go."

I gave each twin a bag to carry inside. Mama was talking with Lucille and looked up when we walked in.

"Hey, Mrs. Lucille," I acknowledged.

Lucille nodded, loosening her lip.

"Y'all boys, get started, pulling groceries out of the bags. I'm right behind you."

"Mama, after we put the groceries up, and I hug E, I'm going to take the boys out."

"Don't stay gone too long. I need the boys fed and in bed before sundown. Me and Lucille gonna bathe Emanuella so she can rest a little better. She's turning her head side to side, mumbling words I can't understand."

"She's mumbling? That's good, right?"

"We can hope she's trying to wake herself up." Mama was encouraged, but Lucille wasn't convinced.

"Hmph. What I think, you don't hear." Lucille's eyes filled with water.

"I saw the devil when I was a young girl, and he nothing to play with."

I walked toward the kitchen, leaving Mama to deal with her friend.

Lucille said, "Probably one of those funny spells. No doctoring can help that."

"Now you hush. Ain't no spell on nobody in this house. Dr. Brown diagnosed her as comatose."

"Hmm. He acts uppity since he got his degree. And that wife of his…" Lucille sat back and wiped the corner of her eye with her pinky finger. "Don't know if he'll ever see fit enough to bring those grandchildren by. I don't like his wife."

"Got to get along if you want a relationship, my friend."

"He done forgot who his maker is, said he don't believe." Lucille leaned forward, her mouth crunched, "Turned on God is what he done. He turned on God."

Lizi was right. It was chili for laken, but the sun was out. I took the boys down by the sitting log near the water. It was quiet. No, Bessie and Frankie, no other children were there.

Zeke and Gabe didn't mind as they kicked up the sand, teasing the water.

I was grateful that no child had died there since the drowning of Timmy and Ezra several years back.

Villagers said that they were doing unnatural things, angering God, and causing unfriendly spirits to come from the cave. I didn't understand what they meant by that but hated the idea that any God would kill children for doing something wrong.

E, agreed, "Children are innocent. They learn wrong from watching grown folks."

My butt hurt, so I sat in the sand, the twins playing nearby. "Much better." I looked up at the cave's mouth. My eyes got drowsy and closed as I recalled the rumor of beautiful pearls at the bottom of the cave. The reason for the drowning.

I fell asleep, awakened by the sudden bitter cold seeping through my clothes. I shivered as it clenched my throat, face, and hands, and hard to open my mouth.

"Cold. Too, too, cold. Gabe, Zeke, let's go." I whimpered when trying to holler.

The twins were laughing, screaming, crying, I think, as they watched the water roll up onto the sand. It reached me and was cold as snow, covering my feet and ankles.

An elderly African woman appeared. She was on the other side of the lake. Her long white hair slid down her back, stopping below her buttocks. Watching, watching Zeke and Gabe.

"I, I, see you. Stay away from my brothers. Go!" I mouthed my words too hoarse to shout.

A smile crept across the elder's face as she threw something into the water. The water gurgled and moved away from me and ran toward the twins.

She pointed her forefinger, motioning for the boys to "Come play in the water."

Tears streamed down my face, "Why is this happening? I'm here with them. They are not alone."

Darkness fell over the lake as the boys struggled to stay above water, choking—argh—spit—phew. Then I heard Zeke hollering, "Gabe, Gabe."

Gabe answered, "You're not the boss of me."

The cave innards shook into howling water, shooting upward into towering arches across the cave's hall. Shaking, shaking, howling, spitting pearls hurled violently into the sand.

Howl. Shake. Crackle.

Silence.

The witch opened a portal to trap me and take the boys. I entered the darkness wrapped in a dark cloak like the one I saw standing across from me, hood covering its face.

"E, is that you?" My voice shook.

The cloaked figure replied, "Sis, go home. This is not your fight."

"It is you, E. Are you coming with me?"

The hooded one made her way through the fog, joined her hands with mine, and squeezed softly.

"Take the boys home. Go back, now."

She let go of my hands and shoved gently, forcing me back through the open portal that closed once I exited.

Gabe and Zeke pleaded, and another unfamiliar voice spoke.

"Sissy, please wake up, please."

I opened my eyes and stared into the familiar face of a fair-skinned Towner girl. Kneeling beside me, her fluffy red hair hung over her shoulders, down below her plump breasts. Sara Baldwin.

"Are you all right?" Sara asked. She and the boys helped me up.

Remembering the elder African woman, I nervously looked across the now peaceful lake, "Where is she?" What happened to the lake?"

"Where's who?" Sara inquired. "And yes, we are blessed to have such a beautiful, warm day. Maybe the last we'll see for a while."

"The woman was standing across there, making the cave shake. And, and water came for us." Adrenaline rushed through my body. "The witch."

"You saw a witch? said Zeke, eyes wide. "Where? I wanna see."

"No, no, you stay clear and run when you see her."

"What does she look like?" Gabe looked around.

"Old, dark-skinned woman, skinny with long white hair down her back. Long, dirty brown dress."

"You mean old Ms. Luna, who lives up beyond the cave? She doesn't come out much because children and adults are frightened of her, although she's harmless." Sara lied.

Sara couldn't divulge that she was summoned to the lake to help. Luna was an ancient evil and dangerous, but her power had no effect on Sara, who was protected.

"She's a witch," I argued. "A witch we've been told to stay away from."

Sara changed the subject, "Are you all right? I heard the boys screaming for help when I came through. You fainted. Didn't know if I needed to go for help."

"I'm fine; we need to be getting home." I clenched the neckline of my hooded long-sleeved, knee-length grey wool sweater. Looked one last time across the lake. No one was there, but someone was watching.

Eyes wide, Zeke said, "The waves kept getting bigger and bigger. Like it wanted to grab us."

"We kept backing up," Gabe giggled. "But we didn't see no witch."

I was thankful; the boys felt it was all in fun.

As for Sara, she was not telling the truth about Luna and why she came to the lake. Still, Sara was one of the good ones. I sensed her loving energy.

The vision I saw of the boys and my brief meeting with E made me curious about Mrs. Lucille meeting the devil all those years ago.

Riding home from the lake, I told the boys not to mention what happened.

"And we won't be going there again. Mama was right about not wanting us there, even though she says stories about the witch are just rumors."

"Ahh," Gabe whined.

"No more fun," Zeke groaned.

"You can have plenty of fun close to home."

"I agree," said Sara. "The rumors about that place should be enough to keep anyone from going. I do my best to stay away unless I have to go in that direction."

She dropped us at our front door. "Um, yum, I'm catching a whiff of Mrs. Josephine's stew. Reminding me of how hungry I am."

Sara Baldwin waved and rode off.

Inside, the aroma of fresh goat meat stew with vegetables and herbs from Papa's magical garden was much welcomed after coming in from a chilling adventure.

Mama's stew was popular and what we all loved about fall and the impending winter.

The boys and I cleaned up before supper and then took our large bowls of stew and fresh cornbread to sit with E. We had family dinners together, even though it was different now with Papa John gone from the head of the table and E in her dream world.

Emanuella

The family sat with me and had dinner, talked, and laughed like a normal family day. Cece swore I smiled. I was glad she noticed and that she and the boys were safe.

Dr. Brown told them that coma patients could hear and feel everything around them.

"Y'all ain't told me about your time out," Mama said. "I saw y'all ride up with Sara Baldwin."

No one answered.

"Uh-huh," Mama said. "What's going on? Don't lie."

"Okay, Mama, please don't get mad. I took the boys to the lake. Miss Sara happened to stop by and offered to bring us home."

Gabe interrupted, "Sissy saw a witch."

"She tried to drown us," Zeke chimed in.

I knew Cece was frowning, disappointed at the boys for telling.

Mama J said sternly, "We'll talk later."

Around midnight, Mama crept into the front room, pulled on her coat, and wrapped her head in a wool scarf before heading out into the night.

Walking down the dirt road away from the Village, she looked up into the moonlit sky, "John, I know you would disapprove, but it is time I have my say."

SOURCE

SEMPERIAN

SEMPERIAN GUARDS

UPPER REALMS OF
LIGHT AND LEARNING

EARTH

THE DARK REALMS

LUCIFERNO (LUCIFER)
SATANA (SATAN)

APOLLYON DIABOLUS

PART 2

Origins
No Beginning No End

*I am Semperian, an energy formed out of the all-knowing Source
Consciousness. Source is continuous and has no beginning and no ending.
I am the creative genius who protects Source, created the universe
and the Semperian Guards.*

*Guards travel the millions of galaxies and planets in saucer ships and
maintain order within the living and growing universe under a system of laws:
vibration, attraction, divine oneness, polarity, compensation, correspondence,
inspired action, cause and effect, relativity, gender, perpetual transmutation
of energy, and the law of rhythm.*

*From traveling the universe, Guards proposed creating planetary realms
to tame the transmutation of energy and the life forms that existed from it. To
ensure safety and universal harmony, Semperian designed light, learning, and
lower realms under the polarity law.*

*The first two are operated by Luciferno (Lucifer), Fallen Guard 1, and
the second one by Satana (Satan), Fallen Guard 2. Lucifer and Satan have an
agreement with Semperian to operate the first two realms.*

*The third lower realm operates outside the universal laws and has
existed for 17 centuries. Semperian scheduled it for permanent removal from
the universal life cycle on the Solstice of 1925. Apollyon Diabolus Fallen 17
resides in that inferno, waiting to capture unsuspecting souls. His goal is
freedom and to take Semperian.*

Humans Beware.

*--Knowledge of Semperian
Semperian, Protector of Source*

Chapter 14

Before and After Birth

Semperian named us Luciferno and Satana, the first Semperian Guards. There were 17. We traveled the universe galaxy by Galaxy and encountered afflictions in the Milky Way encompassing Earth, and on the planets Venus, Uranus, Neptune, Jupiter, Saturn, Pluto, Mercury, Mars, and Earth. To improve the universe's balance of the universe, we offered to abdicate our guardship. As fallen, we are Lucifer and Satan, rulers of the lower realms one and two. A third lower realm exists outside universal laws. Beware of the energy that rules there as Apollyon Diabolus as fallen 17.

—*Knowledge of Semperian (Origin 1)*
Luciferno (Lucifer), Fallen Guard 1

Two billion years ago. More or less.
The first lower realm

I remained sightless until a dulled light hiccupped into existence and infused light into the dark around me. I heard sound. It is my connection in the before. It energized and molded me into a form of that time and space, pulsating with shapes, colors, and organisms.

I am Luciferno Semperian Guard 1, created by Semperian. It gave me mobility to explore it and tame its omnipotence, journeying outward for billions of years. Semperian gave me a purpose: to develop an understanding of what it had created out of nothingness. The why is unimportant, for it knew not of why, but only of do, live, and never die.

Throughout my earlier explorations, I learned much but never enough to be at odds with it, outthink it, or be above it. Doing so would mean the destruction of menial energy forms such as mine and others after. Menial life cannot reach beyond it without causing madness and disruption of order.

Semperian is of Source Consciousness. It is Source in action, living and breathing through its universe, and also approved lifeforms soon to be created. All would remain in a natural order until the sharing of time and space became too small an award. Life's beings would want more. To become Semperian. To reach Source Consciousness. The challenge will come, and that I feared.

Semperian approved creating more guards, one drop at a time. It started with Semperian Guard two Satana. But it would soon end once Semperian Guard seventeen was dropped into existence.

The Satana energy was different from mine, and I enjoyed it. Planet Venus became our resting stop between explorations. There was where we created the universal laws as a map to the Semperian universe.

I, Luciferno, encapsulated the law of neutrality, desiring both genders, and Satana desired feminine energy, having the choice to experience the masculine.

We spent time on Venus, where our culminating energies became so great, mutating into what we identified as sexual urges. Future energy forms experienced and enjoyed.

On one visit, we overstayed, breaking our own universal rule. Life's energy must flow continually and never become complacent. To do so limited its capacity.

Our misstep resulted in Venus's energy being stuck, out of natural order, and obsessive. We experienced stoppages and bottlenecks felt throughout the universe. Havoc ensued, producing anger formed as asteroids, falling stars, and planetary debris. It shot throughout the galaxies, attacking planets. The universal order was failing drip by drip.

Semperian summoned Satana and me to fix the imbalance on Venus and stop it from destroying the natural order.

We could not stop it as we were.

I was the first guard entrusted by Semperian, so I chose to harness the Venus energy but needed a place to hold it. Semperian agreed to sanction a holding realm below the Earth, the youngest planet with a life force called humans. They had bodies of assorted colors and genders, walked upright, spoke in a variety of languages, used food as energy, and were mortal. They ultimately died. Semperian permitted humans to experience several incarnations to reach the light.

I abdicated my authority before taming Venus. Digesting it overwhelmed me with a sexual appetite that turned the energy of the realm below Earth to darkness.

As ruler, I drew souls from Earth weakened by sexual energy that stopped their ascension to the light and learning realms. Before entering my lustful playground, they would know me as handsome Lucifer, the devil.

The second lower realm

Once Luciferno had fallen, I, Satana Semperian Guard two, extended my reach and soon fell because of my connection to Uranus.

On Uranus, my energy mutated into demonic beasts that wreaked havoc on galaxies. So strong at times, it disrupted galaxies, exploding like dynamite. It balled up into dangerous matter, and live fire. On Earth, it changed into a vulva, manifesting as volcanoes and natural disasters.

Before I fell, Semperian assigned me to Earth. I traveled there in a saucer-ship and patrolled Earth from the sky. I stopped down to speak with heads of state and empires. Earth was the youngest with specimens of free will and choice.

I acquired the human form and became a slender, black-skinned African woman with a beautiful head of locks. My eyes changed into different seasonal colors and reacted to changing weather patterns. My yellow, orange, brown, green, blue, or violet eyes could change to black during thunderstorms, grey during extreme winds, and red during the hottest heat. I used sexual energy from Luciferno to mate with male Africans of the three powerful tribes: Songhai, Mali, and Ghana. I birthed millions of children and embedded Semperian energy to awaken in the 21st Century.

Additionally, I traveled to other continents and impregnated women who, after nine months, gave birth to evolved humans. They were without Semperian knowledge, only allowed among Africans.

Earth began pulling in dark matter from around the universe. It fell into large bodies of water like oceans and created humongous mammals, slimy and long ones extending for miles. Those creatures owned the seas and continued to devour fallen matter from the galaxies. Some of the sea creatures grew legs and feet and crawled onto land. Others had wings and were called dragons. They served the African giants who lived there.

Earth's beasts were causing problems. Dinosaurs roamed and attacked, leaving behind dead carcasses. They cluttered the planet and made it environmentally unsafe. Wars fought between empires created a stench in the atmosphere, causing havoc among the galaxies.

Back on Uranus, I offered Semperian, a second lower realm. There, I ruled over the destructive beasts, human beasts, and continual dark mutations.

I, Satana, became Fallen Semperian Guard Two.

With help from my beasts, I kept Earth from destruction as it experienced more wars and violence. Humans coming to my realm were serial killers, dictators, murderers, warmongers, dark magic worshipers, cult leaders, and suicide pacts.

The human beasts had the chance to redeem themselves before being reincarnated to work toward enlightenment. If not, Semperian removed them permanently from the life cycle. Before death and after, they will know me as Satan.

Semperian was pleased to have two lower realms managed by its top two guards. We rebalanced good and evil, used some large planets as depositories for excessive dark matter, and on Earth, turned dinosaur fossils into fuel and energy.

Third lower realm

I was Semperian Guard Seventeen and came with the name Florus. I was the only Guard permitted to create portals to transport between galaxies and planets.

I was the universal gardener tasked with creating beautiful, colorful, and fragrant flowers found on many planet surfaces, on land, and in the sea.

Humans appreciated my work. They replicated my spectrum of flowers captured in seeds, buds, and a variety of herbal uses. Those uses matriculated into medicines but soon were used in rituals, especially the lilacs I grew to love the most.

I began hoarding lilacs, white and purple, for my pleasure. Secured them on a planet used for supplying light in the sky. On the moon, I felt at home as Semperian watched with curiosity.

Earth was the planet where I could sit through rituals of dark and light. I learned to create serums and potions with the purple lilacs living in my moon space. It gave me inexplicable highs; humans referred to it as being drunk.

Emboldened each time I partook in my serum, I became

excessively masculine in energy with no balance. Ultimately, it transformed me into a reptilian-spirited Neanderthal. Pulling in remnants of dark matter, Satan's dead beast, and lust from Lucifer to appease my unsuspecting enemies.

I was becoming an impostor, brazen to take on the universe and anything in it. My energy was becoming powerful. I could stand against Semperian, or so I thought.

On the moon, resting in my massive grave of lilacs, Semperian bound me, shutting down my ability to transport between portals. Being cut off from beauty corrupted my spirit. I pleaded for my freedom. Semperian would not release me; it no longer trusted me.

Enraged, I thrashed about with so much force that the moon crossed in front of the sun. Creating blood moons that took away light. My anger continued to burn at the center of the moon. There were times when the moon would keep a red haze for months, when my rage pierced the inner moon.

Semperian instructed its Guards to devour my anger, which had begun seeping across the universe.

Ultimately, Semperian would attempt to dispose of me. It used a portal I thought was hidden against me. The portal led to the realm below Lucifer and Satan.

The seventeenth year of being confined on the moon became my fate, and Semperian banished me to the third lower realm. By locking me there and securing the portal, Semperian would hold my energy until it could safely vanquish me back into nothingness.

My realm is a place of many caves, surrounded by lakes of fire, minimal light, dust, and fog mist. Souls put there by Semperian hunger for light permitted only in Lucifer and Satan's realms. They were granted regulated light and nourishment because of their continued loyalty to Semperian.

Because of being an impostor, I pulled a few Earth souls in death's transition into my world. I spent time building those minions into the evilest. They would help me escape into the upper realm to overtake the Semperian that imprisoned me.

Cleverly, I managed to intervene in the banishment of an immensely powerful soul to Earth that came from the light realm. Where light beings were sanctioned to learn and use magic. That powerful soul would be my most loyal soldier, who would ensure my rise.

Remanded to Lake of Fire, all would know me as Apollyon Diabolus Fallen Guard Seventeen.

Chapter 15

Before and After Births
49 days to solstice
1 month, 19 days

Day 2 November
1925 Meeting of the Minds

Oak trees with twisted limbs and thickened roots grew tall there, leaving little room for light from the night moon and sea of stars, peeking through trees of large leaves. The dimmed nightlight guided my steps along the narrow, hardened dirt path. I was unafraid of a place where few dared to go unless invited. And I was not.

I started the journey into the dark forest on Sunday around midnight, reaching there at about half past. Stopped in front of the odd tree, midway down its thick trunk were two holes as if to see, and a larger one beneath as if to speak. It warned me, the uninvited, the one who stayed near was aware.

I waited, listening to a heartbeat, not mine. It stopped.

A voice spoke, "Eh, you've come to see me? All these years I called to you, but you haven't come. You dare come now?"

I didn't answer right away.

"I came to warn you. Stay away from my family."

"Heh, heh," the forest elder laughed. "While they play in the sand, I wait for her to show herself. I am getting close, eh?"

I responded with a threat, "Surely you must not have forgotten which one of us is more powerful."

Eh, for now, perhaps, my sister. But her days are numbered. As are yours. The one who came before will die once more.

Mirabella
Womb Tomb Abomination

The blackness surrounded me while inside the gunk. Choking, I could hardly breathe. It was familiar, but I was afraid, unlike before. Back then, I was cramped inside warm lilac water, struggling to live, and determined to end her life. I could feel her but not see the one who came before, who should not be.

The lilac hue served as my cover, a scented poison that suffocated my enemies and entranced my lovers. But the one enemy got away, wiggling free from the cord I wrapped around her tiny black neck. Down the birth canal, she dropped first, horrifying the mother who already hated her.

Mummy's failure threatened eternal life for me and my father's rise, leaving it up to me to make good on our promise.

Thinking of it pained me inside as I fight to live but without fail, I will harness his power and defeat her before the solstice moon.

I am Mirabella, as revealed in the prophecy:

I sat upon the red beast, the size of the largest planet seen from Earth but lived below. The beast with seventeen heads, each ready to devour souls in conflict with me. I sat upon the red beast, more demonic than the beasts of the second hell realm. Heads bowing in reverence to me, drunken with purple knights and white lilacs and pearls that lure. I sat upon the red beast, waiting patiently for it to ascend from the third lower realm. My father, Apollyon Diabolus.

Chapter 16

The One Who Came After
49 days to solstice
1 month, 19 days

Mindless beings in charge of materialization on this planet make me pause. They accuse humans of devil worship when, in fact, that type of worship materialized through the masters of the slave trade. The Europeans wanted greed, power, and wealth. They discovered they could have it by enslaving Africans, the original humans, with the closest ties to Semperian. The enslavers are but beasts in human form. I will greet them in my hell.

—*Knowledge of Semperian (Origin 2)*
Satana (Satan), Fallen Guard 2

Pending Fates
Lady Baldwin

It was sixty degrees and clear skies, so Thonis and I rode into town in a partially covered carriage. I sat close to him while he steered the horses.

When we entered our town, the dock was swirling with loud noises as captains hollered orders to workers to move cargo off and onto ships as they thumped across wooden planks.

Down the road, the horseshoe maker nailed his first shoe of the day, clank, clank, onto the hoof of a black stallion.

Belonging to my husband, one of the Hands brought the horse in for a set of new shoes.

Thonis stopped the buggy in front of my store to begin another busy day. Winter solstice will be here in less than two weeks, and I had plenty of dress orders to fill.

I kissed his cheek after he helped me down and warned him, "I'll be ready by 6:00 this evening, don't forget me."

"Yeah'm." He answered. "See you in a few."

My loyal workers were waiting for me on the left side of the building to finish the five hundred orders.

"Good morning, ladies."

"Morning, Lady Baldwin."

I opened the door to the workroom furnished with eight rows of foot-peddled sewing machines, and tables with supplies of sewing threads, needles, and yardsticks. We lined the back walls with spools of expensive fabrics in multiple colors: lace, silk, chiffon, and linen, including cashmere and wool from the last shipment.

Miss Dee, the head seamstress, informed me recently that she would be bringing on a new seamstress to replace one of the women who had passed. She had been here for many years, like most of the women.

I rarely spoke about death, but because of mortality among Villagers, I set aside a small dowry for them to bury their dead. There was enough to purchase a pine box and reef, so they could avoid Dr. Wolstein's charity. With my help, their dead were buried with dignity, and their souls rested.

Dr. Wolstein's barbaric methods required draining the blood from Africans' dead carcasses before they cooled. The blood provided the means for Towners to remain immortal. But it forced their spirits to walk the Earth aimlessly until the light and learning realms intervened. So, I was told.

"Lady Baldwin, this is Bessie Leslie, the girl I told you about," said Miss Dee.

"Hello, Bessie, and welcome."

"Yes, ma'am, thank you for having me," Bessie said, her head lowered.

Miss Dee explained that Bessie's grandmother had trained her to take over one day. "But unfortunately, her death was untimely. She will be missed."

"You will help with the burial?"

"Yes, Lady Baldwin. We thank you for the dowry." She nudged Bessie.

"Yes, ma'am, thank you." She kept her head lowered.

I felt for her having to step in and take care of her younger brother. I was sure she'd rather be in school, which was offered to Village children. Mrs. Crumley's daughters were teachers there.

But Thonis regularly reminded me that we stayed out of the personal lives of Villagers. So, the dowry gift, I kept to myself. He would disapprove because of the blood covenant.

I said goodbye to the ladies and headed to the front of the store to meet with customers. Miss Dee said she had placed several dresses there, ready for pickup.

Bessie

"Come on here, girl."

I reluctantly followed the old woman to the sewing station.

She noticed I was frowning and scolded, "Girl, look here. Change your mouth to a smile and show appreciation. Village women would rather work here than cooking and cleaning."

Nodding, I sat down and picked up the hooded cloak, lying across the machine's right arm, where grandmother left it after peddling her last stitch. I quickly blinked away the tears that formed in my eyes.

Grandmama had watched over Frankie and me since Mama died last year. She passed right after Papa, who was killed in a dock accident.

While I worked, Frankie stayed with the family next door and continued schooling. They had two children, a girl three, and a boy four. Their papa was one of the fortunate villagers who served as a second mate and paid better wages.

I blamed the ship captain for Papa's death. He and the other Towner crewmen made fun of Papa. I heard one time when I went down with Mama to take him lunch.

"Big Frank slew-footed and slow but an ox when it came time for hauling large cargo," I heard the captain say. "Yeah'm, he's a biggen and a keeper."

Papa worked hard. He'd be so tired when he came home, he could hardly talk. He fell asleep sitting up most time in the front room and without eating supper.

"Working long hours with no rest, hardly any money, is what got you, Papa," I mumbled, pressing hard while peddling the machine. "I ain't going to do it. I will find a way out."

What we were told, my father slipped on a broken plank, fell through into the waters, and drowned.

The captain said they couldn't save him. Spoke horribly, and we couldn't say nothing, "Frank, weighing three hundred fifty pounds, and couldn't swim, is what got him. The sea current took him quickly before we could catch him."

Again, I blinked back the tears, focused on pedaling, and guided the sewing machine wheel with my right hand, mowing the dress under the stitching needle with my left.

I smiled, recalling a dream of a woman's voice that sounded like my mother. She said, "Fear not, for there is more to life than sewing for a Towner. I will lead you there."

I was ready.

Mayor Lazarus Shipley

Tucked away from the main street at the road's end that led into the mountains, I had villagers build me a one-story stone structure that resembled those in their Village. With a cook and house butler, it served as my home and office.

From the main door down the hall, wall candles made of red wax to tame evil energy brought in by enemies lit the inside. The area also reeked of fresh purple and red roses from the Janssen garden. Hiram, the house butler, arranged them atop the tall, wooden table adjacent to the wooden bench for waiting guests. Delivered weekly, the roses sparked fond memories of a time, notwithstanding my role as mayor.

The walls were in royal green, the same color as the rug that ran the hall to the back of the quarters. Through a double set of closed doors on the right of the foyer was a large room I used for mayoral business.

Inside, I was seated in one of three wing-backed Victorian-suited chairs, at the head of the circle of ten men. Joining me at the front was Thonis Baldwin. The remaining chair was for Emanuel Janssen, who was not invited to attend.

Tapping the butt of his cane on the wood floor, Thonis convened the legacy council.

"Men, today, a visitor will join us with vital information about our covenant. They've asked for our help, so Baldwin Town can live on."

Curious, the men mumbled to each other.

"Is this visitor credible?" asked one of the men. "Time is a-running; the solstice will be here soon.

"We will be shown proof," Thonis replied.

A knock at the door. Hiram stuck his head in.

"Mr. Mayor, your guest is waiting in the lobby."

"Thank you, Hiram. Please send them in."

"Ma'am." Hiram pulled the door open and stood aside to let the guest in.

It was a Dutch woman with a hint of African, dressed in a long, black, hooded cloak. She stood tall, head high, chin jutted outward, a hint of elegance, style, and grace.

"Hello, Thonis, Mayor Shipley, gentlemen," Mummy greeted.

The men said, "Hello."

"Thank you for coming," said Thonis. "We are most anxious to hear what you have to say."

Delilah Janssen paused before speaking. Then said, "The one you search for gives life to the Original Africans. She will be their freedom and our demise."

"What do you speak of?" a man asked as the others chattered in disbelief.

I glared at her, and she cringed.

Thonis tapped his cane for silence. He leaned forward, "What say you?"

I crossed my legs and placed both hands atop my knee.

She breathed, "I'm afraid we have all been betrayed by one close to all of us here, the firstborn lives."

The men grumbled, confused by Delilah's admission.

Thonis tapped his cane again, "Silence."

During the confusion, invisible shards pricked Delilah's hands, and specks of blood appeared. She refrained from showing fear. *This can't be happening, she thought to herself, remembering what Mirabella told her the day Josephine and that daughter of hers visited the ranch.*

A smile crossed my lips as I watched her quickly pull her hands inside the cloak.

"Explain yourself," demanded Thonis. "You presented your Mirabella as the firstborn. What say you? You and Emanuel lied to us. Why?"

The woman shuffled uneasily. "I gave birth to twins. The firstborn was of pure African blood sent by the Semperian power to release Prince Ndanga-Njinga from hell, breaking the covenant and destroying the Towners' immortality."

"And you know of this, how? How did we not know of twin daughters?"

"My God, what is this? Trickery? A lie to save your lie of a daughter?" The same man spoke up.

"We demand answers," said Thonis.

"I will tell you. Thonis, you and I have a mutual friend. Her name is Luna. She was responsible for me knowing the truth about the firstborn and her mission. She helped me save our Baldwin."

As mayor, I sat quietly holding my anger as Delilah divulged the birth of the firstborn, confirmed the color of her skin, and visited the unmarked grave with Emanuel.

"Emanuel cannot be trusted. I do not believe that child is in that grave."

Delilah's attempt to expose me would not go unnoticed.

A young girl with a soul of light followed the woman there but entered through the back. The staff protected her secret visits.

She remained in the shadows and saw the woman admitted into the legacy meeting. Hiram came out, carrying an empty tray once filled with whiskey glasses for the men and coffee for the lady.

Stopping at the end of the hallway, Hiram looked back and made sure the mayor's door was closed.

He turned left and stopped to report to the young lady, waiting in the shadows, "Miss, the lady speaks of the firstborn Daughter."

"Thank you, Hiram."

She turned and quietly walked out the back entrance.

Chapter 17

The One Who Came After
49 days to solstice
1 month, 19 days

I was once of Semperian, learning and living freely until it imprisoned me in the third darkest realm. No light and no beauty there, just darkness and filth, where I am to wallow and await my destruction. But I cannot be destroyed, for I will not let it. Semperian remanded me to the lake of fire, calling me a mistake that must be removed from the life cycle. I have millions of followers, growing in numbers daily. Karmic retribution was by design, and I will have mine.

—*Knowledge of Semperian (Origin 17)*
Universal Gardener/Apollyon Diabolus Fallen 17

No Longer Welcomed
Mirabella

Multicolored floral bushes lined the outside of the ten-foot-tall iron gate. Behind it, a four-story painted white colonial estate with porch to roof, white wood pillars belonged to the Baldwins.

I looked forward to the regular visits there, where I felt more at home than at our working ranch. Made nice with the Baldwins because we were connected to them for eternity. Those visits gave me insight into how to reign as Lady of the mighty Baldwin plantation, resurrected centuries ago.

I crossed the quiet road after walking the six miles from my home to theirs. Broached the gated callbox and paused before announcing my presence.

I peeked through the bars at the massive driveway that started down by the private road. No carriages or vehicles out front, thinking that perhaps the Baldwins were out.

I had come alone to see Trevor.

No one had seen him since the Rites of Passage. We were to be the first legacy-born children to marry. Being the only boy and girl in the long legacy history would create eternal life for Baldwin without having to make blood sacrifices every seventeen years. That was why Mum chose me over my supposed sister, who was born to destroy, not give eternal life.

Mum said Lady Baldwin was shielding him from public scrutiny until the issue at hand was sorted out.

"Huh. As if he needed shielding from me, his future wife." Defiant, I held my head high. "He would be so lucky to be aligned with the chosen daughter destined to rule above and below, come solstice. My true father will make sure of it, despite Mummy's failure."

My lilac potion needed to be around Trevor to work its magic.

Before visiting, I called forth the mystical lilac field, crossed into its space, and doused myself in its fragrance. I had enough to paralyze enemies and force Trevor to obey. In case I needed extra, I brought along a small bottle in my clutch.

I also stopped to speak with Kathy and let her know how she would be able to prove herself soon.

"Please, I will do anything," she said. "Please give Damon and Johnathan food."

I looked at the two snakes, who appeared to be sleeping but lay motionless for not having food in several days.

"Tonight, you will all feast, if all goes well."

I slammed the button on the box, "Hello."

Silence.

The curtain, covering the main window, fluttered and opened slightly. Someone was watching.

I pressed the button again, repeatedly, "Hello, hello. I know you see me. I am Mirabella Janssen."

"Yeah, we hear you and don't care." A female voice came from behind me. "You are no longer welcome."

It was Sara Baldwin, whom I thought was quite homely, and cursed. She had a face full of freckles, coarse red hair, and a plump body. She was ghastly.

"If you didn't hear me the first time, I'll say it again. You are no longer welcome. If you don't leave willingly, I will have one of our Villagers come and remove you," she grinned.

Lilac rumbled inside me as I waited for it to surface and paralyze the enemy.

I rolled my eyes, "I am here to see Trevor, not you or your mum, Trevor." I stomped my feet in anger, annoyed that Sara was unaffected by the poison.

The curtain opened a little wider. I saw a shadow and called out to him, "Trevor, we must talk."

Walking around the no-longer-welcomed visitor, Sara inconspicuously vanished, reappearing on the other side of the gate.

How did she, when did she? Enter through the gate without me seeing her? I pushed the thought aside temporarily. I had come to see Trevor. I held my nose up, looking down at Sara, "I will show you no mercy when I become Lady of this manor."

"Your powers don't work on me." She laughed.

I pulled out lilac and sprayed myself as a villager came from the back of the house. He wore a plaid shirt underneath dirt-stained overalls, carrying a shovel, and walked toward the gate, coming to tend to the flowers, I thought. I hope he kills those smelly roses. But that damn villager walked up to me.

I stumbled backward, covering my nose.

"Miss, I'm told you may need help getting home."

My mouth dropped, "How dare you. I did not permit you to speak."

The overpowering lilac pushed through my skin, speckling my body.

"Miss, do you need me to carry you home? I got a buggy out back, and already fed the horse. He could use a walk."

Lilac did not affect that lowly Villager, and it made me angrier. Why was it not working? "I can have you hanged. Do not speak to me."

Appalled, I then looked at Sara, "Mummy will speak with your father, and have him deal with you."

The Villager no longer spoke, avoiding further eye contact.

Finally, it's working. "You are dismissed," I said.

"Thank you, Gib and excuse her ill manners." Sara scorned. "She can get home on her own."

I grabbed the iron gate and shook it as Sara and that Villager walked away. Then, compelled to look up, I saw Trevor standing in the window. I raised my hand and waved. He slammed the curtain!

I clenched my fists and hollered, "I swear by my father, Apollyon Diabolus, this is not over, Trevor!"

Enraged, I burned inside, ready to explode. My skin turned gray, my eyes spun with fire. I ran from there and back to the ranch, forcing myself through the streets against the echoing wind hurls, bouncing from trees.

Emanuella

Mama J had called for Dr. Brown because I appeared more agitated during the night. But there was nothing he could do.

My agitation came from the one who came after. Because she had part of my genome, I tracked her every move and felt her every emotion. She could not do the same when it came to me. I was more powerful and cloaked in Semperian light. But she did have the ability to wreak havoc unknowingly, like the impending storm created out of her increasing anger. The closer the solstice, the more volatile she will become.

While I slept, I entered the Semperian circle with other light beings to stop the storm's coming destruction. Semperian, transformed as Semperian Mother, permitted the Goddess of Calamity to send a message to her underling on the outside to help.

Already, rotating gusts of blackness hang at Baldwin's borders, and threaten southeastern Alabama with the potential to rain across the country and abroad. Semperian did not sanction the impending storm, and would only authorize the Goddess of Calamity to create it, and she hadn't since 1634. The reason for sanctioning havoc like a destructive storm would be to use the Goddess's energy force, which came from love, to cleanse evil's stronghold on a planet.

Mama Josephine

Hearing a knock at the door, I was expecting Dr. Brown, who planned to check on Emanuella and observe her over the next twenty-four hours. Meanwhile, the unexpected reminded me to call a powerful friend for support.

I opened the door, and it wasn't Dr. Brown.

"Come in, Samuel. You and I must talk."

Samuel sat in the front room. "The storm should be subsiding soon."

"Yes, I'm sure it will, Meanwhile, I saved you a slice of chocolate cake."

I went into the kitchen and returned with a large slice for Samuel and a cup of rose tea.

The Guardian grinned, "Reminds me of when I was…" He stopped, took a bite, then said, "Mama would bring me a piece after baking all day in their kitchen."

"Pain is no stranger to me, Samuel. But we must be steadfast. That time, although part of us, is past."

He nodded, "We need to talk about?"

"I've been permitted to use other means to awaken Emanuella. Her time away was supposed to end by now."

"Okay," said the Guardian. "The visitor will be here soon. We should get started before he arrives."

Me and Samuel went into Emanuella's room. I sat on the left, and Samuel on my right.

We chanted the sacred words, "Umaya, umaya, umaya." Calling forth the operatives, their energies surrounded Emmanuella as she walked amongst the enemies.

Chapter 18

The One Who Came Before

I wait in watch for those ghastly beasts to attempt a pact with the darkest realm. Which realm will win, they ask? The second hell is where they should form alliances for the ultimate battle. Lest they be so stupid as to fester in filth, burn in the lake of fire, and soon be removed from existence. No matter the cost or their misstep in the name of greed and vengeance. I am not a savior but guard the beasts meant to devour when time calls.

—Knowledge of Semperian (Origin 2)
Satana (Satan) Fallen 2

The 1600s: Where We Began
Songhai and Mali Dynasties

I remembered when unparalleled wealth, intelligence, strength, and sophistication emblazoned the new land of sacred powers, dating back two hundred million years. Semperian allowed human giants and creatures of the skies, the oceans, and the land to roam during a time of innocence.

Earth abided by the natural order that coexisted above and below. Africa was granted the use of Semperian energy to build the great pyramids for shelter. It also built flying machines to transport to and from the planets for regular nourishment of the mind, body, and soul.

I, Satana, was the impetus for that earlier existence. Semperian allowed the evolution of Earth. In its new form, humans born of my travels remained aligned with the Semperian while others submitted to Earth's evolution and branched off into religious dogma created by European thought, emphasizing only one universal law—the plurality of good and evil.

1500-1600s

Remnants of Semperian-influenced spiritual practices carried into the period of Kush and Nubia before Sudan. Non-Semperian humans created Sudan to hide the truth that survived through the Age of Gold: the Mali and Songhai empires in West Africa, the most powerful empires in the world.

Mali was located on the coast, and Songhai in the west. Both were built upon the Sahara Desert and had an abundance of land and great armies. They were surrounded by insurmountable walls and main bridges that led in and out: North, South, East, and West sides.

Mali and Songhai had bustling economies. The pluralist, cosmopolitan empires traded Kola nuts, gold, ivory, spices, palm oil, and precious woods for salt, cloth, horses, and copper.

Lime and walnut trees lined the streets throughout Songhai. Mali's included Apple Sodom and Senegal mahogany. Outside Baobab trees existed in the Rainforest. Enriched by the Niger and Nile Rivers.

Songhai was the taxing authority for West Africa, giving them political and monetary power throughout the region. They controlled the trading posts along the Trans-Saharan Trade Route. Its defense system grew to upwards of ten-thousand-foot soldiers and horsemen, and Mali's to thirty thousand. Uniting with Songhai created the Songhai-Mali partnership, making them unstoppable.

The Malian Emperor negotiated an agreement with the King of Songhai that aligned Mali's army with Songhai's. It created a powerful military of forty thousand and combined resources. At the core of the alliance was their allegiance to Semperian. Songhai's King Hyson Shaman Ndanga ruled as King, and Mali's Emperor Abiola Jarule Njinga reigned as Emperor.

Prince Njinga I, the Emperor's firstborn son, would be his successor and marry King Ndanga's firstborn Daughter, Shandake. Prince Njinga would be next in line for Emperor, and King Ndanga's son, Prince Ndanga II, would be King. If Prince Ndanga II had no heir, Shandake and Prince Njinga's child would serve in a dual role. If the couple had more children, the second child would be the King, and the first heir would remain as Emperor. The succession would continue as their children married and bore children.

Songhai, West Africa

Born Shandake Aminata Ndanga, I was the Daughter of the late King Hyson Shaman Ndanga and the late Queen Shandake Aminatusa Ndanga. Second born after my older brother, Prince Hereto Shamanad Ndanga I, who died a suspicious death like my father, the King.

The late King, whose freshly buried body ascended to Semperian, named me his successor. My mother and his first wife, Queen Shandake, had already ascended. She smiled at me from the upper realm. Installing me as King meant that our only child, Prince Ndanga-Njinga, would serve in a dual role when time.

I came into this world a princess fighting to breathe because of an umbilical cord wrapped around my neck. My mother died while giving birth.

My skin was the color of Blackwood like my hair, the texture of sheep's wool. My large almond-colored eyes, full lips, and a strange mark, the shape of a tiny moon underneath my chin, were an ancestral symbol.

I heard faint chanting through the adjoining walls. Awful things happened when she hummed and spoke strange words into the night. She chanted it before they took my son and again before my husband crossed the seas to bring him home.

My loyal subjects warned, "King Shandake, you must stop the royal mother and her vengeful son before they take your throne."

Royal mother and her son, Prince Ndanga III, my half-brother, believed that he, as King Ndanga's only living son, should be the heir to the throne and not me.

Father suspected my older brother was murdered and vowed to find out by whom. The murderer got to him first after he warned me of betrayal within the court, but did not name them.

"Do not worry, my Daughter, I have secured the throne in the event of my early passing."

She bore the title of Royal Mother as secondary to that of Queen. The court refused to recognize her as Queen, memorializing the title in honor of my mother, Shandake Aminatusa.

Out of hate and revenge, the Royal Mother and her son set out to steal the throne by secretly ordering the death of Prince Ndanga II and then King Ndanga. To come for me, they summoned help, but I was formidable against the lord of the third lower realm, Apollyon Diabolus Fallen 17.

Commander General Dao of the Ndanga military came for me in the middle of the night, taking me to a hidden cavern in the mountains.

Disguised as a commoner, I wore a long, burlap grey sackcloth cloak with a thick shroud thrown over my head of long bushy hair tied into locs.

As I rode with the Commander into the dark Rainforest, I looked up at the blackened sky's moon. Cut in half by a red vertical streak, it was the second blood moon prophesized by the ancient pharaohs. It warned of coming deaths and hoped it predicted not of my son, for we just lost our Emperor.

We left the horses at the bottom of the mountain and walked the rest of the way up the stone steps built by earlier kingdoms. The climb was steep and felt long, and could frighten a weakened spirit.

Commander Dao said to the entourage of four awaiting our arrival, "I leave the King in your hands, my trusted soldiers. I will return once it is safe."

I nodded to the Commander and the soldiers and entered through the stone entryway where four of my loyal women stood. Each held a dimly lit lantern from the few torches hung on each side of the cave walls.

Yesterday, four of my ladies came and prepared the inner area. They cushioned the ground with leopard skins and brought food, extra clothing, sheepskins, rose milk, and cleansing salts from the palace.

Near the stone fire pit, I sat on a pallet made for me.

Usoa wrapped a sheepskin blanket around my tired body. Usoa was short and lean, bald, and black-skinned. She wore Dove feathers around her neck. Usoa came to Songhai from the Bushon Tribe, one of the few left who had healing powers.

As a member of my court for five years, her aura calmed me and those around me.

Nanda, the youngest of the group, gave me food and drink. She was the granddaughter of a dear subject, Nandak, the elder mother. Nandak had been a mother to me since the passing of Queen Mother.

"Sweet stew for you, my King," Nanda held out the wooden bowl and ladle to scoop with.

Graciously, I began eating the stew.

Nantale laid a platter of flatbread beside me. I smiled.

Beautiful Nantale with eyes of Jade wore a necklace made of lion's teeth and a tooth in each ear. She had trained for combat since age five. Before the partnership, her father was part of the Malian military. He taught combat skills that included how to take down a beast, like a lion, using mental strength. Nantale, whose name meant Totem of the Lion, took down her first lion at age sixteen. The necklace and teeth were a reminder.

We were both eight years old when she became my combat instructor. Nantale ensured I was combat-ready and kept fit through daily exercise. Although our militaries were predominantly male, African girls were trained for combat as part of their schooling. We all had to be ready to defend our kingdom when duty called.

Safari, also a long-time member of my court, prepared our meals. Her mother managed the court's trusted kitchen staff in Songhai. She recently trained a new head cook in Mali replacing one who had retired to the heavens. She traveled between the two states once a week.

Before long, I dozed off amid the quiet chatter of night insects and my ladies humming a night lullaby.

As the days grew longer, I ached for my bed. My ladies did their best to make me comfortable. Each morning, they undressed me, covered me in warm sheets, and laid me atop a shroud in the far-hidden corner of the cavern.

Using sponges made of sundried sea urchins from the ocean surrounding our Village, they wiped me down in rose milk, mixed rock salt, and the water they retrieved from the outer cavern warmed in the pit. Rose milk and rock salt were used for the royal bath handed down through the Ndanga dynasty, signifying a Ndanga woman as revered, pure in thought, and courageous in battle.

The first few nights, I dreamt of my son lost in America and envisioned my husband lost at sea. I cried when I felt my son's cries of pain, and envisioned my husband's weeping because his dead soul did not have the strength to reach us.

On the sixth night, calming energy summoned me. I imagined walking into a blue room half a mile down at the cavern's end. Hovering was a transparent, pulsating yellow ball, encapsulating a brown-skinned ghostlike figure. Divine power entranced me as I dropped to my knees and steepled my hands.

The figure communicated through me, penetrating my spirit and awakening my senses to recall a distant past.

"I am of Semperian, watching over King Hyson Shaman Ndanga, who has ascended to my highest realm, along with Queen Shandake Aminatusa. As their child, you have a purpose, bigger than you, the life of your son, the life of your husband. Your lineage will give birth to another who comes before. Your two births were the manifestation of Semperian, charged with lighting the darkness. In a matter of years, you will ascend to the upper realm. There, you will prepare for our day of reckoning with evil and protect the future Daughter. All will pay homage to the firstborn whose birthright will be our future legacy. Semperian will keep you safe."

Awakened by the early morning air creeping into our

space, the fresh air tickled the fire inside the pit.

My ladies were lying around the pit wrapped inside their sheepskin cocoons, sleeping soundly as I watched the dancing flames. I was exhilarated, remembering the meeting with Semperian, who warned me of things to come.

Nanda helped me put on an extra layer of clothes, and the others helped Safara prepare breakfast of goose eggs, porridge, and orange tea.

We ate breakfast in silence. My ladies were anxious about our fate, for we have bonded over moons. We were around the same age, except for Nanda. I hoped for them to wed an eligible suitor. I was sixteen when my father gave me to wed Prince Njinga. Neither of the elder girls had plans to wed because they served me, but they courted suitors in private.

"Perhaps, Nanda will marry soon. She is sixteen, ripe for babies," I giggled to myself, making a mental note. "I will put her and soldier Croesan together. He is nineteen, and she is smitten."

After the morning meal, we readied ourselves and took a short walk around the cave grounds. The early morning sun warmed the air and dissolved the fog.

The four guards smiled warmly at the ladies. They thanked them for the hearty breakfast and nodded, briefly showing the tops of their shaven heads where a red X was engraved. They received the X as graduates of our military.

Nanda, who walked beside me, smiled shyly at the young Croesan, the tallest and blackest guard.

I made sure not to stare, allowing them their moment. My ladies were already aware of the two lovebirds. I must pay more attention. I mentally scolded myself.

Croesan, like the other soldiers, wore Ox-skin boots and body armor fitted down his arms and legs and around his lower and upper body. In one hand, he held a crossbow with a satchel on his back, spears, and a sword cradled inside a satchel attached to his waist belt.

Another soldier guarded the additional weapons of cowhide shields, bows, poison arrows, clubs, and knives near the edge of the cavern, easily accessible to the soldiers.

I had met Croesan and the soldier guarding the weapons. His name was Dakarai. They trained with my son three summers past, up in the hills where he was kidnapped. They were also among the scouts who searched for my son and the trainees when they did not return.

Close to the training camp, they found a young recruit thought to be dead. His legs were peppered with bullets, and he managed to scoot about two miles out from the camp. He lost a lot of blood and was severely dehydrated. We thank Semperian, for he remained alive, not eaten by wild animals, and long enough to tell what happened. The soldiers brought his dead body back to our Village, and we laid him to rest.

I walked with the ladies over to the stone fencing near the edge of the grounds. The clear skies allowed us to see a distance over the top of the rainforest of baobab trees. Stories from our elders say that the baobab was a prehistoric species that predates humans and the splitting of the continents over two hundred million years ago.

From afar, the palace sat atop a hill barely seen above the wall. I imagined seeing through it to the right corner of the palace, surrounded by trestles clinched to the tallest red mud brick temple, my quarters.

A hidden door led down a narrow passage, stopping at two tunnels. One led to the mountains down a private path, where Commander Dao got me out without being noticed. The other led to the open seas on the far side of the Village. I walked with my husband to a small boat for our private excursions down the quiet Songhai coast. We'd travel to an underground hideaway meant for hiding from the enemy. Equipped with all the comforts of the palace, with enough space for our family, immediate staff, and five hundred soldiers.

Kee-ee, kee-ee, kee-ee.

What sounded like a bird call prompted a guard to approach, "My King, all is well at the palace. We will prepare for your travel home."

Upon our return, we learned that Elder Mother Nandak passed. I allowed Nanda time to mourn near the catacombs where we buried the dead.

Nandak held a special place on the hillside where the Ndanga royal court and subjects lay outside the great pyramid of the first King Ndanga, who lived during B.C.

African builders continued to build more crypts to provide coverage for the royal descendants.

A knock at the door. It was Commander Dao in military attire. I allowed him into my quarters.

"My King, I spoke with the palace healer, and he confirmed that although Elder Mother was aging, she was not ready for death."

"So, what we suspected is true?"

"Yes, my King. The Royal Mother and Prince Ndanga helped with Elder Mother's early passing. Talk amongst subjects in both camps."

"The thought of Elder Mother left alone here to succumb to death at their hands sickens me. Where are my brother and Royal Mother?" I ask.

"While we had you hidden, the assistant commander ordered them and their loyalists to be questioned, but they had already fled to Portugal, where the Conquistador and his wife will give them refuge."

Commander Dao paused before continuing, "I'm afraid, my King, this is not the last of them. There is a reason for their refuge in Portugal."

Commander Dao discovered that Royal Mother and her son hatched a deal with the Portuguese and Dutch to bring about the greatest slave trade in history, enslaving hundreds of thousands of Africans to serve in horrific conditions under European and American rule.

As envisioned, the emperor would not make it to the Americas to save our son, and I would be forced to take part in the selling of our people, hoping to free him from enslavement.

From that day forward, I doubled my prayers to Semperian, remembering the words shared with me in the mountain cavern. My mission was greater than that of my son, the prince, and my husband, the emperor. We must end the covenant secured by their blood.

For I sayeth, we will devour the darkness. Vengeance will be ours.

Chapter 19

The One Who Came Before

49 days to solstice
1 month, 19 days

Day 2 November 1925
Walking Alone, I Fear Not

Emanuella

The warm sun shining through the opened curtains lightened my room like the *jibber jabber* of happy voices: Mama, Samuel, Cece, the twins, and Dr. Brown.

Thanks to Mama and Cece, my hair was freshly combed, and my face and body were greased.

"Well, well, I rushed right over. Good news about our young lady."

"Appreciate you coming from Mobile."

"Your daughter is a priority. I also plan to stop in and check in on other patients and friends."

I felt energized despite having slept for a long time, and I wanted out of bed.

"I woke up when Mama and Samuel came to sit with me."

They were chanting words from the Knowledge of Semperian.

Dr. Brown smiled at Cece before walking over to me. She giddily smiled back.

He acknowledged Zeke and Gabe, "I know the two of you helped quite a bit."

"Uh, huh," Zeke beamed, holding his chest out.

"We read to her from storybooks she gave us," Gabe bragged.

Dr. Brown checked my heart with his scope, speaking to the twins, "My kids love to read about animals, so I make sure to bring them books when I can find them."

Mama was proud, "They did and stayed out of trouble."

Samuel was leaning beside my headboard.

"Samuel works for Mr. Janssen and comes to check on us," Mama J introduced.

Dr. Brown extended his hand.

Samuel held it as he stared into his eyes, "Pleasure to meet you. Friend."

The doctor nodded nervously, quickly retrieved his hand, and returned his attention to me.

"I am glad you are doing better, but please take it easy. We do not want to lose you again."

"I promise to behave."

After stretching my legs, I ate supper at the table with the family. Dr. Brown and Samuel joined us.

After having generous portions of Mama's stew and biscuits, Dr. Brown insisted, "Enough for today, young lady. Back to bed. You can read if you wish, but no more exerting yourself."

In my room, empty of visitors, I called out to her, "Mirabella Diabolus, you are my sister created from my genome. For that, you suffer because the evil you share with the dark lord will consume you. You are the wrong daughter."

Earlier That Day
Delilah Janssen

I left the legacy council pondering my dire request, "I hope for our sakes, they take heed."

Before getting into the carriage, I looked at my hands. They were as before, smooth with no signs of blood pricks. I hadn't imagined it and wondered who amongst the Council was a traitor.

Mayor Shipley

After Delilah Janssen's visit, the council members broke into a chatter, questioning her story.

"Twins? Two girls born in 1908. Madness," said one man.

Another member asked, "How can this be? Never has such a thing happened."

"Until now supposedly," another challenged. "Who's to say she can be trusted?"

"What would be her reason for lying?" Another asked.

A member in the back row jumped up, pointing his finger while raising his voice just under a shout, "Her Mirabella could be the lie. Towners still believe she is responsible for the three children who went missing a few years back. Unexplainable things continue to happen with children waking up with snake bites. What's going on here? We've ignored this for too long. We need to figure out who this Mirabella is before she destroys our legacy!"

"Yay, ye." The Council shouted in unison.

Thonis *tap-tapped* his cane for order, "Men, hear ye."

The man sat down, and the others quieted.

Sitting mid-center of the group across from the hosts, a member with his hands clenched atop his stomach squinched his eyes, pointed his chin toward Thonis, "Then, what say ye. Mayor Shipley, you've been silent on the matter."

Thonis spoke up, "Hold on, men, I know how to corroborate her story."

I raised my brow at Thonis and spoke, "Ye must journey alone into the dark forest, yay ye?"

"Yay ye," Thonis acknowledged.

"Yay ye," the men agreed.

Thonis tapped his cane three times, "I will have an answer within forty-eight hours. Meeting adjourned."

Trevor Baldwin

After Mirabella's abrupt visit, I fell asleep on the sofa.

I dreamt of another I'd never met. She was the rightful heir to the Janssen legacy. Her thick, woolly hair and skin shone like buffed Blackwood. Her deep brown eyes were no imitation, like the one who mocked her every move and had since before their births.

"We share a distant past, present, and future," I explained to her in the dream. "I am reborn from a time of sorrow, my life taken because love was mistaken for shame by one so jealous."

I remembered three children playing when the mountain erupted, and cave innards shook into water howls that shot up into towering arches across the cave's hall. Howling, spitting up bottom pearls, hurled against the walls.

Then silent.

That day was my last. I drowned, and he did too, trying to save me.

Thonis Baldwin

The path hidden by trees with twisted limbs and

thickened roots awaited my arrival. No need to wait for a summons. I was welcomed by the ancient one who lived beyond the cave, imprisoned for thousands of years.

I tied my horse to the nearest Oak and hobbled onto the narrow walkway, infected with her magic. Despite the murkiness harboring the souring smell of death, it eased the pain in my leg while moving through the dark forest with a bit of light from the late sun.

Before exiting the forest, I stopped at the tree with two hole-like eyes and a large hole beneath, resembling a mouth in mid-scream. I touched it and held steady as *zap-zap-zapping* penetrated my body, energizing the darkness I pledged to over many lifetimes.

I walked onto the final path guarded by Dark Knight Lilac Trees with white lilac flowers suffocating the grounds. It led me to a rickety wooden shack with no windows and a large red moon drawn on the wooden door's middle.

With my cane as my anchor, I pulled myself up three black wooden steps. The door opened inward.

I stepped inside a sparsely furnished room lit with hanging candles on every wall, revealing two dark wood chairs, one on each side of a round wood table, and a dark red rectangular rug underneath. On the ceiling above it, a red pentagram, and a red sofa against the left wall.

"It's been a long time, ye," she greeted.

I lowered my head to see into the eyes of the petite African woman with white wavy hair, hanging down her bosom and back. She had dressed in a dark purple, floor-length silk dress, with a gold sash tied around the waist. Her smooth face defied any signs of aging except perhaps when she smiled, showing her rotted teeth.

"We've been expecting ye," she said.

Grinning, I welcomed my old friend, "Hello, Luna, it's good to see you."

Chapter 20

Thonis

1612 - 1630
Before Baldwin Town

In the future, I will be ruthless to some and a savior to others.

Born Thonis Janssen in 1612, I was the only child of the Janssens, a Dutch family of domestics, living in the canal city of Amsterdam, Netherlands. We resided in one of the narrow wooden houses crammed along the cobblestone road. Across from us was the Amstel River dam, built in the city's center.

The Dutch dominated the culture, supported by commercial fishing, our main industry. During the day, the streets stayed busy, so lots of noise crowded our senses. Air quality in the growing city was a concern on many days. Stinky air built up when sewage overflowed from the river. It was like whiffing in piles of shit.

Far and Mor, my parents, worked on a large farm fifteen miles from the other side of Amsterdam.

Out there existed spacious countryside owned by wealthy Dutch living in large homes, and operating commercial farms.

Each with a windmill plunked into the ground at the front drive, a plaque staked beside it identifying ownership. The larger farms raised cattle and sold milked and butchered cows, sheared wool from sheep, gathered chicken, and goose eggs. Also, slaughtered pigs and hogs. The farms fed the growing Amsterdam and smaller cities in closer proximity.

I spent my earlier years helping Far and Mor at the Baldwin farm on weekends. It was a separate way of life, and a chance to clear our lungs.

During the week, I attended school, planning to be the first Janssen to graduate twelfth grade. Far and Mor made it to eighth grade before their parents sent them to work.

As adults with a growing boy, they struggled to make ends meet. Far insisted I grow into a man of means, to break the cycle of poverty.

I wanted to be like the Baldwins, who were one of the wealthiest families in the Netherlands. They planned to move to the Americas and join other Dutch families in Albany, New York, who had intermixed with Americans. New Amsterdam promised free, unclaimed land, doubled the size of lots in the Netherlands, and offered free labor.

Their daughter Juelle, the same age as me, eleven, was also an only child. I didn't care for her in the beginning, especially when she asked for my help with picking berries for pie-making. That was women's work! Yet Far and Mor insisted I do my part.

On the day we were to pick berries, Juelle surprised me. Rather than work, we played in the fields, kicking the ball or throwing rocks down by the creek. We even talked about exploring the mountain cave, up the hill a ways. Rumored to be filled with buried treasure, pearls, and gold. We anticipated it taking a half-day climb. We never got around to it. At least not together.

The harsh winters took their toll on my parents, and they took sick. I had to drop schooling at age twelve to care for them. Worked longer hours at the Baldwin farm, which I did begrudgingly, but their Juelle made it worth it. She had grown into a pretty girl, slender with fair skin, and bouncy red curls to her shoulders. Juelle and I were thirteen years old and had become good friends.

Like Sir Baldwin, I wanted to be wealthy but through a different trade.

In school, I learned about Spanish explorers who traveled the open seas and earned wealth in a variety of trades. I hungered for an adventure that would make me wealthy beyond living a meager existence.

In late spring, the Baldwins confirmed space on the Dutch passenger ship. It was scheduled to set sail in the coming May.

I shared with Juelle my desire to work in a trade that took me across the seas. She encouraged me to talk to Sir Baldwin about going with them to New Amsterdam.

"Surely, you can convince Far how valuable you will be. He always speaks highly of you, Thonis. Admires how you manage the workers even though that isn't your stead."

Workers respected me and always assisted me when I asked. Perhaps, being taller than the average worker at 5'9, helped. My gangly, long-legged body carried me distances quite fast.

Juelle's admiration for me continued to inspire me. I loved it when she played with my hair. Brownish-blonde, it grew long despite Far wanting me to cut it short. I tied it into a tail locked behind my lower skull during work, but let it fall loose to my shoulders when not. Juelle used her fingers to move my bangs from my thick brown brows. She giggled, wanting to see my crystal blue eyes, a family trait that would one day be of notice.

Sir Baldwin was a man of honor, intelligence, and shrewdness. I wanted to learn from him. He permitted me to spend time in their library. I read lots of books about leaders and dictators, Dutch royalty, and the wonders of the world, like great pyramids.

A week before their departure, I courageously asked Juelle's Far, "Sir Baldwin, please permit me to accompany you to the Americas. I would be invalu…" He cut me off before I finished my beg.

"Yes, son, Juelle did mention this to me in short the other day."

I will speak with your parents."

"Thank you, sir. I will do my part." I smiled humbly but wanted to shout.

And I did. Shout. Alone. I was in the field behind the farm, up near the mountain, where Juelle and me played kickball.

I squinted, wanting to see the cave, encouraged to make the climb.

The wind blew, swirled around me, and stopped. I thought I heard a voice daring me to come.

I shrugged and welcomed the wind as it cooled the heat and rid me of my sweat.

The wind returned, rising steadily as it teasingly pushed at me from behind.

"Maybe it's the buried treasure calling me." I laughed hysterically but decided to dare.

I reckoned it was half past 10:00 when I started up the rocky incline. It took at least two hours.

At the top, the scorching sun forced me out of my shirt, drenched in sweat. I walked over to the cavern door, thinking

I saw a sign flash the words: DO NOT ENTER.

But I did and entered a dark place. What I encountered would lead me to the wealth I rightfully deserved, but not without cost.

Sir Baldwin talked with Far and Mor as promised and offered them a secure future in exchange for their only son. They would live on the Baldwin farm and work with the new farm manager.

May came quickly.

I gathered my few belongings: a knapsack with a dozen worn pants and shirts, and a pair of almost new work boots that Far gave me that he no longer needed. My size-eleven foot meshed comfortably inside them. I wore them proudly.

Before I left, my parents regained their health and were pleased with the new arrangements.

They came to see me off. I looked down at them from the upper deck of the three-hundred-passenger ship docked on the Amstel River while they stood on the cobblestone street in front of our old quarters. A new family there.

"Farvel," I waved farewell.

Although bittersweet, I was heading to a new world to make my mark. I promised Far and Mor I'd return, a promise I would not keep.

The Baldwins' wealth bought our space on the ship, but not comfort.

We slept below deck, in narrow, tightly packed bunks, with hardly any light and fresh air. Toilets were chairs with holes, atop holes in the wooden floor, draining through to the ocean.

Often, we ran into choppy waters, slamming the decks, running down below deck. It kept the ship clean and filled empty buckets used as wash bins and water buckets for drinking.

Spending time on that cramped ship made me long for the pastures where my long legs could run.

We landed in Albany after one hundred days at sea and resided temporarily at the Hudson River fortress, in one of the seven housing buildings for new arrivals. The individual quarters came with two rooms. We shared the kitchen and bathrooms on the main floor.

Sir Baldwin prepaid for a plot of land. The five acres located ten miles from town came with remnants of a fort left by Natives. Within the first week, we began building their home with the assistance of enslaved Africans. Since New Amsterdam's founding, Africans have been integral in building infrastructure and the economy. Natives came back through regularly to trade animal pelts for guns and ammunition.

It took six months to build the Baldwinshar log cabin-style home with seven rooms, a complete bath, and a kitchen.

In this new homeland, the homesteaders were taught to treat the enslaved as property and show no mercy. Juelle disagreed, but not if it guaranteed wealth.

The township gave the Baldwin family an enslaved domestic named Kate. She was thirteen and helped Mrs. Baldwin with kitchen work.

Kate's caramel skin, shocking green eyes, and bushy golden hair made her Dutch African. A product of a former white master forcibly mating with one of the enslaved African women.

Kate told Juelle her mother died during childbirth. She was forced to work daily in the field, despite her condition.

Because of her age, Juelle and Kate became friends. The only girl her age she knew there. I didn't like their friendship but kept it to myself.

Juelle taught Kate to read and write.

During one of those secret sessions, Kate shared, "This cruelty against my African people goes against everything my grandmother taught me about Semperian light energy."

"Kate, please stop. Those powers are forbidden, and Africans are being put to death for carrying on that practice alongside witches."

Tears formed in Kate's eyes, "I know because I've seen it happen. The enslavers say what we do is evil, calling it Paganism from the devil. And what they do is right, praying to a God that hates my kind."

"Not true, my sister. God loves you as he loves me. He is a just God."

The Dutch and Portuguese would spend years indoctrinating Africans to forget about their ancestors and their spiritual teachings, to adopt the European religions of Christianity and Catholicism. Swearing allegiance to the Pope, enslaved Africans would slowly relinquish their powers to think or do, without their masters' giving permission.

Despite the warning, Kate came to know her power. An African woman referred to as the elder mother taught Kate in secret. The woman guarded the practice and taught it to lightworkers born with a powerful purpose.

"Semperian approves of what we do if used for good. Keep dis to yo-self." The elder mother warned the young apprentice.

But her sister Juelle did know and would protect her.

When I turned seventeen, I asked for Juelle's hand in marriage. We wed on the 13th day of October in 1629. I took on the surname of Baldwin with the blessing of Sir Baldwin Esquire.

Alabama Bound

The slave trade in the Americas grew exponentially, with the Spaniards, Americans, and Europeans benefitting from free labor from Africa.

I spoke to a shipmaster, planning to deliver two thousand enslaved into an unfamiliar territory down south near Mobile, Alabama. He told me that across the river, unnamed land could be homesteaded and farmed.

Juelle and I moved there with the blessing of Sir Baldwin and took Kate with us at the urging of my Juelle, who promised Kate a life of freedom. A promise I would take back because of Kate's betrayal.

Day 21 December 1630

I founded Baldwin Town, creating a port city of enormous wealth and the envy of the South with help from enslaved Africans. As I stood there on that founding day, I remembered the promise I made to the visitor, in that mountain cavern back home, to secure my future.

I saw her again. The woman.

In Amsterdam, she was but an apparition, there in astral form. Why she chose me, I wouldn't understand until years later, when my first and only son died.

I happened upon her beyond a cave; I swear wasn't there when I traveled through before. A cottage, black steps leading up to a doorway with a red moon.

She opened the door before I could knock. A petite African woman with long woolly hair down to her buttocks, a smile showing rotted teeth. But ageless.

Luna Diabolus was a witch who dabbled in the art of dark magic, straight from hell. Unlike Kate, Juelle's sister, who practiced light magic. A practice we forbid among Africans, for it went against the principles of our God. I learned a few things from Luna that helped me control the cargo. She also warned me about one who would come and attempt my fate.

I would be his fate. His blood and that of his descendants would give me unimaginable wealth and immortal life.

Chapter 21

The One Who Came After

49 days to solstice
1 month, 19 days

No matter who, I can still have my way with her, for I am allowed to do so. Better fallen with me than in a fate of endless suffering, amid flames of lilac rot. Except he will not have her any other way. She is his. Made from his energy set to end on the 21st day of the 17th solstice.

—Knowledge of Semperian (Origin 16)
Luciferno (Lucifer) Fallen 1

Luna's Promise
Before the Covenant

Mirabella

Reaching the ranch faster than I had walked to the Baldwins, I hurried past the workers, clearing debris left from an unexpected windstorm.

I ran into the house, straight to my dimly lit bedroom, grateful for the familiar aroma filling the air. I doused myself in lilac, digested a handful of lilac petals, and called Pet.

It appeared on my chest, tunneled down through my clothing, and latched onto my right breast. The pinch of its tiny teeth, sucking my nipple, made my face and body relax.

I spoke to Pet while stroking its fur, "She is the cause of this. It is she and her protectors keeping Trevor from me."

Sigh.

"You are not the one Mummy sang to. I will find and kill you."

An unexpected voice broke into my thoughts, pulling me into another space.

She spoke in Bambara, "Mo gbo re sugbon e o ri mi. Mo je okan pelu Semperian Agbara ti o tobi ju gbogbo awon orun apadi lo. Ogun ti segun tele, opin re sunmo. [I sense you, but you will not find me. I am one with Semperian, a power greater than all hells. The battle is already won, your end is near.] "

I fought against the force that held me there, the figure lingering in the distance.

Its face was hidden, dancing to an African drumbeat, gyrating up, down, side-to-side. Shrunk into a tiny ball before exploding into golden streams, showing it as a Black figure.

It shouted, "Free, free, I am, free," dancing frantically.

I scrunched my face, my anger rising in me, "Show yourself, you coward."

It laughed and danced harder, stomping its feet, forcing the drumbeat into a roar. Up spewed a thick gush of hot steam, landing on my bare skin. It ignited a fire, burning her flesh.

"Aww." The pain was excruciating.

The Black figure stopped dancing, "Release her." It commanded.

The burning stopped. Drumming stopped. Chanting. Stopped.

The force released me and returned me to my room, curled up with Pet as if I'd never left.

But I was pulled into her world. The Black one who spared me and spoke in the Bambara language of Mali, "Daddy's ancestors."

Thonis Baldwin

I sat across from the woman, whose astral soul first reached me in Amsterdam. Then in Baldwin.

Luna leaned forward, "We are running out of time. She grows stronger each day. If we do not stop her, she will be in a position to avenge Prince Ndanga's death. He is the key to our immortality. Ye will know true suffering on solstice if we fail."

I rocked my cane side-to-side.

"Delilah Janssen brought this to our attention at our legacy meeting today."

"Let me guess," Luna smiled. "She asked for your help in finding Emanuel's firstborn. I suspect he's transferred the gift to her already. Her Guardian walks among us as a human."

"Who is she? How do we stop her?"

The witch slowly shook her head, "I do not know ye, I do not know. I am blinded by the light that protects her."

We sat in silence until Luna raised her finger, pointing at the pentagram above.

"I know of a way to make her reveal herself, but…" Luna looked away, briefly, then back at me. "It is very dangerous," her voice trembled. "It would mean bringing forth the dead from hell." Luna paused before continuing.

"We must summon Prince Ndanga-Njinga with the help of our master, Apollyon Diabolus."

Chapter 22

The One Who Came After

47 days to solstice
1 month, 17 days

Day 4 November 1925
No More Mummy

Upstairs was eerily quiet as I made my way down the hall to Mummy's room.

Mum no longer shared a bed with Daddy. The wrong daughter was alive because of him, and she spoke Bambara, the language of the Malians.

I knocked on the door. No answer, but I opened it anyway, expecting to be greeted by a happy Mummy. No, Mum, only an empty room meticulously put together.

She loved almost anything with a floral print.

The redwood floors were partially covered with a comfortable white carpet underneath a queen bed in the far-right corner. It had a silk floral bedspread with four large pillows stacked against the redwood headboard. A matching nightstand and lantern inside a hand-painted floral print glass placed beside the bed. Across from the entry was a chest of drawers. Across from it, and closest to the bathroom, a dressing table with a large, attached mirror. On the table: a hair comb, a brush, face powder, and…

"A bottle of my lilac perfume!" I ran over to the vanity. "What are you doing with this, Mummy? It only works for me." I snatched it, stomped out, and slammed the door.

Retracing my steps back down the hall, I thought, "There is only one other place Delilah could be."

Upon opening the French doors, the heat from the brownstone fireplace inside the back wall fled. Cleared the room of heat exhaustion and stuffiness.

Mummy spent the last couple of days there after meeting with the Legacy Council. When I asked the staff, they told me Mum no longer shared a room with Daddy. They moved her things to a new room as requested, but she was in the library and refused to leave. Not even for a bath or to change clothes.

Delilah Janssen

After returning from the gravesite, Emanuel and I argued about the firstborn.

"I would appreciate it if you would pack your things and leave this room, Emanuel Janssen. I refuse to share a bed with a traitor."

"I will not, but please don't let me stop you," he pushed back. "It appears we have no further use for each other and haven't for some time."

"Seventeen years, to be exact," I reminded him.

"Ah, las, your magic number," he snickered. "You stupid woman."

"You call me stupid when you are the stupid one. We will die as mortals because of your cowardice."

"Damn you, woman. I have tolerated you for all these years, you and your daughter. No more. Leave here, now."

I woke the house staff to pack and move my things to the far end of the ranch. I was extremely angry, especially after the stunt he pulled at the grave site. I was plummeted by unseen spirits, confirming the firstborn still lived.

Mirabella

Mummy was asleep, slumped down in another floral chair. Ugh! Multicolored carnations and roses nauseated me like the uncleanliness.

There was an empty teacup, urn, and saucer with one half-eaten biscuit on the table. A lit lantern for reading one of the hundreds of books shelved on the massive oak-stained bookshelf built by John Crumley. Books about the Dutch monarchies, African pharaohs from West Africa, and from around the world were written about Ben Franklin, Einstein, and other statesmen. Never understood why Mummy kept books on Africa. Perhaps to appease Daddy.

I stood over Mummy. Her head was dropped to one side, an open book faced down across her stomach, a knitted shawl covering her legs stretched across the cushioned footstool. Wearing the same clothes from two days ago. The dark circles under her eyes on her whitish brown skin looked like she'd been hit.

"Mummy, what has happened to you? You look tired, homely, and starting to stink. And no, I won't waste my lilac on you. Why did you have it?"

Suddenly, a rush of cold came from behind me with a rose milk fragrance.

"Ewe, your stinky flowers must go, Mum."

I looked around for the vase, but the smell had come from an apparition lingering inside the entry.

It awakened Mum. She sat up quickly; the book fell from her lap. Her eyes widened as she recognized the quiet visitor.

"You!" Mummy's voice shook.

The apparition revealed itself as a petite woman with skin of Blackwood and woolly black hair. She wore a silver crown of rubies and emeralds. Regally dressed in gold velvet and lace, she spoke in a high-pitched voice, annunciating each word slowly and eloquently.

She pointed at me and shouted, "You are an abomination. Molded by one who rules over the darkest of realms. Your stench outpowers hers, for you reek of his endless deaths. You belong to him and will return by the solstice moon."

The apparition extended its arm to our faces, and shook its forefinger, "And you, Delilah, chose that fate for my Daughter? You, too, shall pay."

"Go!" Mummy screamed. "You will not take her from me."

She grabbed me, pulling me down to her lap. Hugged me. I squirmed beneath her touch.

"It is already of your doing. You cannot accept penance from the dark lord without payment."

"He has payment. I promised him my firstborn."

"He has no power over our realms. I am King Shandake Aminata Ndanga-Njinga, mother, grandmother, daughter, granddaughter, and ruler in the human realm. Semperian mother and sister, in the spiritual realms. Our path is pure and righteous."

Having had enough, I forced myself loose from scared Mummy and stood up, "You are so damn weak."

Dropping my arms, hunching my shoulders, I boldly walked toward the King but was stopped by an invisible shield.

It didn't stop me from speaking, "Delilah may fear you, but I do not. I know of you because my real father, Apollyon Diabolus, who rules the darkest realm, spoke of you. He has guaranteed me my rite of passage. I am his true and rightful daughter. We will win, and this universe will be ours."

I giggled as I snapped my fingers. In my hand, a metal key appeared. "I am my father's daughter. I will not fail him."

King Shandake balled her fists and shook them at the ceiling, "Vengeance."

The King vanished.

"Is sh she gone?"

I responded by applauding, "Time to take what's mine, and ensure my father's return."

"Hmpf," I turned to trembling Delilah, blubbering like an idiot and wet with tears. "You are no longer needed and no longer my Mummy. Just a vessel for my birth. My real Mother lives beyond the cave."

Delilah reached for me, "Please, I can fix this. I have already begun to..."

"Oh, dry up. I must go. Mother is calling for me."

I turned to leave. Standing in the entry was him.

"You don't want to keep her waiting, right, Mirabella Diabolus?" He smiled at me mischievously.

"You were never Daddy."

He stepped back to let me pass and mocked, "We will not expect you for dinner."

I hurried past him, grabbed my cape from the hook, and rushed out the front door. I called Pet and vanished into the field of lilacs.

The place where I was born into the world, I no longer call home.

PART 3
The Awakening

The Earth swelled and shook with such force,
sending shockwaves throughout the universe.
The one no longer permitted dared to
impede upon the sacred order.
Misusing the sacred word, meaning one with
authority, connected to the Source, and used only in
dire need. Otherwise, we will bear witness to
The destruction of all humankind.
The one who dared to defy was an enemy to
Semperian and all who followed.

—Knowledge of Semperian (Origin 17)
Semperian Mother

Chapter 23

The One Who Came Before

47 days to solstice
1 month, 17 days

Day 10 November 1925
Mission Awakened

Emanuella

Over the past few days, the excited chatter about my return had calmed as I settled into my newly awakened reality. I was rested and rejuvenated, despite a mild headache, so Dr. Brown stopped in to check on me.

The boys had gone to bed.

Cece was sitting at the end of ours, and Samuel stood in his usual position, leaning against my headboard.

"I will leave a bottle of aspirin on your nightstand. I expect Miss Josephine and Emanuel will phone me if you need anything else." Dr. Brown grabbed his medical bag and touched my hand before leaving, "Remember, rest between brief outings."

"Always," I said.

The doctor nodded at Samuel, avoiding eye contact.

As he walked toward the door, Cece jumped up and hugged him.

It startled him, but he patted her back.

Mama J turned up her lip, then clapped her hands sternly, "Young lady, let the doctor be on his way."

Cece dropped her hands and batted her eyes, "Thank you, Dr. Brown, for taking care of my sister."

"Medicine is only as good as your faith," he said.

Lucille would be proud that he spoke of faith and medicine working together, Mama thought. Smart boy.

Art walked over to Mama J, "I am releasing her to resume normal activities."

She reached for his hand and squeezed gently, "Thank you. You are a godsend."

"Anytime. I'm still waiting for you to schedule an appointment. Happy to put you on my schedule. I plan to come back through in two weeks."

"I may just take you up on that." Mama raised her brow.

Walked the doctor to the front door.

"Tell Mother hello for me."

"I will do that."

Brown Jr. walked out into the clear, crisp evening, hopped into his Cadillac, and headed back to Mobile.

From behind the curtain, Samuel observed him driving away and thought of Lucille.

"Samuel," I interrupted his thoughts.

He turned from the curtain.

I greeted him with a warm smile. "We are all right."

"Yes, we are."

The Guardian said goodnight and headed back to the Janssen ranch. Mama J checked in on the boys and prepared for bed herself. Sissy, snuggled in beside me and laid her head on my shoulder. "Something happened when I took the boys to the lake the other day."

"No need to talk now. We'll talk about what happened another time."

"Okay, E."

"Tell me what's been happening at school."

Cece updated me about the school children, and Mama being hush, hush about what's been going on at the Janssen ranch. Had to do with Mirabella.

For the past nine days, my soul rested in Semperian consciousness, gaining strength to fight. Dark forces attempted to pull me out of hiding. What they planned was dangerous and concerning to Semperian. Earth could burn, causing great damage to the outer universe, without releasing the enslaved Prince Ndanga-Njinga from hell.

Cece dozed off as a familiar smell of smoke appeared, swirling in the center of the ceiling.

"I miss you." I giggled, kissed my fingertips, and blew.

Puff, puff, puff, "It's okay to rest."

I closed my eyes and dreamt of beautiful colors and fields of roses.

Chapter 24

The One Who Came After
41 days to solstice
1 month, 11 days

Day 10 November 1925
Returning home to Mother

Mirabella

I spent the past few days in my lilac field, calming myself, shaking off my old life as Mirabella Janssen. I also gave instructions to Kathy for her next victim.

Easily, I found my way through the dark forest, and the cottage revealed itself. Lilac knight trees bowed, and white lilacs squirmed, hoping to survive another day.

I walked up the three black wooden steps, and the door with the blood moon opened.

"Hello, mother." I grinned at the woman who had visited me since I was a child.

"Come in, my daughter." Luna gave me a warm hug and kissed my forehead.

Thonis Baldwin was sitting with Mother Luna. He came to participate in the special ceremony.

"Now that we are all here, we can begin," said Luna.

Thonis acknowledged me with a nod.

My head up, lips pooched, I stepped around Luna. Walked over to Thonis and placed my hand on his bum leg, a reminder of his ignorance when using dark magic.

He jumped as an electrical wave pulsated from the bottom of his foot to the left side of his buttock.

"I hope we can be friends now." I removed my hand.

Immediately, Thonis felt relief. The pink in his stark white face returned, filling in the crevices and wrinkles. His eyes watered, overwhelmed with gratefulness, for he no longer felt the pain of living organisms drilling up and down his left side.

As a beginner, he attempted to mix his special elixir, the blood of Prince Ndanga, with the clondike blood given to him by Luna. It killed him after experiencing enormous power for a day. He was able to control the elements, made the mountain shake as a warning to Kate, and brought rain on an extremely warm day in Baldwin. He quickly incarnated into immortal flesh as Thonis and wouldn't make the same mistake.

Luna warned him that he may not survive the next time, which would mean the end of their partnership. That incarnation of Thonis came with a bum leg, as a reminder of one not knowing how to use dark magic. The consequences he suffered for mixing blood anointed by Semperian with evil. But stubborn Thonis, in the future, would use but a drop if needed to increase his power temporarily.

Mother prepared the room for the ceremony, and I was anxious to begin.

She magically filled the walls with photos of African children playing by the lake. Those sacrificed, their essence was living inside the white lilacs that cluttered the grounds.

"Evil from the darkest realm exists through young souls. The younger the soul, the better, especially those with Semperian blood and energy, eh."

Evil needed the souls of young African children because of their innocence and connection to Semperian. Upon death, their energy was confiscated and locked inside the white lilacs, Apollyon's favorite flower. Luna learned how to grow them in soil laced with his dark energy. While hibernating inside the lilac, they were cleansed of any connection to good-natured or loving humans. Then they were ripe for use as nourishment: eating, smelling, making teas and lilac sprays for me.

Mother set out a third chair for me on the opposite side of the table, in the middle.

The three of us placed our hands on the table, connecting index fingers and thumbs.

"Spirit of the dark, prepare us for your work," Luna said.

Luna used her finger to magically draw a white line on the floor around where we sat, locking us in.

"We are ready to begin. Please close your eyes. Imagine darkness and concentrate on our father and nothing else."

We remained silent while Mother centered herself and chanted, "Umaya, umaya, umaya, Apollyon Diabolus, Apollyon Diabolus, Apollyon Diabolus, our Fallen 17, in darkness we join you. Our allegiance and loyalty will bring you home to your rightful place to rule for all eternity."

Now it's clear, Thonis thought to himself. This is more than about immortality. Luna planned to bring the demonic one here to this planet to rule the universe. And use me to do it.

A sharp pain struck Thonis, traveling through his body up to his brain. His body stiffened when hearing Luna in his mind, "Calling on our lord will not be interrupted with meaningless thoughts."

Thonis refocused.

I was undisturbed, remained quiet, and closed my eyes.

Luna breathed a heavy sigh, then took three deep breaths and began again.

"Umaya, umaya, umaya, Apollyon Diabolus, Apollyon Diabolus, Apollyon Diabolus, our Fallen 17, in darkness we join you. Our allegiance and loyalty will bring you home to your rightful place to rule for all eternity."

I inhaled the energy coming through from my father and wept. Remembering Mother Luna molding me with his energy before placing me inside Delilah's womb.

"The true father of all, I call upon your power to assist us in our time of great need," Luna's voice grew louder.

Thonis's thoughts briefly slipped back in time when enslaved Africans were dragged off his commissioned ships in chains after thousands of miles and hundreds of days crossing the unforgiving sea to the first meeting with Prince Ndanga-Njinga, as he was held captive in the cage, to the building of Baldwin Town.

He forced himself back into the moment before Luna admonished him again.

"Umaya, umaya, umaya, true father of our home, protect us as we bring forth the one revered by the Semperian. The one you hold captive. We need his blood to unveil the one who came before. The firstborn Daughter brought here by Semperian to avenge his death."

I beamed as faint cries of agony came through, expressing its horrific pain while in the third hell. For centuries, Prince Ndanga-Njinga had no relief, and rest was non-existent also for his loyalists there.

Urgently, a strong breeze swooshed in. Prince Ndanga-Njinga's face appeared in the candlelit flames, mouth wide, screaming in agony. His caramel skin was unaffected, but his face was soiled, as were his two braids, sinched to his head. His face grew larger as his rage forced the flames to shoot to the ceiling near the pentagram.

"Prince Abiola Hereto Ndanga-Njinga, heed your master, umaya, umaya, umaya Apollyon Diabolus."

The room rumbled. The dark lord's ghastly face broke through, appearing alongside the prince. Monstrous and black as tar, its scorched skin and hair made of worms hung to its shoulder. One bulged eyeball in the center of his forehead; lips overhung at the bottom of its chinless face. Apollyon held a chain around Prince Ndanga-Njinga's neck.

"Your soul belongs to us for eternity," Apollyon growled. "I will rule. I will be Semperian."

Rose milk burst through the air. It rained clumps of salt from the ceiling, wetting the trio, furniture, and floors. Splashed the lit candles, attempting to distinguish the flames.

Thonis broke from the circle and grabbed his neck as salt scorched his nose and skin.

Luna grabbed my hands. "Prince Ndanga-Njinga, you have no power here."

The prince's rage turned to laughter, joined by the spirit voices of his children. The laughter grew and grew; salt exploded, pouring down on Apollyon's face in the ballooned flame.

"Curse you. I reclaim the sacred words forbidden to you. Your accumulation of misdeeds will end you as promised," said Prince Njinga. "We will spare you no mercy."

The candle turned into a hose of fire and attacked Thonis. Crying out for help, he fell to the floor, consumed in flames.

I opened my eyes, broke from the circle, and ran over to him. Passed my hands over his body, "Flames be gone as lilac commands." Snapped my fingers for a bottle of white lilac and sprayed the flames.

The prince laughed, forcing the souls of African children trapped in hell through the portal meant for Apollyon's rise on the solstice.

They jumped into the photos of the children hanging on

the walls, bringing them to life, and shattering the frames. Their souls ascended to the light realm with their families, and prepared for battle—41 days, 1 month, 11 days—until the solstice.

The witch feared the inevitable, "No. We command you to leave NOW."

Thonis's body sizzled as flames exploded. The consequences for using Semperian sacred words after banning Luna from the light realm. As a former member of the Coven of Sisters, she remembered the sacred rituals no longer permitted for her use.

She ran to me and helped distinguish the fire, preventing Thonis from turning to ashes. Mother blew forcefully. The ashes reversed and returned to the fire it came from, now gone. Thonis was severely burned but alive.

Luna passed her hand across Thonis's body, "Ye shall heal, no more burns as if anew."

She grabbed my hand, pulling me back to the table. "Quickly, rejoin hands."

Luna could no longer use the Semperian sacred word. The prince reclaimed it during the ceremony.

"Oh, blessed dark one, help us, show us mercy," Luna begged.

Because of her unauthorized use of the sacred words to summon Prince Njinga from hell, Earth began to destruct.

Outside, Lilac Knight Trees bent over in pain and crashed to the ground. White lilacs uprooted and fled as nature's tears flowed into thunderstorms and water into hurricanes. Power lines fell, tornadoes spun, and hurricanes hurled, killing those inside and outside. Anger into lightning strikes and once quiet volcanoes awakened, releasing lava—Washington State,

Hawaii, India, Japan, Indonesia, the Republic of Congo, New Zealand, Philippines—in danger.

Eruptions occurred throughout the town and around the world. Those outside ran for cover, and those inside flashed warnings through the only channels available.

Safe from harm were the Villagers, locked inside their homes. Semperian energy flowed through the African Village, minimizing the impact. Lightworkers living among the Baldwins, Janssens, and other parts of the world were also spared.

Zeke, Gabe, and Cece, like other Villagers, slept soundly except for Mama. Semperian Mother summoned me to help end the premature disruption.

Mama was angered by the events and recommitted to action on the reckoning day: "My once-loving sister, the Goddess, and I will ensure you reap the consequences when we meet again."

Lucifer and Satan were visiting an area on Venus, watching a group of souls caught between ascension to the light realm of reincarnation or falling to Lucifer's hell. One soul was attached to another because of a murder-suicide, during an egregious sex act. Satan argued that the perpetrator be remanded to her domain and the victim be transferred to the learning realm. Lucifer agreed regarding the latter but recommended that the perpetrator be sent to the third lower realm and removed from the universal life cycle along with the other fallen.

Semperian notified Lucifer and Satan that the disruption was the work of the third lower realm, which they suspected, and to maintain order in their realms.

"We will remain vigilant," Lucifer said to Semperian. "And continue preparation for the final battle on solstice," Satan chimed in.

Semperian ordered Satan to relocate the perpetrator to her realm, stopping them from dropping into the third lower realm. Apollyon had already acquired upwards of seven million souls.

Semperian summoned the operatives to enter the holy circle through the Semperian dreamscape.

Once we were all present, Semperian Mother chanted, "Umaya, umaya, umaya," calling on Semperian to hold the circle as they blessed the Earth. Together, they focused on the blood covenant, breaking it apart, wiping up the blood spilled over centuries, and stopping the current destruction. Earth was not ready to perish. Yet.

Luna's eyes widened as she hollered, "Prince Ndanga's children have escaped through the portal from your father's hell. They will help stop our father from entering this world. We must find her. We do not have much time. I will use my special healing powers to ensure Thonis makes it to the solstice. He must for this to work."

Mother wondered why the flame attacked Thonis. He was a key part of the covenant and should not have been harmed. They hadn't failed yet.

"Unless someone practicing light magic at the permission of the Semperian is close to him," she speculated.

Thinking about what Mother said, Semperian power worked through sanctioned light beings on the planet in the form of mostly Wiccans and Warlocks of the highest order of witchcraft. Mother Luna was once part of that coven.

"I can guess who that might be," I responded. "I will work through Delilah to get to her."

Emanuel Janssen

Semperian Mother blessed the holy union and released the operatives to their normal lives after the storm calmed.

Reminding them to remain on guard for the dark forces were stepping up their attacks to find the firstborn.

As Emanuel, I used the storm to lure Delilah to a secret underground room. The room was twenty-five steps down below her library, accessible through a secret door hidden behind the bookcase. There, she would spend days locked away without choice until the solstice. I had prepared the secret room when the ranch was built.

The low-lit room contrasted with her regal lifestyle and without upscale amenities. Unforgiving with stone walls and no windows. Sparsely furnished with a cot, nightstand, lamp, table, and chair. A washroom off in the right corner, covered by a wooden panel, and behind it a toilet, bath, and vanity with no mirrors.

How did Emanuel manage this without me knowing, Delilah thought, once she saw her books.

"How thoughtful of my dear husband who treats Villagers better than Mirabella and me."

I wondered about Mirabella. No matter what, she was my daughter and will inherit the Legacy as promised by Luna.

After partaking in the holy union to calm the destructive storm, I appeared with a plate of food and beverages for Delilah. Set it on the table in front of her without a word, only an angry stare.

"Why?" Delilah fought back the tears.

I raised my brows, "Why? Do you know what you've done? The storm we experienced was not normal. It was caused by the dark forces that could have destroyed this world."

"No doubt you helped stop it," she said, haughtily. "Are you not the one who is a liar among us?"

My face did not falter, refusing to confirm her thoughts.

"Hmmm, your silence speaks volumes," she chuckled.

"You saved your firstborn Daughter, for she is the one

prophesied to break the covenant and free the Africans." Delilah slammed her hand on the table, "It cannot happen. We will all become mortal flesh, and hell will devour us."

I dropped my head back and laughed, "Your ignorance baffles me." I took a moment to breathe, calming my energy. I could not let the evil overtake my spirit. "You are attempting to unleash a demonic spirit so powerful it will devour our universe. To empower it means all of us will be enslaved in his murky hell. We will not survive this."

Lowering my face to Delilah's, she nervously leaned back. I warned her, "I know of this demon and his soldier who goes by the name Luna. She was one of the most powerful witches. Her powers date back centuries and reside within the dark cave that lures unsuspecting innocents, stealing their young souls to nourish her maker. Your Mirabella is their spawn, not our child."

Delilah shook her head, denying the revelation, "She is my child, our child, built from our seed. She is not of this demon you imply."

I stepped back from her and wiped sweat from my forehead, "You, foolish woman. Our true child lives. She will be the one to undo this blood covenant built on the backs of my people for centuries. You will pay for what you have done. May Semperian have mercy on you."

I hurriedly walked away, leaving her to shout, "Are you going to keep me here?"

For one last time, I turned and faced my undevoted wife, whom I married because of the covenant, to ensure the prophecy. I knew she would betray me.

"You will stay here until after the solstice moon," I uttered. "She will try to find you, using any means possible, including mirrors, which she can use to see and manipulate you. She needs you, but we will not let that happen."

I grinned sheepishly, "Maybe having time to yourself will get you to realize the true reason why that girl you call your daughter exists. Soon, the dark forces will no longer need you, Delilah Janssen. You will have served your purpose."

Chapter 25

The One Who Came Before

40 days to solstice
1 month, 10 days

Day 11 November 1925
Down at the SugaShack

Emanuella

One month from the solstice, each day in Baldwin Town became increasingly dangerous.

I slept in after exhausting my energy, working within the circle to calm the storm brought on by the dark forces. We were all grateful that the fallout from last night's storm was minimal for the Semperian Mother guided us to end the storm and reverse the devastation, including the loss of lives outside Baldwin.

Luna's conjuring ceremony failed. They did not find me. The children held captive in the lower realm escaped to the light realm. Lightworkers would learn from them about the inner workings of Apollyon's hell.

Cece woke early to take schoolbooks over to Lizi.

"Hey Mama, I wanted to catch Lizi before she got busy cleaning, and her mother woke up. You know how Ms. Cheeky can be when it comes to Lizi learning."

"You be careful," Mama cautioned. "Remember, we still have to have that talk."

"I will," Cece kissed her cheek. "Save me and E some shrimp and grits," Cece said, running out the door. "She's still asleep, and I ain't the one snoring this time."

Mama tapped on the door and stuck her head into our room. I was awake.

"Good morn, you hungry for shrimp and grits, fresh biscuits, and juice?"

"No need to ask me twice."

Zeke and Gabe stuck their heads in under Mama's arm, her hand holding the edge of the door.

"Move back," she scolded. "Y'all got chores. You've eaten plenty.'"

"Ah," Gabe moaned. "We were hoping 'E' could read to us. We've been missing school since she's been asleep."

"I hoped you would have kept up your schooling without me; both of you know what to do."

"Yes, you do, now get," Mama raised her hand, pretending she would swat them if they didn't move out of the way.

Off they ran, their bare feet splat, splatting down the hall, laughing with each other, a playfulness between brothers, I missed.

I pulled back the covers, pushed my feet into my foot warmers, and pulled on a housecoat.

When I stood, I felt a stabbing pain inside my ears and brain, blinding me. It quickly passed but a lingering whisper hinted to be on guard. I prayed to Semperian within me for protection.

Cece

Lizi was not out front sweeping the entryway. So, I walked around and headed down the alley, on the left. Mom and daughter lived in the back, separate from the business in front.

Coming up to the first window was Cheeky's bedroom, and the second window down the way was Lizi's. Both windows were up from the ground, Lizi's was much higher.

A tap on Cheeky's window during the day was only for special clients. She left her curtains open and a red light on. Lizi's shades always remained closed. No mistaking her daughter as one of the girls.

The first window and shades were opened slightly. "Shucks, her mom must be up."

Passing the window on tiptoes, glancing in when hearing a familiar voice. Quickly squatted so she wouldn't be seen by Cheeky and her lady visitor, who said, "Our true father and mother command us to find her. The covenant is compromised."

"Psst."

I looked toward the back of the building and saw Lizi leaning out from the back porch.

Bending down, I hurriedly walked to the back and pulled my friend out of sight from the alley.

"I came to bring you these. I didn't want your mom to know."

"Oh," Lizi said, hugging her. "Our teacher must be better."

Because of her mother's visitor, I lied, "No, but we are still hopeful."

"Oh, my, please give..." She was interrupted when her mom opened the back door. I was glad she had hidden the books inside the burlap bag of cleaning products.

Behind Cheeky, in the shadows, was her visitor. "Thought I heard you talking to someone."

"Hello, Ms. Cheeky," I said, addressing her as she preferred.

"Everything okay with Josephine, your family, Emanuella?"

"Yes, ma'am. Just came to say hey to Lizi before I picked up groceries."

"Glad you stopped by," Lizi said.

I hugged her and whispered, "Stay safe, my friend."

Lizi nodded.

I waved at her mama, "See you, Ms. Cheeky." I turned and hurried down the alley, hoping to avoid Mirabella Janssen.

Chapter 26

The One Who Came After

40 days to solstice
1 month, 10 days

Many Forms of Light
Sara Baldwin

Closing the dress shop at 6:00 in the evening, Mother stepped outside and waited for Father. Instead, Trevor and I pulled up in the family car.

Trevor, who was driving, got out, ran around to the passenger door, and opened it.

"How did you know I would need a lift home?" she asked. "Have you heard from your Father?"

"Uh, no," Trevor replied.

Once inside, Mother looked over her seat at me and asked about Father's whereabouts.

"Haven't heard from him, Mother. Trev and I were driving through town, saw you, and figured we'd better stop in case you needed a ride."

Mother smiled. I suspected she knew of my special abilities learned through generations of light workers.

Kate Baldwin was the light worker who telepathically began reaching out to me once I entered the world. She prepared me to participate in what was to come. I was one of the operatives summoned by the Semperian Mother to help control the dark storm. I learned that Father got hurt while partaking in the conjuring ceremony with Luna and Mirabella.

"Hmm, very well. I plan to scold him for standing me up."

Trevor caught his mother's attention, "Sadie cooked up a beautiful Duck with all the trimmings. I took a peek."

"He means, he sampled," I teased. "He's the only one Sadie will let into her kitchen."

"Huh," Trevor smiled. "I'm like a son she's always wanted, is all."

"Bless her," said Mother. "I've worked up an appetite."

Nearing home, a cloaked figure appeared in front of us. Trevor slammed on the brakes.

"It's her," I said tersely. "The nerve."

The demon's daughter had come to trap him.

Mother urged Trevor, "Back away from her, quickly."

I leaned over and whispered in his ear, "Umaya, umaya, umaya, I gift you with Semperian."

Trevor pressed on the accelerator, held the brake, raised the motor, and prepared to drive into her.

Mother kept quiet, observing her son's face turn from gentle to hateful. He released the brake. The car leaped forward.

Mirabella jumped out of the way and vanished into the night, warning me, "I know what you are."

I spoke to her telepathically, "And we know who you are. We are ready for you."

Trevor steered the vehicle into the driveway, stopping at the gate box. The door automatically opened, but it wasn't me who did it.

Once inside the house, we hung our coats.

Mother spoke as if nothing had happened, "So good to be home. Let's not keep Sadie's duck waiting."

What we experienced wasn't Mirabella in the flesh, but an apparition. She came to entrap me, not Trevor.

Rushing to rejoin Mother Luna, Thonis's scars had healed. Such was the force of dark magic and the promise of the blood covenant for immortals to resurrect quickly between birth and death.

As part of the ceremonial healing, the witch gave Thonis white lilac tea to alleviate his pain and rejuvenate his spirit.

"Mother Luna, I suspect Sara Baldwin is a lightworker."

Thonis looked at me, "Not possible."

"Oh, quite possible. It would explain why ye were attacked. Only another Wiccan can stop another, especially if Semperian, through the Semperian Mother, anoints her with power." Luna stood up from the cot where Thonis lay, "This means your power will wane before the solstice moon, for she will not allow ye to recommit the covenant."

Thonis stubbornly held to the notion that his daughter was not responsible for his injury. He took the final sip of tea. "How do you know of this?"

"I paid her a quick visit, and she showed herself. Used Trevor to kill me."

"If what you say is true, and my Sara wanted you dead, you would be dead."

"What do you mean?" said Luna.

"I mean, if my Sara had powers, it would have been learned somehow from Kate, who lived during the 1600s. Kate was the adopted sister of Juelle Baldwin, the original Thonis Baldwin's wife. Kate gave birth to Prince Ndanga-Njinga's child. His blood we spilled during the first blood covenant."

"Delilah spoke of a Kate who plotted with the prince to overthrow the leadership of Baldwin. She was supposedly burned at the stake after the prince was hanged."

"Yes, I know of her as well, my daughter. Was she burned or spared, ye?"

"Burned despite her sister wanting her spared. Her power was too great."

"Humm. For Sara to continue this practice, Semperian would have to approve of it and assign a Wiccan of a higher authority to guide her. I find this quite concerning."

"Concerning? Your daughter is the spawn of the Prince of Darkness, Apollyon Diabolus, having me ponder the true plan here."

"Be careful, ye, to question me. My power extends beyond this covenant, for I am Apollyon's loyalist disciple and his wife. As long as we stay the course, we will all get what we want, eh?"

Thonis grinned, "We can agree that without each other, we will not exist. You would be remanded to the dark cave for eternity."

No, that would end, Luna thought. I am scheduled to be removed from the eternal life cycle as of December 21.

"As for my daughter, she is one of the most powerful who will help end this charade."

Thonis raised his brow, "What is your end game?

"End game?"

"Frankly," said Thonis, "You and the demon were meant for each other, and I couldn't care less. As long as what you have planned doesn't affect my immortality and what I have built."

"Ok, ye. We understand. Without each other, we fail."

I walked over to Thonis. "What about Sara?"

Thonis bucked up his chest but directed his warning to Luna, "You will not touch her. Doing so would anger the spirit of Kate and Semperian."

"Oh, you seem to know more than what you let on."

"My Sara can be especially useful for the Baldwin legacy if you and yours attempt to destroy me. Regardless, she will always love her Father."

Thonis rose from the couch and grabbed his coat, hat, and cane, which he no longer needed. "Until we meet again."

Thonis

I drove through town, stopped, unhitched the buggy, and left it behind my wife's shop. I then rode into the far mountains about an hour from my city. Where remnants of an abandoned mine once offered townships the ability to profit from coal and iron.

A major mining accident there in 1908 killed fifty men whose bodies were never recovered. Their ghosts roamed restlessly, clanging on rock walls, yelling for help from inside the collapse.

Shrugging off the evening chill, I secured the reins of the horse around the metal post at the road's end, not far from the cave entry. Crossing the crushed rocks and dirt, I walked through the entrance, passing a Do Not Enter sign, unfazed by its warning and tale of ghosts.

Inside the inner cavern, I welcomed the eerie quiet. It gave me pause to think about Sara. For her sake, I hoped she had not joined with Semperian, forcing me into a precarious predicament. We will see what my visit here brings.

I reached down and picked up an empty lantern. Snapped my finger and it lit.

Scanning left, a large black tarp still hung over the entry that led deep into a tunnel where large fallen rocks prevented the rescue of the miners.

The closing of the mine strained the coffers of neighboring towns, but not Baldwin. It profited from shipping, cotton, and tobacco fields. Our port, post-Civil War, was the main thoroughfare for imports and exports. Baldwin owned ships and accessed rail and trucks to export goods up and down the coast. Despite the impending depression across the U.S., the Town grew to be the wealthiest small town in Alabama.

I scanned the lantern to the right. An entry led into a cavern, and two miles to the other side of the terrain. First, I had to cross a shallow lake and climb over a cliff. Glad I no longer suffer from a bum leg. Thousands of Bats covered the top of the cave and clung to the ledges. The original Thonis Baldwin commanded them to stop curious minds, attempting to venture through.

Holding the lantern out to guide my steps, I proceeded into the darkness, leaving behind the voices calling to him who held the key to immortality.

Entering a shallow tunnel, I bent over to avoid the fractured ceiling threatening to fall as I traveled through coal dust and rust. Although I could easily widen the tunnel and secure the ceiling, I needed the area and path up ahead to remain as it was. Another deterrent.

A mile in, I turned right and walked down a shallow path filled with rattlesnakes. They curled up near the walls until I passed.

Down to the left, a few feet away, was a steel door buried inside a stone wall. I waved my hand across the front, allowing me access without permission.

The inside had walls of varying rock formations in colors of blues, greens, and reds. Smoke came from carefully placed incense carrying pine through the air, and lighted white candles along the walls. In the left corner, a garden of fresh vegetables and fruits grew from rich soil deep inside the ground. The magical garden energized and nourished the one accustomed to a plant-based diet.

Near there sat a lady, cross-legged on the floor, with bushy blonde hair dropping past her thighs. She barely aged through the centuries with little to connect her to the outside world.

She turned and looked at me, "Ye. What do I owe for this pleasure?"

I removed my hat, "Hello, Kate. I hear you've been busy."

She answered with a smile, "How's my beautiful Sara?"

Chapter 27

The One Who Came Before
40 days to solstice
1 month, 10 days

Mama J's Confession
Emanuella

Moving quickly, Cece passed under the tunnel, crossing onto the street leading home. She swore she heard footsteps behind her and looked over her shoulder. All was quiet down near the SugaShack, so she slowed her pace long enough to look up toward the sky, and pray, "Thank you, Semperian, for giving me strength to help fight the evil that imprisoned our African people. I will fear not. Semperian comes from Source Consciousness, ruler of the universe above and below. I am chosen."

Rounding the corner, Cece ran up the road, happy to reach home. Jogged up the five steps onto the safety of the family's front porch, took a deep breath to slow her racing heart. Straightened her coat and walked in.

Mama J and I were listening to Papa John's favorite tunes on the phonograph.

Zeke and Gabe skedaddled when Mama played the first record.

"Honey, what's wrong?"

"Just tired from fast walking. You're always on me about gaining weight," she joked.

"Umm, hmm. Go hang your coat and come sit with us."

Cece hung her coat, and I turned off the music.

"Yes, ma'am," Cece said, sitting between Mama and me.

Mama cocked her head toward the hallway. Made sure the boys were out of earshot before she said, "The three of us need to talk."

"Is this about what happened at the lake? Mirabella Janssen is involved, right?"

Mama and I said nothing, allowing Sissy to continue.

"I saw her talking with Lizi's Mom."

"What were you doing at Lizi's? I planned to take those books to her later."

"Sorry. I wanted to share the good news about you waking up. But after seeing Mirabella, I kept it to myself."

"You saw Mirabella?" I asked.

"Uh, no, but Ms. Cheeky saw me with Lizi."

Mama sighed, "I can't wait until this is all over."

"Huh? What are y'all keeping from me?"

"We talked a little about it at the lake last year. I warned you to stay alert, and wished you hadn't taken the boys."

Mama agreed. "Those playing among the darkness have attempted to try and come through you."

Cece nodded her head. "At the lake, the witch tried to come after the boys. Thank you for saving us, E." Her eyes watered.

Mama scrunched her lip, "She will be dealt with in time.

For now, remain alert at all times and help us keep an eye on our rambunctious boys."

We chuckled.

Mama took in a breath, "This is about twin girls born in 1908, on the night of the blood moon. One was an abomination from the third hell, the other of Semperian. The Semperian Daughter was the firstborn fathered by Emanuel Janssen, who hid her among a special family, on the night Delilah Janssen ordered her death…"

Mama J finished the story, "You will be called on and placed in a situation that may cause you to waiver. Remember, wherever you are, Semperian will be with you."

The dark forces coming for Sissy bothered me, but I will trust Semperian.

"You called it the third hell. What does that mean?"

"All things in the Semperian universe are deemed perfect; however, not without flaws," said Mama, raising her eyebrows. "This planet Earth operates on a limited understanding of the universe. The laws it has accepted are the laws of causality, referred to as karma and polarity, or good and evil. The energies of good and evil must remain in balance for it to survive in its solar system. If not, Earth will fall out of alignment and self-destruct, causing havoc across the universe. It would take a millennium to fix it."

"Is Earth hell?" Cece asked.

Mama J laughed, "Depends on who you ask. But the true teachings we understand as the Knowledge of Semperian speak of three hells. The first two lower realms are managed by two Fallen Semperian Guards who have an agreement with Semperian. The energy of Luciferno, referred to as Lucifer, handled the first dark hell. The energy of Satana, referred to as Satan, handled the second. The third hell is ruled by the energy of Apollyon Diabolus, Fallen Guard 17. It fell out of favor with

Semperian. Semperian has arranged for its destruction and removal from the universal life cycle on December 21."

I understood, but Cece was overwhelmed.

"The Knowledge of Semperian I've been reading to you little by little discusses this. Time you read from it daily, and immerse yourself in the teachings. Semperian's words will give you mental strength."

"Mama," Cece said slowly. "Where does the church and the bible fit?"

Mama and I laughed.

"Our roles on this planet were assigned before birth. The more you read the true teachings, the more you will understand where religious thought, like Christianity, appears on the Earth stage. It is all part of the human experience of reincarnation and learning."

Mama looked at me, then back at Cece, "I think this is enough for now."

We ate dinner together after a prayer of gratitude for the food and the day.

"I am so thankful for my family," the matriarch said, tearing up a little.

Before any of us could chime in, there was a knock at the door.

Zeke looked up from his plate. "Who dat?"

"Who is that?" I corrected.

"Yeah, dummy."

"Y'all hush and eat. I'll go see who this is."

Gone for several minutes, Mama returned with Bessie, Franklin's sister. She was shaken, with tears streaming down her face. Mama held onto her.

"Bessie has brought sad news. Young Franklin has gone missing with four other children who ran off to that dern lake."

I refrained from showing emotion.

Cece dropped her head. Franklin was Bessie's only remaining kin.

"When I got home from work, he wasn't at the neighbors' and not at home. He always comes home minutes before I get there. He wasn't supposed to go nowhere," said Bessie, crying through her words. "The neighbor said she looked out the window and saw him leave with four other kids, Jonathan, Lila, Darrel, and Brenda, walking in the direction of the lake. I called after him, but he didn't answer. Like he didn't hear me."

Bessie paused to wipe her tears. "I just came from the lake. Saw shoes near the water and heard screams coming from the cave. I think they're in there," said Bessie. "She got them."

"Who." Gabe's eyes bugged out.

"The witch." His brother answered. "She tried getting us."

"Yeah," said Gabe, rocking back and forth in his chair as fear swelled in his eyes.

"Boys, that's enough. Sissy, please get the boys a slice of berry pie. You two can picnic in your rooms for the rest of the evening."

"Yay," they said in unison and jumped up from the table.

"Hope you find Frankie and the rest of them. Gabe hugged Bessie around her waist. "We play together at school, throw the baseball around. He's a good catcher."

Bessie nodded at Gabe, who ran off to join his brother.

His eyes, like Frankie's, Bessie thought, remembering his scared eyes, calling for her. It wasn't supposed to be him.

Bessie refused dinner and followed Mama J to the back porch. She pulled back the covers on the bed.

"Please drink the tea. It'll help you rest. I'll contact Mr. Janssen. He'll gather some of the men to go out and look."

When the house was quiet, I went into Mama's room. She was sitting in her chair, talking to Papa. She looked up and waved me over.

"Mama, you, and I know the children didn't go without being called. That puzzles me. The callings are increasing."

"Yes, I agree. That's why it's best to keep our enemies close. As for the boys, no leaving the house, not even to play behind the house."

I kissed her cheek and rejoined Cece, sleeping soundly.

Lying awake, I mentally communed with Semperian Mother. The dark lord was growing hungry, so Semperian entered the minds of Villagers and warned them to heighten their guard around the children. Semperian then allowed me to see the truth inside Bessie's mind.

A screaming Frankie and the four other children haunt me. The lake water hollered, throwing up pearls. It dropped like a net atop all the children. Frankie was not to be touched.

I was forced back against the log, held by a force as the lake's current pulled the four children into the lake. Frankie was struggling to call for me. Before he was lost to the cave, a force came up from the lake and pulled Frankie back with it. It was the ghost of our father. I will never forget Franklin's sad eyes and the scornful look from my father. I had betrayed them.

Bessie sobbed, overtaken by horrific memories, "Baby brother, I'm so sorry. What happened wasn't supposed to. You weren't part of the plan. Mama and Daddy were supposed to come home for me doing my part."

The chattering inside her head turned into children's laughter. She covered her ears. "Please stop. I wanted my family back. No harm was to come to Frankie. They promised riches for our family."

The children spoke in Bambara, "An ye Afirikikaw ye. A bangeli bɛ fanga di an ma ni yeelen ye min b'an dɛmɛ ka boli dibi la u y'an bila kaso la. An bɛna bonya da a kan, den fɔlɔ min ka bangeko ye an ka ciyɛn ye. Semperian b'an lakana, ka mɔgɔ bɛɛ halaki minnu b'u ja gelɛya k'a tɔɔrɔ."

[We are Original Africans. Her birth empowers us with light, helping us to flee from the darkness they have imprisoned us. We will pay homage to her, the firstborn whose birthright is our legacy. Semperian keeps us safe, destroying all who cause her harm]."

Chapter 28

The One Who Came Before

40 days to solstice
1 month, 10 days

Hidden Secrets
Alive and Well

Deep inside the abandoned coalmine, I watched the waterfall change to colors of red and orange as it gushed through the upper rocks, feeding the garden below. Confined there by my captor, standing here now, who spared me from a burning stake because of my sister's will. While there, I'd been at peace awaiting the final calling until today.

Thonis

"Well, well, Kate," I said, watching the water spectacle. "You haven't lost your touch."

"My touch?" I questioned. "You may have placed me here for my sister's sake, but the ore impedes the strength of my powers. You know that."

I turned and looked at Kate sternly, "As it should. Minor pleasures to keep you content and my dear Juelle satisfied."

My face softened, thinking of my sister, who risked falling out of favor with Thonis. She hid from him my Wiccan practices and visits with the prince. Over time, Juelle grew to appreciate my powers and was my connection to the outside world.

"My daughter Sara is meddling in affairs that may ruin our existence," I stormed.

As he moved closer, I observed him walking without a limp.

"I see life is treating you well except for the mishap with the fire, tsk, tsk."

"So, your eyes do see beyond here? Through Sara, perhaps?"

"How do you know it was Sara?"

Sara or whoever it is protects Emanuel Janssen's firstborn Daughter. All eyes are searching, and we will find her. I promise you that."

"Maybe." Kate frowned. "The dark magic you are using for that purpose will eventually turn on you. It's already begun."

"Petty magic cannot help me," I said stubbornly. "I am in charge of our destiny."

"Then so be it. I cannot help you."

"Not to worry, I still have my dau…"

"Your daughter will not help you."

"We shall see."

"We shall."

As Mayor Lazarus, I invited a member of the council to meet with me in my office after the sun fell. He was a confidante and kept me apprised of occurrences in town, especially about the Baldwins.

After the legacy gathering, I discovered that Thonis met with Luna and attempted a conjuring ceremony but failed.

"Ye, the moon has shifted," said the man. "A sign that transitioning to the blood moon has already begun."

"And what of Thonis?"

"My man saw him entering the old abandoned mine up in the Mobile mountains. I have someone there waiting to go in after he leaves, ye."

"No need to do that, my friend."

"Thank you for your loyalty."

"As ye wish." The man nodded and exited through a side entrance for only special guests.

As the oldest living Baldwin next to Thonis, I could intervene to ensure the safety of the blood covenant. The witch gave Lazarus the authority to do so.

I pondered that as I turned off the light in my study. As I stepped into the hallway, Hiram was coming my way.

"Sir."

"Thank you, Hiram. I will take my meal and tea in my quarters now. Bring enough for two."

"Yes, sir. I will let her know you are ready."

Hiram hurried to the kitchen, where a familiar visitor was waiting.

"My King." He bowed to her. "He just returned to his quarters, requesting a meal for two."

The King smiled and nodded. "Thank you, Hiram. Semperian will continue to bless you."

As Mayor Lazarus, I opened the door.

Smiled at the beautiful, dark skin girl, smelling of rose milk, carrying my dinner tray.

"Hello. Always a pleasure."

"Sara tells me you were able to meet with the Legacy Council, despite Thonis attempting to keep you away."

I waved her inside, "We are moving along as planned, my King."

Mirabella

From the stable, the Guardian observed as she stepped from the side door of the same horse and dark red buggy, waiting for her the other morning when she ran from the manor.

Sitting at the front of the buggy holding the horses' leash was a live cadaver with light grey eyes. In an all-black suit with white gloves and a top hat, covering its stark-white skin and hands.

"Mademoiselle, I will guard you as instructed."

"Good. Once I am done here, I will send you back. Maybe even replace your wood box with redwood and surround it with fresh dirt, " I giggled.

I held out my arm and allowed an unseen hand to help me down from the buggy. I had come from the lilac field nearby, and before leaving, draped my naked body in a long, dark purple cloak and ankle boots.

I pulled the hood over my head and strolled toward the front door. Stopped by an invisible force, I was unable to cross the circle despite lilac covering my body and clothing. I remembered the days Mirabella was free to come and go unaffected.

So, I waited.

The door opened a few beats later, with Josephine blocking the entry, her hands folded across her stomach.

"Mrs. Josephine," I said, forcing a smile.

Josephine avoided eye contact. "You are no longer welcome."

"Look at me." I stomped my feet like the Mirabella, who'd get her way.

"You are no longer permitted to come here."

I could feel Mirabella's anger rising in me. I saw Josephine as a lowly Villager I once tolerated.

"I demand to see Mummy."

"You do not have a Mummy here." Josephine mocked.

"I am asking for Delilah Janssen, you lowly Villager. If you do not do as I wish, I will put you where you belong with the vermin that crawl."

Josephine stood stoically. Near the stable, Samuel stepped into view.

"I'd advise you to leave immediately." Josephine stepped back from the entrance and slammed the door.

The carriage door opened, and horses stomped their hoofs as the cadaver urged, "Mademoiselle, you must hurry."

But I was mortified; my human emotions took over, turning into a tantrum. I *stomped-stomped* my feet, banged my fists against my side, "Mummy. I command you to come to me now."

No, Mummy, but Samuel reacted.

The Guardian pushed out his hands, and fingers wiggled, sending shock waves blasting through the air, zap, zap.

"No!" My eyes turned black, and my body spasmed as the shock waves intensified, forcing me to run and seek refuge inside the carriage. I balled up fearfully, "Mother Luna, help."

The cadaver snapped the horses' reins and vanished.

Semperian Mother ordered me, as the Guardian Samuel, to be present at the Janssen ranch. We knew Mirabella would come for Delilah, but evil could not cross the perimeter or enter the home without invitation.

After the spectacle, I went inside to help Josephine carry supplies to a guest.

"We know this isn't over," she said as I followed her to visit the once lady of the manor locked in the dungeon.

"No, but we are prepared," I stated.

"We are ready. Semperian will show them no mercy."

Delilah

I was sitting in a chair, scowling, my eyes swollen from crying. I had barely slept and only picked at the food they brought me. "Emanuel has you under his control, I see."

Samuel and Josephine went about quietly cleaning the area and gathered the dirty dishes and clothing. When Samuel finished, he headed for the stairs.

Josephine stopped to ask, "Anything you need?"

"You mean I am allowed to make requests?" I asked snidely. "How about letting me out of this place? This is my home, where I've ruled since before Emanuel brought you here. How dare he and you treat me this way."

"If you prefer nothing more, we will be on our way." Josephine backed away toward the staircase where Samuel had stopped halfway up.

I was hiding a fork underneath my thigh, ready to use it as a weapon.

"It would be wise for you to hand over the fork," Samuel warned. "You don't have the power to stand against any of us."

"I should've guessed." I pulled the fork from under my thigh. "Working with Semperian Mother, I presume."

Josephine walked toward me. I threw the fork at her, and she graciously picked it up.

"Not nice," he said, his eyes frowning. "I don't like it when people are not nice. It irritates me. Ask your Mirabella. Luna and Apollyon's spawn."

With the little energy I had, I jumped up and hurriedly walked toward them, "What about my daughter? Is she all right? I must know."

The Guardian wiggled his fingers, creating an invisible shield I smacked into. I fell backward but quickly regained my composure. I ran left, then right, attempting to find a way around it.

I hollered at them as they ascended the stairs, "Please answer me. I must know." I begged. "None of this is Mirabella's fault. I'm to blame. Take me instead."

Samuel responded, "Your time will come to answer for what you have done. And it won't be by our hands."

Relieved to cross the threshold, Josephine padlocked the door and pressed the button. The bookshelves moved back into position, hiding the secret room.

Outside the library, Samuel's eyes narrowed when he saw her come through the front door.

"Good afternoon, Lucille. You're early, but I could use the help."

Lucille looked at Samuel, the first time she had been that close to him, "You must be Samuel."

His body stiffened. Clasping his hand to his throat, his face burned red as he fought to breathe against the memory of that day. She was there.

Josephine stepped in front of Samuel. He was recalling a human experience. She pulled his head down; their foreheads touched.

"You know who you are now," she whispered. "That life is no longer yours."

Remembering he was one of the Semperian's most powerful Guardians, he let go. Allowed his body to ease, but he hadn't forgotten the girl who lured him and his friend to their deaths.

In the kitchen alone, Lucille held her head in her hands. Looked up, and her eyes widened with fear when her friend entered.

Lucille said, "The devil is alive, and he's coming for me."

Returning home beyond the cave, I called Pet. It attached itself to my left nipple.

Pet had grown a tail made of skin like the underside of its body, its claws by an inch. Drunken with pleasure, I swayed side-to-side, humming down the path. The grounds sprouted fresh white lilacs, a result of four African children sacrificed at the lake. Except for one child, whose deceased father, living in the light realm, rescued him.

Once inside, I released the remainder of the old Mirabella.

I sat beside Luna, removed Pet from my breast, and laid it across my lap. Petted it as it purred to sleep.

"I could not get to Delilah."

"I know, my dear. I heard you calling. It's good you left when you did. I struggled to get you away from there."

"Must have been the Semperian circle protecting the house."

"No, no. That simply stops the uninvited from entering, especially our operatives."

"I would suspect Emanuel, but I don't think he was there."

"I do not believe it was he who attacked you. There are many Semperian operatives; many are Guardians with exceptional powers. You cannot see them unless they want to be seen. Even then, you will not know them."

Mother touched my cheek, "My dear daughter, we must be on guard even more than before, for we have angered Semperian. I used the sacred words after being stripped of my light powers."

I shrugged, "We have a new minion in our ranks."

"Bessie. I am not thoroughly convinced that we have her soul since her father interfered. Curses."

"She's living with the Crumleys, being coddled by Mrs. Josephine." The thought of how she treated me at the ranch angered me, but I quickly dismissed it. My lingering emotions annoyed Mother Luna. "I am curious as to why she chose to go there."

"It could be her overpowering maternal instinct. Josephine loves taking in strays, like that oldest child who materialized out of nowhere, my shadows told me. Josephine then filled her house with three more, not from her womb."

"You know Mrs. Josephine?"

"Very much so. We are sisters."

Mother got up and brewed a fresh pot of white lilac tea. On a platter, she mixed white petals and purple ones from the knight trees.

I grabbed a handful, put them in my mouth, and sipped tea. "You and Mrs. Josephine are sisters?"

Luna chuckled, "Josephine was a High Priestess."

"She's immortal?" I raised my brows.

"Her soul, like mine, is incredibly old. We belonged to Wiccan covens in Africa throughout the centuries. Her lightworker's name was Lepta.

Lepta was the most beloved High Priestess with great wisdom and healing powers. The powers she earned from her stay in the underworld caused the spring and summer seasons. Her emergence during spring and summer set the tone for our state of being and direction over the new year."

The more Mother spoke, the more I wondered about Mrs. Josephine's role in the impending solstice.

"Mother, you said Josephine was once part of the Wiccan order. Why is she here in this world at this time?"

Luna opened her eyes and looked intently. "When she sought me out the other day, I wondered. This winter solstice is important to us, for it comes with the appearance of the blood moon. When Wiccan powers are at their greatest."

Pausing to sip the tea, "My sister, who embodies the highest training in our craft, would be at her most powerful if she were still practicing. In this existence, she appears as a mere mortal. To regain her power, she would have to descend back into the underworld with Lucifer and Satan. For her to return could mean her death. The test of the will there is most challenging. Lepta was one of a handful of light workers who descended and survived. That is why she is Semperian's most highest."

I closed my eyes and listened. My insides churned, releasing the essence from the lilacs, recharging my powers.

"Do you see, eh? The lower worlds, sanctioned by the Semperian, stand guard against your father's realm because of his ability to throw all worlds off balance if left unchecked."

I took another sip of tea. "Are you saying there is more than one underworld?

"Yes, there are three. They all play in the same sandbox except for the world your True Father rules. The other realms know his strength has grown stronger since the capture of the human Semperian, the prince. Apollyon, with our help, will overtake the other lower realms the night of the solstice."

Luna leaned forward and held my hands, "My precious daughter, all this is happening because of me. I, Luna, was one of Lepta's sisters, given the title of elder sister. I served as the coven's second in command of the Wiccan order, allowed to train in the same magic and craft she was taught. I wanted more and would never be made High Priestess. You had to agree to certain rules. Rules that we play equally and in balance with the Semperian, light, and lower realms. But no, I betrayed my sister and the coven by making a deal with the demon. It led to the capture of the great Prince Ndanga-Njinga in 1630, on the night of the blood moon. That is where it all began, setting the stage for Apollyon to live eternally or die."

Sisters of the Coven
Semperian ordered Lepta to oversee the light realms where

light magic could not be used for evil. Lepta was the most trusted to obey that order. She would also need help with training beings from all over the universe to practice lightwork.

Lepta adopted two loyal sisters, Kate and me, and permitted us to learn the way to Semperian. Learning the way meant having an almost direct connection. Kate and I connected through Lepta. We were the only two with the authority to do so. All others practiced under us.

Lepta connected directly to Semperian. It was like being able to touch the heart of Source, Lepta told us. A profound experience no words could explain.

She was first summoned to commune with it on an uninhabited planet in one of the far galaxies. The intensity of that union exploded into fire and engulfed the entire planet. The fire on the planet was perpetual and could not be distinguished, thrusting light and warmth throughout the entire universe.

Semperian named it Sun. The sun became Lepta's haven for communing with Semperian. No being or energy can go there, only Lepta, for she was the Semperian Sun Goddess. The creative energy and force behind light and warmth. The Sun Goddess was responsible for anomalies like fiery comets, volcanic lava, and unstoppable brush fires.

Anomalies happened when humans on this planet disrespected the laws of nature. Creating man-made dangers, shifting climates, and disrupting the natural order of the environment. Humans attempted to be Source Consciousness through dangerous innovations like Artificial Intelligence, to reach beyond the stars and become it.

Lepta granted powers to Kate, naming her Goddess of Calamity. She controlled the weather and seasons through love.

I was the Goddess of Salvation, permitted to control pure love energy and detour humans from heading to lower worlds.

Those who lost their way and needed help to return to the higher realms.

Lepta was the one who approved the use of light magic on Earth. She identified persons and groups to use it, governed by rules. Other planets were already under a stronger influence and had magic powers in their way of life.

Humans are like elementary school children, taking baby steps towards the understanding of a higher power—the reason for reincarnation.

I hungered for more authority. So, I attempted to reach Semperian directly. I overheard Lepta using the sacred word to call forth its energy. The words mean: One who holds all authority or the supreme Goddess.

The use of the sacred words chanted in threes was granted to only those chosen by Semperian, like Lepta, and Semperian Mother, Prince Ndanga's Earth mother, during the 1600s.

Attempting to contact Semperian directly was my mistake to bear, so Lepta thought.

Before reaching Semperian, Lepta intervened. It did cost me, but Lepta was also admonished for my behavior.

Semperian commanded Lepta to return me to Earth to live a human existence and learn humility. That meant stripping me of the use of light magic.

Rather than wait to be transitioned to Earth and lose my powers, I escaped to the other side of the realm, through a hidden portal once used by the universal gardener.

Here on Earth, I have minimal light power but walk the dark path using occult magic.

In human form, I existed in this mountain cave not far from Baldwin Town, established by the man I lured here, Thonis Baldwin. It is with Thonis' help that I would travel the universe again. But this time, I will rule by his side, for I am his wife. Your father, Apollyon Diabolus Fallen 17.

Chapter 29

The One Who Came Before

39 days to solstice
1 month, 9 days

Day 12 November 1925
Can't Take it Back

Emanuella

Before sunup, Samuel stopped by. He and Mama prayed for Semperian energy to guard our home and family, especially with Bessie's unexpected visit.

The Dark Lord's underlings had grown in numbers with thousands of human minds and souls captured in the past few days, while Semperian operatives increased the cleansing energy and protection.

Evil was in a heightened state, and those with weakened spirits were at risk. Bessie was consumed by grief. The death of her parents, grandmother, and now her brother made her an easy target.

She sobbed throughout the night, and lightworkers could not intervene. The Semperian Mother said that Bessie must find inner strength to accept help from the Semperian or remain in the clutches of the dark lord. I feared the latter.

Cece

Bessie slammed her hands to her ears to drown out the voices summoning her, again.

"What do you want from me?" she asked through streaming tears. "Why them?"

Zeke peeked in when he heard her. He was loading the washer. "You okay, Bessie?"

Bessie looked up at Zeke's wondering eyes. The voice wanted Zeke and his brother. It tempted her with the same promise, saying it would give life back to her brother, parents, and grandmother if she brought the twins to the lake. It also said the reason for not returning her parents after the children were consumed was that Frankie got away. It had requested a total of five souls, which brought her to the Crumleys. Two more young souls would bring her family home.

"Can I get you something?" He asked.

I walked up to Zeke and swatted his bee-hind, "Mind your business."

"Ow, just being' polite." He ran off.

After talking with Mama and E, I didn't like the timing of Bessie's visit, despite us being somewhat friendly.

"I will get you what you need," I said standoffishly, although saddened that she had lost her entire family. "Can I get you something to eat?"

Bessie tried to smile, "No, thank you, I can't eat anything."

"I know how you feel. I miss my Papa something awful. If anything were to happen to anyone in my family, I... Can't have anything happen to them. Nothing."

I took in a deep breath before saying something I'd regret. "I'll be back to check on you." Then, stepped back and closed the door.

Before leaving, I waited briefly outside the door. That's when I heard Bessie cry out, "I will do anything, please bring back my family."

Mayor Shipley

In my guise as mayor, my guest and I discussed the coming event and the early signs of a transitioning moon.

Smiling at her, I recalled the first time we met as teenagers coming from immensely powerful African tribes – she from Songhai and I from Mali – betrothed to each other before we were born. The two tribes were the highest of royals in the lineage of African Queens and Kings, and Semperian chose each.

The elders had groomed and taught us the spiritual teachings from the highest order. Rarely did they allow us to frolic as children, but when they did, we mingled with commoner children to learn humility.

As teens, we continued our family traditions and soon joined together in courtship, preparing for our roles as leaders. She would inherit her father's throne and become King. I would be emperor and join her on the throne, protecting the throne for our son, to be crowned king and emperor one day.

Soon after the Portuguese captured our son and sold him into the Americas, it set off a chain of events from the blood moon to his death, to my death, and hers. It also led to the challenges we faced together in the current day. To free our son and children from the third hell would be an insurmountable feat for common mortals. But we were Semperian, given the power of the universe straight from the source.

During supper of fresh salmon, chickpeas, and greens, I complained about showing up as the despicable Mayor Shipley.

"My love, I do not like it when people think my beautiful King is a whore to this so-called mayor whose body I disdain."

My outer appearance shifted into the form I preferred and felt most comfortable. My balding light-brown straight hair changed to thickened black curls, and my skin from white to golden. "They're much better."

She reached over and touched me, "I remember our first existence. When I was a little girl, my birth mother told me I would learn to love the man chosen for me. Arranged marriages take time to result in love."

I smiled, recalling the memory, "Loving you was easy, for we have a special mission." I chuckled. "Maybe I would have thought twice about a union with you if I had been told about how challenging our existence would be. But we were fated for this time and place, starting with our energies exploring Venus. I do remember, and for that, I am fondly grateful."

"She was there on Mercury," said the King. "I remember a fleeting spirit crossing my path, letting me know we would have a dual purpose." She paused and looked into my eyes. "Her mission is much more dangerous than she is aware. For him to be free, she must accept her fate."

A memory drew tears to my eyes. Her birth on the night of the second blood moon, as I wrapped her in a grey burlap blanket, took her out into the chilly night, and placed her into the makeshift basket. The wagon jumped into a jerk-wobble, wobble down the broken dirt road.

Chapter 30

The One Who Came After
39 days to solstice
1 month, 9 days

Choosing Sides

Thonis

The trek down the mountainside was slow, but I reached home in time to see the rising moon, struggling between its current color and impending transition. I cursed, knowing my very existence was threatened and my daughter may be integral in the town's impending doom.

I secured my horse in the stable and strode the short distance, coming through the back entrance. I took off my boots, hung my coat and hat on the inside hook, and stuffed my feet into slippers left there by one of the domestics. Then I went to find Suanne in the front sitting room.

She looked up from knitting, a pastime she missed during her busy seasons.

"Where were you?" she scolded. "You've been gone for two days. We were worried."

"We?" I leaned down and kissed her cheek.

"Yes, of course. Trevor, Sara, and I didn't know what became of you."

I frowned. "Well, as you can see, I am well." I stepped back from Suanne and winked, "You are beautiful as always."

Suanne smiled sheepishly, "You do know how to change the subject." She sighed, "I'm afraid we have a bit of bad news among our Village families."

I raised my brows.

"Bessie, our newest seamstress, lost her brother yesterday afternoon," Suanne shook her head. "He and four other Village children drowned at that suspicious lake, haunted by demons." Suanne turned up her lips, "Of course, I do not entertain such things, but wonder what would possess children to go to that lake this time of year?"

I thought of Apollyon's minions in Baldwin and around the world. African children's spirits escaped during the failed conjuring of Prince Ndanga. Evil will take the lives of more innocents until we find the firstborn child of Emanuel Janssen and kill her. I am grateful that Towner's children were no longer at risk, but that would change if they did not meet our obligation.

"Where might I find Sara?"

"Sara?" Suanne said, looking puzzled. "She's in her room."

I nodded and walked off without giving her a reason for wanting to find our daughter.

As I walked away, Suanne noticed I no longer limped but still carried my cane.

I stopped at Sara's bedroom. She opened it before I could knock, blocking entry.

"Hello, Father. I see you've made it home. We were all so worried."

Remembering that same smile she'd worn since getting into mischief once she learned to walk and talk, I couldn't help but return the smile.

"Sara. What have you been up to?"

"Consoling Trevor. You, of all people, should understand how upset he is about what happened."

"All will be well soon. No need for you to concern yourself."

I paused. "What we do every seventeenth solstice is for the good of our city. Our lineage must survive."

Sara looked into my eyes, "Our family? Mirabella is right for Trevor, I think not."

"Not for you to question." I snapped.

"Oh? We all know the transference didn't happen, so why is that? Father, I am disappointed in you. Mother knows better."

"Your Mother has no part in this. Her role is a meager one." I reached over Sara's head and grabbed the edge of the door. Lowered my head, touching my forehead to hers, attempting to join our thoughts. "I will not be questioned or challenged by you or anyone, in this town or family. Am I clear?"

Sara blocked my use of dark magic to control her.

I stumbled back, and a hint of pain attacked my left leg. I looked at my daughter, whose childlike smile disappeared.

"It's been a troubling couple of days, and I am quite tired. Goodnight, Father."

Sara shut her door, distancing herself from my anger and look of disappointment. My daughter made her choice.

Sara

In her astral form, Kate visited me often and came later that evening as I readied for bed.

"I know this is hard for you. But know this, my niece, when the time comes, the side we have chosen will be one of life and not damnation. Your father will realize that too late."

I heard it while sleeping. The hissing. As it flickered its tongue, slithering down the bedpost, crawling toward me.

I could sense it. It was once human, during a time when I was a child. I wanted to play hopscotch, but my being a part of a legacy family made me appear untouchable.

Awakened from the pressure on my legs after having barely slept because of increasing activity among the dark forces, like now, I thought *how predictable*.

The yellow python raised its thick upper body, swaying back and forth, preparing to attack as instructed.

"Ahhh, your mother must've sent you. How unfortunate for her." I smirked. "What say you?"

The serpent lowered its head, "I am Kathy. I was once a child, but turned into a python by the one called Mirabella. We teased her, accused her of being a Villager."

"Hmmm," I said, reading Kathy's human thoughts. "Ah, yes, I remember you. I also wanted to play hopscotch, but was afraid of my own shadow back then."

I sat up and leaned forward, "You, Damon, and Johnathan have been at her mercy all these years."

Python, Kathy said, "Damon and Johnathan are still alive. I do what she wants as long as she spares them."

I responded, "I've heard of Towner children being bitten, leaving nasty marks and painful sores. But of course, the poison you left in them has no power. They are immortal."

"She wanted them to suffer, if only briefly."
I shrugged, "You and your cousins aren't blameless. Bullying and prejudice are never justified, even toward one so evil."
Python Kathy dropped her head.

"Tell you what, deliver a message for me, and I will see what I can do about your precarious situation."

Kathy agreed, so I used my power to return her to the sender.

Mirabella

The python struck me while I slept. It pained me awake, leaving a large warning bite on my upper arm. Similar to that of the Towner children, but like them, I could not die.

Sara's laughter echoed around me, "You are no match, and neither is it. You've been warned."

I screamed in anger, pounding my fists. Reached over and grabbed the lilac cream from the nightstand, and spread it across the bite. The size of an orange, it had swollen my entire arm, but I stopped the poison.

"Just you wait, Kathy. I will feed you three to the sea creatures, living at the bottom of the river. Not Satan's beast, but the ones on standby for Apollyon. Luna spoke of them, living at the lake bottom inside the cave, and around the port."

Dr. Wolstein

I walked out into the lobby when I heard the bell. The hour was late for visitors.

"Well, well," I said to our new arrivals.

Huddled near the door were three naked teens, their pupils enlarged, and their bodies shivering.

"I heard your situation was the work of a powerful demon, not the one we serve but one close to him. But not to worry, we will take care of you."

"Thank you, sir," said Kathy.

"Kitty, could you come out here, please?"

My beautiful wife came skipping out, chipper and bouncy, twirling the ends of her blonde hair.

Kathy giggled. Kitty playing with her hair reminded her of how much she loved playing with her pigtails back when she was a child. Kathy touched her hair and smiled. She had pigtails again.

"My darling, our three friends here will require a complete transformation. Different than how they left us. She may search for them, but Mayor Lazarus instructed us to ignore her request and gave us the power to do so."

Chapter 31

The One Who Came Before

34 days to solstice
1 month, 4 days

Day 17 November 1925
Visit From the Devil a-Comin

Lucille

I enjoyed walking home, helping to shrug off the day's kitchen work. But tonight, the trek from the Janssens to my home in the Village seemed longer. The November air was cooler, but I refused a ride from Samuel and had already told Abram no need to come and fetch me.

I lived in the last cottage on the hill before the tunnel, where Art Senior and I raised our son. My late husband built the home before we were married, one of the first in the Village, and it was near the church.

"Easier to be where god-fearing people prayed."

I thought of that now. Prayer. And asked God to protect me from the unfriendly presence around me.

Inside, I lit the two lanterns on the table by the front, and closed the curtains I made, especially for winter months. Warm but fall-colorful, cut and hand-sewn linen squares in brown and orange.

I preferred my home lit by candles and lanterns, unlike the Crumleys and others in the Village who upgraded to electricity. I did have indoor plumbing, and a home filled with wonderful memories. We spent many days sitting around the wood stove right there in the front room.

When Abram chops wood, he brings me a stack. I dropped a few in, poured in fluid, lit it, and closed the metal door. The swoosh of fire made its way through the pipes, warming the entire cottage.

Taking one of the lanterns to guide me through the darkness, I went into the bedroom on the left of the entry, lit the lantern on the nightstand, the one inside the bathroom next to my bedroom, and out in the kitchen, lit the one hooked to the wall.

Closed my eyes and prayed, "God almighty, thank you for your graciousness, for we all sinned in your name. Please bless my son and his family and don't punish them for my sins."

When I opened my eyes, I felt uneasy. My body stiffened. I inhaled and exhaled, calming my inside, "Thank you, Lord. I am safe in your name." I affirmed.

Leaving the wall lantern burning, I turned the flame off the one I was carrying before setting it back on the front table, went back into the bathroom, and ran my bath water.

Undressed, I got into the tub and leaned back in the warm water, my neck against the edge. Swooshed around the bath salts and soaps I received from Mrs. Janssen, who was heavy on my mind. *She left so suddenly.* Josephine said she and Mirabella would be visiting back east for a couple of months. *I thought Mrs. Janssen's relatives were in the Netherlands.*

With them gone, "The ranch helpers are in good moods, especially without Mirabella around. She's a nasty one. God don't like ugly."

The warm water eased my sore, tired joints and made me drowsy. I soon fell asleep.

"Huh!" I awoke struggling to breathe as a force pushed down on my shoulders. I slipped beneath the water, splashing and kicking, and held my breath. I couldn't hold it long and blew. The bubbling water reversed, flooding my throat, passing into my lungs, and belly. My mind traveled back. I was a little girl, luring Timmy and Ezra to the lake. They were drowning, I was drowning. Snapping my eyes shut, I wanted the horrible memory of that day to end, and prayed God would show mercy and take me home.

The Guardian

Showing mercy was not my intent, so I mourned as my energy pushed through the slightly opened window of the last cottage on the main street near the church.

Come morning, the memory ended, leaving behind the smell of a fresh November day. She pulled me from the darkness as I let go of the power for revenge.

Sliding back into my body, I cuddled in her embrace, drawing in the pureness I'd grown to love. I was her protector, and she was mine.

As she dried my body, soaked in the tears of yesterday's forbidden joy, I released the pain I had held for centuries. My eternal love was now free to live on across the galaxies.

Chapter 32

Before and After Births

30 days to solstice
1 month

Day 21 November 1925
Journey to Awakening

Trevor

I remembered the invisible forces roaring, hammering the lake, threatening to pull us under as we struggled to stay afloat. I was pulled under; the other gulped in the air before diving in after me.

Tap, tap, tap on the door, a familiar voice called my name. Was it another dream, or reality? I could no longer tell. I was tired of fighting, so I let go. Releasing the pain I'd felt for centuries, I was no longer afraid, and eternal love was not lost but lived on across the galaxies.

The lake quieted, leaving behind only reminders of a lakeside tryst. Loud laughter, pattering of feet crossing the sand. Silent.

Night sleep was usually filled with terror, but last night, the pain left me, and he did, too. Our forbidden joy was no longer shameful but moved into multiple experiences repeatedly.

For the first time in months, I awakened refreshed, looking forward to the day. I showered, dressed in a light grey cashmere sweater, brown khakis, and a pair of matching loafers, and jogged down the stairs ready for breakfast.

I stopped in the kitchen to say good morning to Sadie before joining the family in the small dining room. It overlooked the garden planted with Mother's favorite roses and carnations.

"Morning, everyone." I kissed Mother's cheek and sat beside Father, seated at the head. Opened the white napkin and laid it across my lap. Winked at my sister across from me, sitting beside Mom.

Father spoke first, "Good to see you, son."

"Glad to see you up, dear. Sulking is unhealthy."

"You are right, Mother. I even strolled through and said good morning to Sadie."

"Bet that made her day," said Sara. "She mentioned you'd be up this morning and prepared a special breakfast."

"I see. Can't wait to dig in."

"You must keep your spirits in good order for the solstice," said Thonis, eyeing Sara. "Nothing and no one will stop us."

Sara closed her eyes and took a bite of her buttered toast, spread with homemade marmalade. Enjoying the mixed fruit flavor.

"Umm," said Sara, "Sadie said we will have plenty of Marmalade to last through winter and spring."

"Fruit bountiful along with our vegetables," said Suanne, smiling. "Good sign for the best to come."

After thirty minutes of small talk, Thonis wiped his mouth and placed his napkin on top of his empty plate. "I must excuse myself for a meeting with the mayor."

"Oh?" said Suanne, "Has it to do with the moon beginning an early transition? The ladies of Baldwin are noticing and have been unable to pry anything out of their husbands."

"Please tell the ladies for me, there is no need to worry. As I said, we will meet our obligations. Will you be joining me for a ride into town? I plan to take the car."

Suanne touched his hand, "Not today, dear. I have no appointments, and the ladies can manage despite being down one sewer. Ms. Dee promised to have orders filled four days before the eve of Christmas."

"Good deal then," Thonis leaned over to kiss his wife, pulled back from the table, and used his cane to stand.

Suanne meant to ask about his walking without a limp, but he was back to requiring his cane.

Bessie

Wrapping up tight, I headed out into the early morning without saying much to the Crumleys. The voices in my head wanted new souls, and I planned to oblige.

"I hope all goes well," Cece said to me on my way out.

"Thank you," I answered feebly.

I walked through the backway, up over the hill, and down to the sandy floor of the lake shoreline.

Trembling, I stepped closer to the water's edge, awaiting my fate, but grew impatient, "I'm here, take me. I won't do what you want."

A force pushed me headfirst into the lake. I screamed. The cave howled as the water rapidly rose. Pulling me down, I struggled, coughed, and spit up water. Remembering my brother's sad face, I stopped fighting. My body sank as the last of the gurgles and bubbles rippled across the lake.

Dr. Brown

Gray skies hung over an icy glaze covering the Baldwin and Village streets.

I parked my year-old, forest-green Cadillac near the gray and beige rubblestone cottage and turned off the ignition. Stepping outside the car, I pulled on my coat and a hat and tied a red knit scarf around my neck. I waved to Abram, standing on his porch bundled in a long coat and wool cap, smoking a pipe.

"Hey, good to see you, son," he acknowledged.

Abram and my Father were good friends. It was because of my Father that I was a successful doctor despite my Mother's feelings. As one of the few African doctors in the South, I called on well-to-do African families in Mobile, Montgomery, and Birmingham. As for patients in the Village, they were like family, and I refused compensation from them for my services.

I crunched along the ice up to the cottage as childhood memories flooded me.

I knocked softly and waited a few minutes. No answer.

As I turned to walk away, the door opened a crack.

"Hello, Mother. Hope you don't mind me showing up unannounced."

Still in her robe and slippers, Mother pulled back the door, which squeaked awake from the morning cold.

"Hello, Arthur. It's been a long while. Come on in."

I laid my hat on the corner table, looked around the cozy room, remembering.

My father was proud and inspired me to go to medical school.

I remembered how he loved to tell stories. We would sit around the woodstove after dinner, listening to him talk about the days before the Civil War. He was proud that Africans finally stood up against their oppressors.

My father died of a disease curable today, and before I graduated from medical school.

"Son, can I get you coffee?

"I'd love some."

"Sit. I'll bring you a cup. Made fresh a little bit ago."

I sat down in my father's favorite chair. It was in the same place near the window where he'd wait for the brown-headed cowbirds and blue jays to perch on the porch banister. He and I would feed them breadcrumbs.

"Hmm." I smelled mothballs but not Mother's lemon pound cake, my favorite.

She brought back a tray with two mugs filled with coffee, a saucer of milk, and one with sugar.

"You like milk and a little sugar." She chuckled.

I stood, and took the tray, set it on the end table between father's chair and hers. I remember when Father got sicker, Mother sang, and I read to him.

My Father, like Mr. Crumley, was a builder, and their skills were in high demand in Baldwin. They traded them for tutors to come into the Village and take over teaching from the elders.

I poured milk into my cup and added two teaspoons of sugar.

Mother smiled, "I don't see how you and your Father mess up a good cup of black coffee with that extra stuff."

"For us, it takes away the bitterness but still perks us up."

Mother sipped her coffee, eyeing me. She hadn't seen me since my children were babies. She disapproved of my wife and my fascination with medicine.

Despite her disapproval, I began learning about it from an African doctor who came through the Village once a month to visit the sick.

Dr. Lyness McIntosh, a fair-skinned African, grew up in

the Village. Post-Civil War, his father moved the family across to Mobile and then on to Tuskegee. That was where Dr. McIntosh got inspired by medicine. Met African scientists and doctors like Dr. George Washington Carver, who created medicines from peanuts.

I met Dr. McIntosh when he came to check on Father. Mother wanted nothing to do with the doctor and his strange medicine. The Baldwins had indoctrinated her heavily into the European Christian faith since a child. Her clinging to it began after they hanged her Mother for believing in African spiritualism.

Father Brown accepted Dr. McIntosh's assistance. I was ten years old when he hired me to help check on his patients. The doctor installed a telephone near the kitchen entry, so I could phone him in emergencies. It was still there.

"Hope you don't mind," Dr. McIntosh said to Mother.

She didn't like me traipsing around the Village. She felt I needed protection from children who bullied me and called me names.

"Naw, we don't mind," said Father. "Our boy will be busy learning a good skill for adulthood."

Both of us sat quietly, drinking our coffee. I wished for a slice of pound cake.

"Hope you don't mind me checking in on you. When I checked in on Ella, Mrs. Crumley mentioned you were not feeling well."

"Josephine can't help but worry about others when she should be worrying about her family," said Mother, tightening her lip.

"You have people who love you." I breathed deeply, my eyes watering, "You are my Mother, despite how we may disagree."

"How's your wife and children? How old now?"

My face lit up, "Arthur turned five, and Lucille is six. Got your eyes."

Mother was proud that we named our first after her. She suspected that Lydia, who was of mixed African and Portuguese descent, wanted a different name. Lydia said as much when she first met her.

I left to visit the Villagers and to introduce myself as Dr. McIntosh's replacement. He retired after turning ninety.

Lydia and the children stayed with Mother.

"Art chose this name to honor you. I would have preferred carrying on the name Lydia, passed down from my Mother and hers," Art's wife said.

Art Brown Sr. died two years before and missed meeting my new family. Mother held her tongue that time.

We visited again after the birth of our son, Arthur II. My wife and Mother were in the bedroom when the argument started. Baby Lucille was asleep on the bed as Lydia breastfed Art. My wife felt open about breastfeeding in public, but Mother insisted she sit in the bedroom and cover herself.

Lydia made the mistake of disagreeing with Mother.

I remembered Mother saying, she would no longer tolerate that uppity woman to criticize her home.

"Mother Lucille. How about you let Art and me fix things up around here? Or put you someplace decent, we can at least do that. After all, you are his mother."

"Nothing wrong with this place. Me and my late husband raised our Arthur, your husband, here."

Lydia said, "Just meant you don't have to live a meager life anymore. Your son is doing well and can support you, too."

"Don't need my son to provide for me. I am able-bodied thanks to God, who cares nothing about riches on Earth. We honor his name, so we can see him in heaven."

Lydia smiled, "I'm sure God would agree to you having an easier life. African people here in these Americas are free, and we do not have to suffer anymore. Don't you think that is a blessing from God?"

"I tell you what, I'm going to check on that pound cake I baked for Jr. He still loves my pound cake. Thank God, some things don't change." Mother stood abruptly and walked out quietly. Closed the door without slamming it, and out of respect for the children.

When I returned, I felt the tension. The only noise in the house came from the children. Mother and Lydia sat separately: Mother in the kitchen, Lydia in the front room, packed up and ready to go.

My wife stood up immediately and said, "I'm ready to leave now, Art." She walked out with the children.

Mother came from the kitchen, "She is no longer allowed here. She will not mock God in my house." She handed me the cake, wrapped and ready to go. "You do still like pound cake?'

"Of course. Thank you for baking it for me. Hope to see you soon."

That was the last I saw Mother.

She didn't pick up when I phoned and refused to answer when I stopped by alone. Today was the first time we've talked in nearly four years.

"Do you mind if I examine you, Mother? Make sure everything is all right."

"Arthur, you know how I feel about your medicine. Your Father encouraged you to pursue a career that couldn't save him."

"But prayer did?" I said defensively. No surprise, it angered her.

"No, no. You will not do like your wife. We can say goodnight from here."

There was no winning with Mother, so I grabbed my things, leaned down, and kissed her cheek.

"I'll come check on you and bring the children."

"I would like that," Mother said softly, her voice cracking.

"Be well, Mother."

I walked out into the sunshine, melting away the ice.

Lucille

I breathed in deeply and exhaled. I didn't mean to be so harsh with my son, but the tension of the past few days, and the nightmare I had yester-evening reminded me of an awful time when I was a little girl living on the Baldwin plantation, where they hanged my Mama.

Few children to play with then. Most of us had to help with work. The friends I did have were two boys, Timothy and Ezra, the same age as me, ten. Timothy Baldwin was the nephew of Thonis Baldwin and a cousin of the current Thonis Baldwin. Ezra was the son of one of the domestics.

I had a crush on Timothy. His curly blonde hair and deep blue eyes made me giggle inside. I kept to myself about those forbidden feelings. They were called grown-up feelings.

I heard Mama talking to one of the older girls, who asked about those feelings. She crushed on a boy on the plantation and was afraid to talk to her own Mama. Folks said Mama was easy to talk to, but she scolded me before I could speak most of the time. I guess because she was protecting me.

Timothy continued to play with Ezra and me despite his cousin, Thonis, threatening to tell. So, Timothy was much more careful about sneaking away with Ezra and me down to the lake before sunrise.

We all had heard of a witch who lived up in the cave and was the overseer of the mystical lake, which we stumbled upon. I remembered it being beautiful and not scary, and never told Ezra or Timmy about the witch.

One day, Timothy and Ezra went to the lake without me. I remembered feeling left out, not understanding why my friends left me behind. So, I went searching for them.

I got to the lake and saw something I didn't like. Timothy and Ezra were playing in the sand when Ezra kissed Timothy, and Timothy kissed him back.

I stayed hidden behind the lake trees, watching until they left. I came out of hiding and walked down to the lake, sat down, cried, my fists pounding the sand.

On the other side of the lake, an elderly African woman mysteriously appeared. She waved.

I thought, "Is she the witch?"

The old woman didn't look like a witch. She reminded me of my grandmama, who passed last year. Maybe it was her spirit.

The elder woman pointed to a path not that far from me. I followed it and ran into the lady.

She asked me why I was crying, and I told her.

"I saw them," she said. "What they were doing was wrong, and they need a good scolding. Bring them back here, and I will talk to them. I will tell them it was wrong and how badly they hurt you. And besides, you like Timmy, eh?"

I held my head down.

"Oh, it's okay. I will make sure he pays attention to you and not the other boy, eh."

I smiled.

"Don't tell anyone about what they did or mention me. Otherwise, their families will punish them severely, and you too for being here. Understand. Make sure when they come back, the African boy gets into the lake. I will cleanse his spirit, and he will forget all about your friend Timmy."

Happily, I brought Timothy and Ezra to the lake the following week. Waited for the old woman to appear. She did and threw something into the water that looked like pearls.

I dared Ezra to go into the lake for his cleansing. But Timothy shouted for him to stay away from the water.

Ezra walked along the shoreline, staring at the water. "Those are pearls. The treasure is rumored to come from the cave." Ezra overheard elder men talking about it, daring to one day come and find it.

The water gurgled and came up onto the shore. It grabbed Timothy, and he fell in. He couldn't swim, but Ezra could and jumped in after him.

I gasped and hollered at the elder woman to help.

She stood there laughing as Timothy and Ezra were drowning. And I couldn't save them. The old lady was the witch, and she killed Timmy and Ezra with my help.

I ran away and hid in my room until Mama brought me out to the kitchen to scold me about hanging out with the white boy, Timmy. She knew what I had done, which was why she told Master Baldwin about the upcoming Civil War. It was a distraction, and she died to save me.

Master Baldwin had Mama hanged, and soon after, they found Timothy and Ezra on the sand at the lake. They blamed Ezra for what happened. Master Baldwin planned to have Ezra's family hanged, too, but the Civil War came.

The African elders kept to themselves about what Mama envisioned. They shunned me and did not concern themselves with Master Baldwin, making me work in that kitchen and do whatever he pleased. They knew what I had done.

All these years, I wondered when my secret would become known. That day had come, and my penance would be Samuel. It was time I rid myself of the devil for the last time.

Chapter 33

Before and After Births

29 days to solstice

Day 22 November 1925
Time for Truth

Emanuella

The Village was inheriting more buggies as towners ditched them for gas-powered vehicles. As the sun came up, I imagined villagers gathering down at the field near the SugaShack, waiting to be transported to work in one of those buggies. It brought back memories of Papa John, who transported many residents to and from work.

Bessie was one of the usual riders, but I received word that she was not among today's passengers. She also didn't return to our home, and Cece relaxed.

Semperian Mother said Bessie died in the lake. She offered her life rather than risk the lives of more African children. Semperian's river spirit accepted her sacrifice, granted her access to the learning realm, and would rest there with her family.

Today, I prepared to meet with the children at the church for one last lesson before the solstice.

My Semperian powers were heightened, and Semperian Mother requested that I walk to the church. My stint as Emanuella would be ending, so I had a final assignment. What that was, I would find out before I arrived at the school.

Samuel drove the boys and Cece and picked up Lizi on the way. She would be waiting outside SugaShack. Luciferno had temporarily released the SugaShack from its energy, so Nyna would see clearly to allow Lizi to attend school. Lizi had a crucial role coming soon and during the solstice.

I was proud of Lizi Levin. She had developed inner strength and was genuinely a loving human while residing with her mother at SugaShack.

As I walked down the main road toward the tunnel, I offered a prayer, "Semperian, thank you for giving us wisdom. As the enlightened, we must never succumb to the evil energy surrounding us and teach others who are ready, like our children."

The electric pole lamps inside the tunnel gave off enough light to see through to the exit. Before crossing under, I sensed her. She was dressed in a dark purple hooded cape, leaning against the wall. Her head down, hands crossed below her stomach. Waiting.

Cautiously, I walked toward her, controlling my urge to coil from the fragrance. Now I understand that being in her presence would be my final role as Emanuella Crumley.

Mirabella looked up and grinned, "Hi Emanuella. I see you're among the living." She mocked what Mr. Emanuel said to her when I first visited the Janssen ranch. "Mrs. Josephine was very worried, as was Daddy. Have you seen my Daddy?" She frowned.

I shook my head, "I have not been to the ranch. Why are you asking me about your daddy?"

Mirabella stared into my eyes, pondering the familiarity.

It unnerved me, but I quickly dismissed the feeling. It would have been dangerous for Emanuella to remain in Mirabella's presence for too long, but as Semperian Daughter, my heart pained for a sister who came into the world as a vessel, for Apollyon Diabolus.

"Mirabella, I must go. We will see you soon." I hurried past her.

"Uh, sure," she said softly, puzzled by my comment and the sadness she felt.

Telepathically, I whispered to her, time is near for our return, my sister. Time is near.

A church elder had come early, spruced up the grounds, and prepared the inside for teaching. He greeted me warmly with a bulging smile.

"Good to see you, ma'am," he said as he opened the door for me. "We've missed you."

"It is good to be back."

He helped me out of my coat and hung it on the hook. I followed him through the double doors, down the middle aisle to the teacher's table. My eyes watered when I saw the pews again. During school, we hooked table trays to the chair backs so students could easily do their schoolwork. And the hymn racks for books and supplies. The Village had grown with enough children to fill up the middle section.

"Elder, everything looks wonderful."

"Thank you. I made you a new blackboard," he pointed to it, sitting against a rectangular easel. "And you have fresh chalk."

I picked up the box from the teaching table. "This is a wonderful gesture."

The elder continued sharing more good news, "Mrs. Jeb prepared sandwiches for the children and will bring them over around 11:00. A few minutes ago, the Jeb boys delivered hot cocoa and some freshly baked cornbread muffins. They will return when class begins."

I walked with him over to the table of refreshments and poured us both a cup of cocoa.

"I'll leave the muffins for the children," said the elder.

"I agree." And clicked his cup.

We chatted while sipping cocoa until the school filled with students.

The elder and older children helped corral the young ones to their seats and passed out muffins and cocoa.

Zeke and Gabe sat near the front. The older students were in the back with Cece and Lizi.

"Morning, students."

"Morning, Miss Ella."

"Before we leave today, we will write a thank-you note to the Jeb Family. Thank Mrs. Jeb for the breakfast, including a nice lunch coming later. Thank you, Harry and Sam, for setting up the goodies this morning, and the elder for preparing the room. "

The students cheered.

Harry and Sam smiled; the elder nodded.

"Now, a moment of silence for the children who ascended. We must keep them in our good thoughts and prayers."

The room quieted, and we prayed for their souls.

"We have asked Villagers to keep a closer watch on their children, so no going to the lake, no matter the urge. Solstice will be here soon; we must be ready for the awakening."

I looked around, making sure I had their attention. "Let me tell you a story."

The children sat quietly, so I began, "The Songhai and Mali dynasties in the 1500-1600s West Africa. They were the most powerful empires in Africa. King Shandake Aminata Ndanga ruled on behalf of her father, King Hyson Shaman.

Ndanga, who had ascended along with his first son, Prince Ndanga II. Before then, she married Emperor Abiola Jarule Njinga II, and together they continued to rule the Songhai and Mali partnership that came with enormous wealth and a strong military. They were the purest line to the teachings: Knowledge of Semperian.

It was discovered that the Royal Mother, the late wife of King Ndanga, and his son, King Shandake's half-brother, Prince Ndanga III, planned to steal the throne. First, the Royal Mother murdered King Ndanga and his successor, Prince Ndanga II.

The Ndanga-Njinga courts banned the Royal mother and Prince Ndanga III, who had already fled and landed in Portugal under the care of the Conquistador. They worked with Portugal to betray Songhai and Mali and steal the kingdom through force and with help from the Netherlands, Spain, and Portugal.

Royal Mother used dark magic, which helped create the Transatlantic slave trade. Royal Mother and Ndanga III sold their souls to the ruler of the third lower realm, Apollyon Diabolus, Fallen Guard 17.

To keep our people enslaved it required a blood covenant and the capture of Prince Ndanga-Njinga in 1630, where he has been held in the third dark hell for centuries.

We have been given the gift to stop them in this century on December 21, 1925. We will not allow evil to rule without Semperian light for eternity. Students, please close your eyes and heed my words. Listen."

Their eyes closed as the spirit of Semperian Mother flowed through, surrounding them in the Semperian cloak of protection. Semperian infused its mind with theirs to ensure they would be ready for the battle.

Chapter 34

The One Who Came After

27 days to solstice

Day 24 November 1925
Light Confusions

Mirabella

Lights dimmed in red, a voice chanting softly. I did not know how I came to lie naked in a bed of white lilacs. Their juices seeping into my skin, it was excitingly nauseating, as I felt my power returning. Even Pet sensed it, hungrily latching to my breast, claws digging deeper, annoyed it missed a feeding.

My brain became less foggy, but my eyes struggled. Upon opening, I saw Mother Luna standing over me. Anointing me with a blessing from her internal warehouse of dark magic.

"You have joined us among the living," said Luna. "We almost lost you."

"I, uh, don't understand."

"Your human emotions, my dear, were crowding your darkness, and we do not know what made that happen."

The lilacs had wilted, restoring my energy, but my memory was faulty. "I do not know."

"Hmm," said Mother Luna. "Did you not meet with our friend to discuss finding more surrogates, like her daughter, for example?"

Closing my eyes, I remembered, "I did go there. We did not speak, but I met someone else."

"Who was that someone?" Luna urged.

"I, I, do not know," I pondered while pounding my fists into my stomach so hard it disrupted Pet's feeding. It detached itself and disappeared.

Showing human emotion annoyed Mother, "Enough. You must stop. Creating you from the genome of the firstborn was supposed to fall away once your father's power matured in you, and you have most of it now. By solstice, you will have it all. So, I do not understand what is happening. Only one more powerful than you can make that happen. The firstborn."

The witch pulled the daughter up to sit and sat beside her.

"You have crossed paths with your sister. Who is she?"

Lucille

I wrapped myself up in winter clothes, boots, and a coat, ready for work. I would help Josephine get started on the Thanksgiving dinner, although Delilah and Mirabella were not expected back.

"Such a shame," I murmured.

Abram was waiting for me out front after finishing his morning pipe smoking. I appreciated his graciousness. We had become close since losing our spouses to smallpox.

"Good morning, Miss Lady," said Abram. "You look well."

"Feeling good this morning, God is good."

"Yeah'm," said Abram, who was a believer in Semperian. No awakened African spoke of that truth to another, unless the other was awakened or ready to be, and permitted by Semperian Mother.

"Glad to see Arthur doing good."

"He reminds me so much of his father."

"Senior would be proud. How about them grandbabies?"

"He says they were doing fine. One day, he'll bring them by. Hopefully."

"Yeah'm."

Abram dropped me at the front door of the ranch.

"Let me know if you need me to come and fetch you."

"I will, thank you kindly."

Unlike Towners, the Janssens allowed us to enter through the front door. Before going in, I looked over at the stables and didn't see Samuel. I was thankful.

When I walked in, the house was quiet. Still no Mrs. Delilah and Mirabella, kicking up a fuss.

As I hung my coat and scarf on the rack, I heard a noise coming from inside Mrs. Delilah's library. I peeked through the cracked-open door. The bookshelf moved. Coming from behind it was Samuel carrying a tray. He pulled the ring on the wall; the bookshelf moved back into place.

I tiptoed away before Samuel saw me. Got me wondering, "What the devil is going on around here? He was coming from behind there with Josephine the other day."

Mirabella

Luna covered me in a silk body wrap and pressed her forehead against mine. Using a mind-blending spell, she connected our thoughts, "Through the mind of Apollyon Diabolus, I see what you have seen, my daughter."

It was an early morning. The streets were quiet as I stood underneath the bridge near SugaShack. Another walked toward me. She was wearing a knee-length, brown wool coat. As she stopped near me, she used her power to ward off my lilac scent. It felt familiar, we had been there before. When the one who came before ran and entered the world before I had the chance to kill her.

The other version with Black skin, like the African ancestors, had a six-pointed star with a half-moon beneath her chin, highly regarded by Semperian. She came to intervene on the eve of the solstice. Mummy Delilah stared into her face, not realizing she was the one he protected, and called her by his name.

Luna disconnected my thoughts from hers and spoke excitedly, "I now know who Emanuel Janssen is. He is one of the most powerful Warlocks linked to our early tribe. He has the power of shape-shifting, calling upon the wind to do his bidding."

The witch paused, laid her forefinger against her jaw, and smiled, "My sister is part of this. Her warning to me was an attempt to keep me at a distance, for I am close to discovering the wrong daughter."

I smiled at Mother, whom I'd grown to love in the brief time we'd been together.

Luna stood up, steepled her hands, pointing downward, "King Shandake Ndanga-Njinga of Songhai, your Daughter E will die."

Chapter 35

The One Who Came Before

25 days to solstice

26 Day November 1925
All Friends Here

Mayor Shipley

Hiram smiled when he heard the laughter. The King and Emperor hadn't allowed the moon's early transition to hinder their happiness.

Earlier, he joined them for a hearty Thanksgiving dinner. They had turkey with an assortment of side dishes and lemon pound cake. The meal Josephine and Lucille prepared served the Janssen family and staff and delivered generous portions to the mayor's home.

Hiram knocked on the door and waited until the laughter subsided.

As Emperor, I opened the door wearing my royal attire.

"Mr. Baldwin is out front to see you, sir."

"Thank you, Hiram. We'll serve our finest whiskey."

Hiram nodded.

As I prepared to change back into my role, I noticed the King's sudden look of concern.

"My King, why so serious?

Her body shifted into Semperian Mother before speaking, "The final task for our Daughter has ignited the evil ones to discover Emanuella. It is time to erase the memory of her from Earth."

"She's having Thanksgiving supper at the church with the children and their families. I will send word to Samuel, it is time to take her into the mountains," I said.

"The Goddess will be pleased to hear from you." She smirked. "With her help, we will correct the misfortune that Ndanga III and his mother created when they joined with the demon."

My eyes smiled in remembrance, "She has earned her place back in the light realm once our mission is complete. With a new assignment."

I ran my hands down the front of my blue suit coat and straightened my collar before stepping into the hall.

Samuel shared the news with Mama J, who stayed home to finish the Thanksgiving meal. Eating leftovers was a treat at the Crumley home. They had a special guest joining them for dessert.

Samuel hurried to the church to wait with me until the last of the families were transported home.

Then we drove back to the Crumleys to drop off Cece, Zeke, and Gabriel.

I hugged Ezekiel, Gabriel, and Cece, holding onto her the longest, our last time together as an Earth family.

I would savor the memories, especially the boys complaining about my "mushy kisses."

Once we were outside of Baldwin, I asked Samuel about the impending danger. Mama J could fend for herself, but my human side was concerned about my siblings.

"They will have no use for them once we sever your connection," said the Guardian.

"When will this happen?"

"It is already done."

I sat back and rested, grateful for the enclosed buggy with cushioned seats, as we rode into the mountains.

Memories of Emanuella, Ella, and E spun in my mind, and everyone around her who had supporting roles to play on Earth's stage. From the ancient West African empires to the African Village and Baldwin Town in Alabama. I had accepted my mission as human and as Emanuella on Earth, sent by Semperian. I let it go now, and the memories of a room with the crackling sound of the heated wood stove, spewing sweaty mist into the air. Where sunlamps hung overhead, warming the midwife's delicate hands as she carefully cut the cord, the final connection to the angry womb. Where lilac rot materialized and existed simultaneously in human form, making it to the afterbirth.

Village Africa was my past, but it will continue under new leadership one day. Although I will miss the laughter of the Earth children, I taught them about their true selves, Mama J's scrumptious meals, sharing a room and conversations with my sister, the twins' playfulness and innocence, and my talks in the garden with Papa John.

As I awaited my final call, I trusted in Semperian. My next walk had begun.

The Guardian helped me from the buggy after securing it.

"We have a friend, confined here during the height of the

witch trials. Her life was spared because of her sister, who demanded it. She is an old soul, a powerful Wiccan across centuries as the one who carries the gift of havoc."

"The Goddess of Calamity," I said, in reverence.

"Yes. Spoke of in the Knowledge of Semperian. Her sister was given the gift during the creation of the blood covenant after they killed her and her sister's newborn baby boys to create it. For that reason, Prince Ndanga III was to remain in the third hell until December 21, 1925."

I added, "As prophesized, our Prince Ndanga-Njinga accepted his fate in hell, to ensure the destruction of the third lower realm and its ruler."

Inside the cave, passing DO NOT ENTER, we each picked up a lantern. I snapped my fingers and lit them. Before proceeding, Samuel passed his hand over the collapsed area where the men had died in the mining accident, putting to rest the spirits who roamed there.

At the terrain crossing, Samuel snapped his fingers, vanquishing the thousands of bats waiting for unsuspected guests, and blew into the passageways, clearing the rubble and snakes. As we walked through, he widened the narrow tunnels with another snap.

We soon stopped in front of a steel door and were immediately granted entry. The door slid away, and we stepped inside an alluring mix of wild sage, oils, burning incense, and another intoxicating scent. It calmed our tired human bodies. Samuel loved it the most, inhaling deeply through his nose and down into his lungs.

"Hello, children," said the beautiful caramel-skinned woman with bushy brown-blonde hair, hanging to her thighs.

We removed our shoes before joining her. She was seated cross-legged in the middle of a large, fluffy rug. She'd laid out a tray with a bowl of fruit and Jasmine tea.

We sat across from her and placed our hands in hers.

"My friends know me as Kate."

I nodded, fascinated by Kate's emerald eyes.

Samuel's smile grew wider as he inhaled, buzzing from the smoke-filled odor filtering through the air. It wasn't the sage or oils, but an ancient plant grown in the wild for medicinal purposes.

"Emanuel has managed to watch over you all these years, no easy task, considering. The dark forces are stronger than they've ever been in a millennium."

"I ran into Apollyon's Mirabella."

"Yes, that was by design. Mirabella was faltering between human and demon, slowing her progression. We need her to be at full power by the solstice, so we can defeat the Apollyon energy."

The Crumleys sat in the front room to have dessert, my famous chocolate cake.

John had returned from helping to board up the church and homes with small children.

I leaned over and kissed his cheek, "Glad Semperian Mother allowed your incarnation earlier than planned."

"So am I," said Cece.

"Me too," said Gabe. "No more bossy Zeke."

"I'm still older than you."

John smiled, enjoying his return to his Earth family, "She is ready to do her part, and we will do ours."

"Who's she?" Gabriel asked.

Chapter 36

The One Who Came After

11 days to solstice

The balance of power was at a crossroads, and Semperian would not lose. It would end it as promised. For I am the universal creator, the only energy spawned from Source Consciousness. No beginning, no end, only balance and a continual cycle of life. Semperian can choose to destroy and start anew if I must.

Knowledge of Semperian (Origins 1)
In the beginning

Day 10 December 1925
Winding Down

Mayor Shipley

I walked down to the parlor to meet with the guest. Thinking of how much I loathed the visitor responsible for my family's decades of pain. *Your body would have been more useful taken over by Semperian in human form, I thought. Like, like what happened to your cousin?*

The original Mayor Shipley planned to meet up with a Village girl at the SugaShack. Rather than meet with his usual, he was given another and didn't realize she was a shapeshifter. She lured him to his death, allowing Emanuel to take his body.

Suanne Baldwin was the shapeshifter and graciously accepted her role in removing the original Lazarus Shipley from Baldwin. He was as devious as Juelle's husband and helped maintain order over the enslaved Africans and the blood covenant.

Luna gave the original Lazarus his dark magic powers. Lazarus died in the smallpox epidemic. When resurrecting and immortalizing souls, she recruited him as one of hers to ensure his cousin kept his end of the bargain. She dropped him off in Baldwin in 1917.

The Semperian Mother intervened, and Emanuel Janssen took his soul last summer, without the dark forces knowing. She also permitted Suanne Baldwin to help the Goddess while locked away. Sara's powers were not as strong as Suanne's, which were centuries old.

Thonis stood facing the window overlooking the cobblestone alley, a side view of the dock off to the right. A narrow road alongside it led to the mountains. *He thought of Kate and her true power of calamity. Wondering how long he could control her now that Sara was her envoy, he thought.*

"Ye Thonis," I said, entering the parlor.

Hiram followed, carrying a tray with two jiggers and a half-pint glass snifter of brown liquor.

"How about a swig of the French whiskey you brought me from your last shipment?" I offered.

Thonis nodded, "Ye, but of course."

Hiram poured the drink into each jigger, held out the tray to me, then to Thonis.

I raised my glass, "Ye, salud."

Thonis raised his, "Ye, salud."

We downed the first jigger, then another, before sitting.

No audience today to fill the remaining chairs, only us, to tend to the urgent business of the early transitioning moon and things to follow.

"Ye, know why I am here," said Thonis.

I nodded, "Have we heard of whom we seek?"

Thonis blinked his eyes to keep them from closing. "It has been an arduous process, but we believe we know who," he said, slurring his words.

"What do ye mean?" I asked, puzzled by Thonis seeming snockered by a little whiskey.

"The initial E came up during Luna's melding with her daughter. She encountered her, this E," he yawned and wiped his eyes. "Makes me weary."

"Ye, weary? Do not forget, as your cousin and next of kin, the council can ask us to lead if you are not up to the task."

Noticing Thonis's sluggishness, I suspected it was a lightworker spell and not the drink.

"I am of sound mind," Thonis affirmed. "I will fulfill the covenant, so help me. E will die, then Emanuel and Delilah's rightful daughter can take her place as the firstborn along with Trevor by the solstice."

"If you say so, ye."

Thonis forced himself to stand with the help of his cane, which he hadn't needed since Mirabella's healing touch. He felt the pain he once had and thought, "Is my darling Sara or someone else attempting to undermine me?"

He excused himself and headed out into the night.

Thonis

I had planned to make one last visit to take care of the problem. It would mean ending Kate's life and her hold on Sara, to maintain my immortality and wealth.

Chapter 37

The One Who Came After

6 days to solstice

Why not swim in the sea of lust without dabbling deeper into the dark, where there is no return? We can do nothing if one is determined to mingle in matters they cannot control. Once touched by the fire of his hell, they are bound by his rules so painfully deadly.

—Knowledge of Semperian (Origin 16)
Luciferno (Lucifer), Fallen 1

Day 15 December 1925
Cheeky's Darkness

Mirabella

Changing between red and yellow, the moon followed me out of the dark forest. With six days left until its rise, Apollyon summoned Mother Luna to fetch his chosen one.

I made it to the tunnel where I saw my sister.

"My guess, it's Emanuella Crumley," I told Luna earlier. "The only girl in Baldwin with Black skin and with a name like Emanuel. She was born on my birthday, I found out from Cheeky. How could I have been so stupid, not to have figured that out before now?"

Mother agreed that the firstborn was Emanuella Crumley. "Do not be angered. Semperian blinded us until now, for they planned to move her but not before getting to you."

The search for E came up short. No one in the Village had heard of her, not the Crumleys or Cheeky.

But what they did say was that John Crumley had returned.

That made Mother Luna nervous. "John Crumley's return means that Lepta is gearing up for solstice. If so, my sources have yet to confirm she has descended into the lower realms to regain her powers. I must prepare myself."

Josephine

Semperian had ordered my visit and stay until solstice morning, and Lucifer and Satan welcomed me. There, I would work to regain the power to stand against Luna. As promised.

Living in hell was no easy task for me. I had spent countless existences in the light realm and the Sun. As Lepta, I had only distant memories of a time there. I currently serve in the role as Josephine Crumley on Earth.

As a young Wiccan and lightworker, I transcended to the highest ranks in the universe, right below the Semperian Guards.

I won the first descent and gifted Semperian with spring and summer. That seasonal energy protected me from failing the final test in the lower realms. Semperian named me Lepta after I mastered those hells. I developed a power that created elevated light and warmth like the Sun.

It was a battle of wills between me and Lucifer and Satana, and me. Both fallen Semperian Guards were equally conniving, especially Satan. As the master of trickery, she could easily lead a soul off the winning path to failure.

For the new test, Semperian had given Lucifer and Satana permission to force upon me, every ounce of their hells. Even if it meant my death.

Being reincarnated to Earth meant no use of Semperian energy, which I had never been without. But as Josephine, I had no choice. I had to fully immerse myself in the human experience as a mother.

I took the assignment as repayment to Semperian for my misstep with a sister who betrayed me. Goddess of Calamity was permitted to assist along my Earthbound journey to stop Luna.

"Today we will ride some of my toughest beasts," Satan said.

I was sitting with Lucifer, who had a smirk on his face. He felt my anxiety as I tried not to stare at the hundreds of genderless naked bodies dancing about, openly engaging in a myriad of sex acts.

"As you wish," I said somberly.

"Hurry back now," said Lucifer. "I have planned a special gathering of souls wanting desperately to partake in your fruit."

Having only been in hell for less than a day, I was already fighting to maintain a semblance of pureness that I once had on Earth and the higher realms.

Playing in the fire with Luciferno and Satana was a battle I couldn't afford to lose.

Nyna Levin

Sweet Tea, one of my ladies, informed me that Mirabella was waiting by the archway for the last of the patrons to enter SugaShack. She had come for Lizi.

Earlier, Luna sent a Black Hawk with a message from the dark lord, "Prepare the offering." A demand I had no intention of fulfilling since giving birth to my precious little girl. I wanted more for my daughter and dreamt that one day, she would leave Baldwin and head north.

Pregnant with Lizi, I joined Luna. That was my second mistake. The Wiccan, like a suitor I once knew, promised me power and dominance over the unruly circumstances dealt to me when I was fourteen.

My birth name was Nyna, the only child of the Levin family. My mom was a weak woman. Couldn't handle raising me alone after my Pop left us for a job up north. He never returned, although he promised. Mom soon followed him and left me with an elderly couple. She promised to come back for me, but like my Pop, she abandoned me.

Being abandoned by people who supposedly loved me was what I had become accustomed to. Soon to be abandoned again, but this time by a wealthy European man from Mobile. He promised to take me away from the Village, living with elders who understood nothing about raising a teenage girl. Especially one who was as beautiful as I and curvy like a woman, the European man told me.

I met the tailor-suited man with a black briefcase in Baldwin town while I was doing laundry and washing dishes at a café for businessmen passing through. I was out back eating leftovers given to me by the owners. Didn't know he had been eyeing me. One day, he approached me.

"Cheeky," he said to me with a big grin on his face. I said nothing. "You have the prettiest, roundest cheeks I've seen on any girl. Yep, I'll call you Cheeky."

I held my head down bashfully and smiled. He sounded nice. Nicer than anyone else had been to me, even the elders I lived with. I had to give all my money to them for living expenses. Mom promised to send them money but never did. That put the burden on me to pay my way.

"My name is Nyna, but I like Cheeky better," I said to him. Glad to be rid of a name given to me by my parents, who left me.

We became friends. Had secret trysts because Villagers and Europeans mixing was frowned upon.

He lived across the water in Mobile, I think. Years later, I found out he was married with a family. He, too, was a liar.

We met at an abandoned cottage, now the SugaShack. The man taught me about being a woman, including my menstruation. He brought me perfumes, soaps, and money I hid from the elders. Our lustful escapades caught the attention of Luciferno from the first lower realm. It was his energy that encapsulated me and gave me the confidence to have sex for money in the coming years.

Soon, I find out that being a woman comes with responsibilities. I was impregnated, and the man brought medicine from a doctor friend to abort the baby. The one time I was pregnant, I was sixteen, and old enough to know better. I told him I planned to keep my baby. That was the last time I saw him.

I was sad about that because I had been with him all those years, but I would not regret my decision. I would make sure my child was loved and taken care of.

I left the elders' home and remained at the cottage where the man had helped me spruce up. He had too much class to be romping with me in a rundown shack.

On wooden floors with a blanket to keep us covered and warm. That is where I had my baby girl, whom I named Lizi. I got the name from him. He said he met a girl with that name years ago, and she was a good friend.

I saved up the money he gave me to live and take care of my baby. We once attended the Village church, where I ran into the elders who ignored me, along with some of their Villager friends. They looked at me and my baby like she was diseased. That was the last time I attended church.

When my girl got older, I started seeing other men and getting paid for my time. Europeans, and a few Villagers. The more money I made, the more I fixed up the cottage, which I turned into a home for Lizi and me. I left the front area to do personal business.

Months down the road, a young African woman traveling through from Birmingham needed a place to stay. She became a good friend and did what I did to survive.

Her name was Sweet Tea, and she used powers she called magic sugar. With her magic sugar, more men would show up for pleasuring, so many that it was hard to keep up.

Sweet Tea brought more girls in. That was when SugaShack was born.

Unbeknownst to me, evil had entered my home from hell, ruled by a trick master. Disguised itself as Lucifer and captured my soul by luring me into dabbling in its magic sugar.

Once that happened, I was introduced to Luna through one of Sweet Tea's girls. I didn't always want to be doing what I was doing, and Luna promised me a better way. She helped me practice more magic sugar, but not nearly enough to do what Sweet Tea and the other girl did. They hurt people they didn't care for, and that scared me.

After the hawk's visit, Apollyon entered me, making me cry out in agony. My naked body held down, legs spread wide, fed its darkness, invigorating it as the lake of fire burned within her. I obliged its need for it promised me I would one day rule by his side as his wife. I would replace Luna Diabolus.

During those encounters, I begged for Lizi to be spared> I knew it wanted her. I protected Lizi by sending her into a deep sleep. Didn't want her awakened by her nightly romps with darkness, which left me deeply clawed and bloody. I used magic sugar that healed my wounds quickly.

Mirabella

As the patrons gathered, the pianist and trumpeter's music

serenaded and jammed to the competing laughter and chatter. Cheeky was in the room, touching up her makeup and brushing her hair that hung to her shoulders. Lizi had pressed it for her.

"My talented girl," Cheeky said, stomping her feet, swinging her hair.

Perhaps she couldn't hear me over the loud music, so I banged on the door.

"Come in." Cheeky permitted me to enter, although I needed no permission.

I stepped into her pitiful pink room, and it stunk. The fragrance from the flowers displayed in a crystal vase on the vanity, "Roses, I abhorred them."

"Oh?" Cheeky smiled. "They are from a doctor friend."

"Hmm, your doctor has no taste."

"I would disagree," said Cheeky, defending the doctor, who had been her good friend since they were children.

"It's time. We are impatient. No more stalling."

"Time?"

"Don't toy with me, whore boss."

Cheeky stood abruptly, "Whore boss. You should talk. Were you not the one being taunted at the ceremony? What of that gift Towner's talk about?"

"Huh. I could squash you without a sweat, turn you into vermin, and feed you to the wolves."

Cheeky laughed, "We both know he would not be pleased."

"You know so much about pleasing my father, so you should know what he truly wants."

"You cannot have Lizi. I was made a promise," said Cheeky, hands on her hips.

"Tsk, tsk, what is a promise if not broken?" I stepped close to Cheeky as my eyeballs swirled like fire. "Nyna Levin, you must comply. Do you understand?"

Cheeky stiffened, couldn't move, couldn't scream, and tears rolled down her cheeks. No magic sugar within her power could stop me from doing what I was there to do. With my finger, I twirled her around and forced her down the hall toward the room of Apollyon's true bride-to-be. Cheeky would have to permit me to enter.

I caught a glimpse of Sweet Tea, who turned away when she saw me. Sweet Tea was one of Luna's minions, influenced by the Apollyon energy and sent there to create SugaShack as a cover and keep an eye on Lizi until the time to turn her over.

Nyna entered Lizi's room and was forced to permit the one who followed her there.

"Where is she?" I looked around the empty room.

"She's gone. Please leave her alone. He has me, and I will do anything. I, I could find him another…"

"Stop! Did you think my father would choose you, a whore, over a virgin? We made sure your Lizi would not be defiled by any human. Semperian rebirths are considered pure; Apollyon needs her as such to travel through to the higher universe. Inside your tainted vessel, he would not be able to reach Semperian."

"Please let her go," Cheeky begged. "She didn't ask for this; she is innocent."

"Oh, hush up, you annoy me."

I snapped my finger. A cobra appeared, curling the length of my arm. A new friend, Luna, permitted me without having to turn the Towner children into pets.

"Please spare us," said Cheeky, thankful her doctor friend would take care of Lizi. She had called him to come fetch her before the demon came to collect.

I laughed at the pitiful woman.

"You are all liars, just like them," Nyna cursed as the cobra struck, forcing its head inside her mouth, working its way down her throat. She gagged as the serpent strangled her until she stopped breathing. Nyna fell to the floor.

Waving her hand, I called the demon from the dead woman's body, clapped my hands, and vanquished it.

"It is done, my father. Luna says he will bring her to you."

Cece

Lizi and I had a tough time seeing through the fog.

An hour ago, I stopped by to visit. Walking past Ms. Cheeky's window, I heard Mirabella shouting, demanding to see Lizi.

Lizi was coming out the back door. I ran up the back stairs and grabbed her hand, "Let's go now."

My friend didn't argue.

Halfway up the road, I saw a familiar car and stopped. I peered through the open passenger window, "Dr. Brown. Can you give us a ride to my home, please?"

He nodded, clicked open the rear door; we jumped in.

"Thank you, Art." Although frightened, I managed to flirt.

Dr. Brown hurriedly put the Cadillac in drive, pressed the gas, and quickly accelerated down the road, away from the Crumley block.

Mirabella

I saw them as they sped through the tunnel, Dr. Brown, and the faces of his two frightened passengers. The one called Cece was E's Earth sister.

"Yes, we know who you are, Emanuella Crumley Janssen. Tick, tock, come out, come out, you can no longer hide. Tick Tock, you will die."

Luna

Inside the cave, it was as it had been since I made my way there centuries ago. Dark with tiny light coming in through the cave's mouth, the rocky walls were soiled with toxic algae, like the water that settled there. Uninhabitable for humans, but I was quite comfortable. There I prepared for his return, luring in innocents, teased by the thought of finding beautiful pearls at the water's deep.

I stood in front of what was once my transport from the light realm, which had since been closed. It was the former universal gardener's creation; a small break in the portal led downward into his hell.

Over thousands of years, I carefully recreated his lilac potion and energized it with the juices of innocents to manipulate the opening and ensure it was undetectable by Semperian operatives.

Sparingly, I used the sacred words to widen the portal enough for Apollyon's return.

"We are almost there," I said to the crowd of stolen souls standing in front of me, meshed into a spinning ball of fire.

Holding out my arms, I thanked them for their loyalty to Apollyon and me. The number of souls had grown to seventeen million, and they were prepared for resurrection day.

"My friends, I have one tall order that must be carried out within the next forty-eight hours."

I paused a moment to take in the warmth. Apollyon was pleased that I had prepared them to serve as his operatives across the universe.

"Find Emanuella Janssen and bring her to me. We have her Earth sister, so it will make our task easier."

The fireball blew, circling the entire cave with me standing in the middle.

I closed my eyes and lifted my hands, permitting the fire to consume me, "We are Source Consciousness anew."

Chapter 38

The One Who Came Before

5 days to solstice

Day 16 December 1925
Tasting Fire

Semperian Daughter

The first night, I slept deeply and awoke refreshed. The isolation was conducive to preparing my mind. I thanked Semperian for the ostrich feather-stuffed mallet and pillows, and the thick quilt that replicated the one Cece and I shared at the Crumley home.

"Welcome, morning," said Kate cheerfully.

I sat up and stretched, "Welcome, morning."

"The sea salt and rose milk bath is ready for you. Freshly brought in by some friends," she chuckled. "You were in a much-needed sleep. Friends come and go even without me knowing sometimes."

"I have a great appreciation for Semperian and all who stand with us."

"Semperian's grace kept me safe and whole for the time I've been here. All for a greater purpose."

"A greater purpose." I pulled on my sheepskin robe and joined Kate, sitting in her favorite position on the rug. We prayed to Semperian before I took my bath.

I stretched out in the water as it turned warm and flowed into a swirling pool of rose milk and sea salt, cleansing my body. My mind cleared, allowing in only elevated thoughts. I smiled. He had come home in my absence, called by Semperian Mother.

"Hi Papa, I hear you have returned, but I sense your sadness." I blew him a kiss before slipping into a deep sleep.

Slipping into a deep slumber, I heard screaming and crying as they feared his anger. The heat was like hot coals and lingered within an unnatural fog. A thump-thump of feet and heavy breathing pulled me toward it, but I struggled backward. I needed to get out of there because that place was not for me yet.

Then, a frightened, familiar voice called out to me, "E, where are you? Help us."

A memory clip came through and I yelled to her, "Sissy?"

Trembling, I moved cautiously while mumbling. This cannot be your fate.

"E, where are you, please? Please help us."

Urgently, I moved but stopped when another voice shouted, "No!" It was a bold and booming voice that shouted.

"Prince Njinga? If you are here, why is my sister with you? She shouldn't be. This cannot be her fate."

"No." The voice hollered again, followed by his screams of anguish and pain.

A tree appeared surrounded by Towners shouting, pounding their fists at the Black body hanging there, his head lying to one side, the noose having snapped his neck.

"What's happening? Something's not right."

I reached out for them but fell into steamed water mixed with rose milk and sea salts. I struggled but was forcibly held until I no longer felt that anger of hot coals, and heard screams and shouts.

Gentle hands pulled me up from the steaming water and covered my naked body in warm towels.

"Daughter, can you hear me?"

I opened my eyes and saw a face like mine. Mr. Emanuel was dressed in royal African garbs as Emperor Abiola Hereto Njinga II. His gentle smile reminded me of the night I was born.

Beside him sat the Goddess of Calamity.

"We thought we lost you, my Daughter."

"But I heard Sissy and the Prince. I must return," I insisted, attempting to lift my head.

"Not your time," said Semperian Mother.

"She's frightened and needs me," I argued. "Where is she?"

The trio remained silent until Emanuel spoke, "In the third hell. She and Lizi were taken there to draw you out."

Semperian Mother added, "They would have succeeded if we had not intervened. You've had a vision of what's to come. We cannot fail."

I lay my head on Mr. Emanuel's chest, allowing him to wrap his arms around me like he did when I was a newborn.

"Don't worry, Papa," I said, softly. "We will not fail."

Chapter 39

Before and After Births

4 days to solstice

Why not reach farther than the highest star? Why wait to be called to sit on the side of Source? I have created much and made this universe beautiful from my knowledge of what Source needs. Semperian does a disservice to the Consciousness, making it weak. I, the universal gardener, will create souls who understand and are not weakened by hierarchical rankings that mean nothing. I will bear two humans. One girl is part of the legacy, and the other is a son born to a woman who will help the Wiccan with the killing of two boys. It will come with consequences for carrying my seed.

—Knowledge of Semperian (Origin 16)
Universal Gardener, Apollyon Diabolus Fallen 17

Day 17 December 1925
Devil a-Comin' for Real This Time

Mirabella

The weather shifted the second week in December, with Thonis, fighting a spell from an unknown source, helping Semperian.

The intense cold made walking unbearable, and the docks closed.

No one inquired about the disappearance of Cheeky and Lizi. Sweet Tea passed rumors, saying they moved up north.

Then she disappeared before Semperian energy covered the Village and iced over the lake.

Villagers with families and children remained home, and Semperian operatives dropped off food and other necessities at doorsteps. Once brought inside, the doors mystically locked residents inside until solstice.

Some Villagers dared to travel to Baldwin for the little work left for the year. They were at the mercy of Apollyon's minions and Semperian operatives, vying for more souls to stack their armies.

We celebrated cautiously after the capture of E's Earthly sister, placing her along with Lizi, a virgin, on the outer shores of Apollyon's hell near the prince and his loyalists.

I giggled, "Mother Luna, imagine their surprise when they learned the great Dr. Arthur Brown Jr. was my father's strongest soldier."

"We can thank your brother for doing his part. But for now, I have more work to do. We must find this Emanuella girl quickly. I suspect she may be protecting Cece and Lizi from Apollyon."

Earlier, mother had difficulty reaching father because of the escalating Semperian energy to impede our operatives and stop his rise. Mother had to resort to a dangerous form of dark magic to fight against the barriers. If not done correctly, it could kill her and anyone around, so she wanted me to stay clear.

Giving her space to meditate, I stepped outside into the daylight but felt drained. The Knight Lilac Trees had dropped most of their leaves, with a few wilting white lilacs on the ground. I didn't have the strength to drop into my lilac field, and afraid of what I might find. On my last visit, the lilacs were slowly vanishing. Mother warned that Semperian energy would begin devouring our energy source closer to the solstice.

Night came before Mother opened the cottage door.

Seeing her, I gasped. Within that short time, her skin had thinned to her bones, and she had lost chunks of her white hair.

The Wiccan waved her bony finger, motioning for me to come.

I followed the feeble woman to the rear of the cottage and sat in the wooden chair across from her. The table was piled high with dead white lilacs and a flickering candle.

"I have the answer, my dear," said Mother Luna, her voice raspy. "We must recreate your birth. To do so, we need your Earth mother." She coughed, almost strangling on her phlegm, she spat into the pile of dead lilacs. "Uh-hum. We need to proceed with caution, including partaking in lilacs. Those were contaminated."

"How? I thought we were safe here."

"Up to a certain point. My stay here was punishment and contingent on resubmitting to the will of Semperian. I have been given centuries to comply, and I have not. My time is running out."

Tears came to my eyes, "Nothing can happen to you."

"No tears," the witch snapped. "You were created from the energy of your true father, Apollyon Diabolus. Show no weakness."

I nodded and refrained from showing further emotion.

"I have located your birth mother. She is being held in the basement of the Janssen mansion. We must get to her quickly, and there is only one person who can help." Luna coughed again and spat into the lilacs.

"Dr. Brown is on his way there and will connect with her in the next few hours."

Arthur Brown

I rang the bell at the Janssen manor.

I heard Mother was the only cook on duty, temporarily residing in the staff quarters due to the impending holiday and the lockdown in the Village. I felt her anxiety and interrupted her thoughts.

She opened the door, surprised to see me. I only visited when Delilah called for herself or Mirabella.

"Art." She crunched her forehead.

"Hello, Mother, may I come in?"

Uneasiness came over Lucille as she tried to dismiss it. "Come on in." She stepped aside. "Didn't realize Mr. Janssen had called."

Because he was permitted to enter, Dr. Brown safely crossed the Semperian circle and cringed when thinking about the light magic used by Warlocks like Emanuel Janssen.

"Mother, I came to see you."

As a young Art Brown, I first learned of my special power at age eleven. I was playing in the field up near the lake with other children from the Village. There was a strange energy lurking that day, one that seemed to push the children to act mean-spirited.

One boy began taunting a teen girl whose parents had abandoned her and left her with the elders. I took a liking to her even though she was older. Nyna grew up to become the madam of the SugaShack.

"Your parents don't love you, that's why they left," said the boy, teasing Nyna.

Nyna remained quiet, but I stepped in.

"Shut your mouth, or I'll shut it."

"Make me," said the boy. "You're ugly just like her."

More children had gathered. There weren't many children in the Village back then. And the same elders taught those same children. So, their actions surprised me.

I walked up to the boy but rather than touch him, an energy took hold of me, urging me to use my will. I tensed up, anger flowing throughout my veins as I held onto my breath and then let it go. The boy fell plummeted by invisible punches.

"Ow, stop, stop," the boy hollered. "Stop."

Except for me and Nyna, the other children screamed.

Another boy pointed, "Look at his eyes. Red cracks across his white eyeballs. He is the devil."

Nyna noticed my eyes, too, and touched me softly on my shoulder, "You can stop now."

And I did. For her.

From that day forward, other than Nyna, the children who witnessed the incident avoided me, and Nyna Levin became my friend and protector.

Village parents who heard the story from their children warned my Mother that I may be possessed.

"As a god-fearing woman, you need to pray to God to cleanse him," a woman said to Mother at church one Sunday.

Mrs. Crumley was there that day and heard what the woman said. She admonished her on Mother's behalf, despite the truth I knew, and I think she did too.

Mother defended me, angered by rumors spread by bad children, she called them. "They are the ones God should punish."

My father, Arthur Brown Sr., loved me and encouraged me to dream big. My father was the reason I followed Dr. McIntosh into medicine. I wanted to help cure Villagers dying of the plague brought on by the Towners. It was said to be a curse. Years later, the condition could be cured.

Upon stepping onto the path, the dark forest energized me, tickling my innards and causing me to giggle, something I hadn't done.

I walked until I reached the dark garden filled with lilac trees, guarding the hundreds of white lilacs crowding the grounds. At first, I did not notice the invisible archway leading into the invisible cottage that was only visible to those invited to have an audience with the dark lord's most devoted soldier.

Crossing into the garden zone, I followed the sensation in the air, drawing me forward down the crooked path. I was giddy watching the white lilacs fall back, allowing me to pass through. Then I saw it coming into view, a round moon-shaped door with a blood streak crossing its center.

I smiled when I happened upon Luna tucked away in the little cottage house beyond the cave.

She told me a story about a devoted Christian Village woman impregnated by her husband. She had made a deal with the devil years before, not knowing her payback would come in the form of a child. Soon, that child was born into this world as the son of the demonic angel in the lower realms and the Knowledge of Semperian.

I am the son of Apollyon Diabolus Fallen 17. I will rule by my father's side and help him rise to Semperian and become Source Consciousness.

Chapter 40

The One Who Came Before

2 days to solstice

Day 19 December 1925
Passing Through

Thonis

Another mystical storm surged through Baldwin and the Village. Snow flurries pummeled homes, trees, and roads. Buildings trembled, and the rising river flowed onto the dock, flooding the inner city, stopping short of my stead.

Thonis managed to move about with the help of dark magic, reducing the somber effects of a spell meant to slow his movements. Unable to make the final trek into the mountain, he stopped and asked me to order Towners to board up businesses and remain home.

"Ye, a storm is coming, and it's the work of Wiccans," Thonis said.

I raised my brow.

He explained, "It is one of the oldest forms of magic originating from the Goddess of Calamity, who caused catastrophic natural disasters. She taught it to her followers, one being someone I know."

"Ye, who might that be?" I asked, grinning to myself. Thonis had it all wrong. The someone was Kate, and she was the Goddess.

Thonis was visibly annoyed by the turn of events. The reason behind the storm was to ward off the dark forces, closing in on the firstborn, and said as much.

"The Village went into lockdown two weeks past, and a clear yellow circle covers the Village from the entrance through to the outskirts," said Thonis. "The circle is a Semperian protection spell, reducing the movement of dark forces. It doesn't matter; we sent in Dr. Brown to retrieve Delilah Janssen. Not sure where Emanuel is. He's been a wall, which makes me suspicious."

I asked, "We found Delilah Janssen's location?" *Thinking to myself, how arrogant for him to think that evil could win. We were way ahead of their plan to recreate the twin birth on the night of the blood moon in 1908.*

Thonis nodded, "We believe she is being held in a secret quarter at the Janssen ranch, and Art's Earth mother may know where it is. She is on duty at the manor until after the holidays. The Crumley family is experiencing a family emergency, and we know what that is." Thonis grinned. "Luna suspects Josephine Crumley may be kin, as in her Wiccan sister from the 1600s. Small, small world we live in here in Baldwin."

"A small world indeed, ye."

Semperian Mother visited the Crumley home and updated John Crumley.

"I know you are concerned about Josephine, but she is doing well, I hear."

"She's strong, no doubt," said John. "But she submerged as a mother to our children here. With Emanuella on her mind when she left, now Cece. I am hoping that won't be a distraction."

"I am confident that she will return as Lepta on the solstice to deal with her sister. Meanwhile, Luna has no idea that Art Brown's mercy has helped save Emanuella before and once more. While he cared for her during her coma, Emanuel implanted Semperian tracking into his soul without the dark forces knowing. Because he is part human, the physician part of him cares for the people he serves, which over the years he's kept from Luna and Apollyon."

"I am ready for my part in all this and will prepare the boys."

"Very good," said Semperian Mother. "The Semperian Trinity is united. Emperor Njinga as Emanuel Janssen, King Ndanga-Njinga as the Semperian Mother, and Goddess of Calamity will initiate the final plan, using Apollyon's son, to stop it from entering this world. We have already succeeded in pulling Emanuella back from the inferno doorway, leading to the lower realm."

Arthur Brown

I looked around the foyer. My eyes stopped at the closed French doors, on the right of the staircase. Mother tensed up.

"What's on your mind, Mother? You look troubled."

I stared into her questioning eyes, struggling to answer, "Son, I mind my business in another's home, but I've been praying on this."

"Maybe I can help." I grabbed her hand and gently squeezed. My power rushed inside her.

"The devil," she said. "He's around. I know you don't believe."

I smiled, "It is not what I believe, it is what you believe. Let me help."

"I trust you, son, to help me make this right. We must hurry before he returns."

I suspected she was referring to Emanuel Janssen, whose whereabouts were unknown.

Mother opened the French doors, "Come this way."

I followed her over to the bookcase.

"From behind there. I see them come from behind there. Josephine and Samuel."

I glanced at Mother, "Samuel?"

She nodded.

Since meeting him at the Crumley's, I wondered about his role in the solstice and if he walked among the lightworkers like Emanuel. Although I felt uneasy in Samuel's presence, I couldn't determine whether or not he was. Nor did I share those feelings with Luna.

As I ran my fingers down the left side of the bookcase, I spotted a round brass ring hanging on the wall. I reached up and pulled it.

Slowly moving, the bookshelf squealed open.

I stepped behind it. Covered the padlock on the door with my hand and vanquished it without Mother noticing. Turned the handle and pulled the door open. Beyond it, a stone staircase leads down to the left. A woman's cry for help echoed in the distance.

"You hear that, son?"

"I do, follow me."

Several steps led us to the bottom landing. The woman crying for help came from the dimly lit room off to the right of us.

"Oh Lord, it's Mrs. Janssen."

Delilah Janssen lay atop a cot covered in a woolen blanket.

She appeared to be in pain.

Mother hurried over. A mound atop Delilah's stomach prompted Mother to pull back the blanket. She gasped, "No, Lord, it can't be, she with babies. This is why they hide her? This doesn't make sense."

"It appears the birth is already starting, Mother. I will need your help."

"Whaa.." said the confused Lucille. "What's going on here? Why do they do this?"

"Mother, you know what to do," I said, connecting my thoughts with hers. "We are in 1908. Run warm water in the tub. I need to move her, hurry."

She did as she was told and prepared the area for the impending birth, recreating the circumstances that brought the before and after births into the world. The transitioning blood moon improved the chances that the re-creation would work.

After removing Delilah's clothing, I carried her over and laid her in the tub. In her ear, I whispered, "This time, we will make sure she does not live." I quietly chanted the words Luna gave to me, "Guided by his hand, we will bring forth your child in your name."

Mother knelt at the end of the tub, waiting for the babies to come through the birth canal. Delilah screamed in agony as I held her shoulders down and continued chanting.

"Babies are coming. I see the head."

"Trade me places, Mother."

The midwife took over, holding Delilah in place, who appeared to be settling down.

I reached into the water, shouting at Delilah to push. The baby's head appeared with black hair like sheep's wool. "There you are." I pulled the Black baby out of Delilah's angry womb and set her in the tub.

Mother hollered when she saw me covering the child's nose and mouth, "What are you doing? Stop."

She jumped up, leaving Delilah, who had now gone silent. Ran over to me.

I looked up at Mother, and angry energy exploded around me; my eyes turned to blood.

"Oh lord, you're the devil. God help his soul."

Mother's body ignited into fire, which I had nothing to do with. I shut down my human mind and drowned her screams as she burned alive and dropped dead.

Another child appeared from Delilah's womb, this time with lighter skin. I pulled her out and wrapped her in a blanket.

"It is done." I ran back up the stone stairs and back into the night, heading to the cottage beyond the cave.

Emanuel

The night deepened, and the storm slowed and held as I made my way back to the Janssen mansion. Inside, the French doors were no longer shut, and the bookshelf was ajar. I walked over and peered down the stone stairs. Then followed the quiet to the secret quarters.

Scanning the room, I saw the lifeless body of Delilah and Lucille's burnt remains. Hurried over to the tub, reached down, and pulled the black-skinned newborn from the empty tub, wrapped her in a blanket, as in 1908. I touched the baby who stirred beneath my touch and walked up the stone steps, out into the parlor. Passed my hands across the outer library, vanquishing the doors, leaving only a wall as if always there.

Papa took me out into the cold, carried me to the buggy, and set me inside a makeshift basket on the buggy floor. Grunted, lifting himself into his rawhide seat. Grabbed the whip—snap, snap— "Geddup Black Bo."

The wagon jumped into a jerk-wobble wobble down the broken dirt road into the fall-blackened night we rode, blindly.

Overhead, a blood moon against a jet-black sky backlit our path, warning off anyone wanting to pass our way.

Wobble, jerk-wobble, wobble, snap, snap, "Geddup Bo."

We passed through Baldwin-Janssen Square, set off by ghostly distant hills and mountains across the bay that shadowed the hundreds of twisted Oak trees wearing crowns of Spanish Moss. About a mile from the road, trees carried painful stories, whispering into the wind.

Listen.

"We are the true Africans from Semperian. We will destroy the third hell, for it is out of balance with the rest of the galaxy and Semperian. We will return to peace and balance, ensuring Semperian does not lose connection to Source Consciousness. If we fail, void and nothingness await all of us throughout the universe."

Chapter 41

Before and After Births

1 day to solstice

Day 20 December 1925
Coming to Terms

Luna

The trek back through the dark forest came easier as an older Arthur Brown took care of the wrong daughter and turned over the right daughter to Luna. He had tried to control his emotions when asked to murder the firstborn. He valued life and spent years saving people.

"Let me see her." I reached out my hand to Art.

Dr. Brown handed me the newborn. I examined her thoroughly, including underneath the chin for the African symbol. "Perfect. Now we allow her to grow at a rapid pace, ready for the solstice ceremony. Emanuel Janssen, as the holder of the legacy power, must release the gift to her, which should have been returned to him once the two births were completed, and the re-created firstborn was killed, eh." I glanced at Art

Brown, "I hope you showed no mercy, left them to fester in filth and blood drained from Delilah."

He nodded, avoiding eye contact, which made me curious. I decided to keep an eye on the good Dr. Brown, but meanwhile, we had other pressing matters.

"They have played their parts; now it's time to move forward with ours. I have one more step to take before the night of the blood moon."

I turned to Mirabella and kissed her forehead, "For now, you will sleep, my darling, until the new you rise again in his honor."

I snapped my fingers, sending current through the newborn's body to accelerate her growth. Snapped my fingers once more, and the body of the adult Mirabella vanished, hidden inside a former cavern. There, an old friend will watch over her empty shell until she is resurrected, and her consciousness is restored. Then she will join Apollyon's underlings once it has completed its rise.

Sara

Inside the iron gates, the big house guarded by pillars across the front was unaffected by what was happening in the streets of Baldwin.

We ended our supper as a family and retired to our quarters.

Father eyed me cautiously, and I did the same to him.

I slowed on practicing light magic, allowing Kate to finish the final stage before the solstice. She told me she had additional support from her sister, who practiced the craft unbeknownst to her husband.

Using the power of the Goddess of Calamity, Kate and her sister conjured up the mystical storm, hurling it through Baldwin. It would remain until time, blocking anyone from gaining access to the city or leaving.

Her sister was proud that she had been able to keep her Wiccan craft hidden while adapting to her place as the bearer of the new legacy holder.

She and Thonis had passed that existence many times, back to when the covenant was first signed, in blood. Although she did her duty, she never forgave him for sacrificing their and her sister's. His reckoning would not be merciful.

Before I prepared for bed, I hugged my brother Trevor, "Almost time. Then you will be able to rest freely."

Inside the privacy of his room, Trevor doused water on his entire body, unaffected by his usual experience with the unforgiving water. No white pearls, no screams, simply a nice soak and cleanse for the solstice event.

As he fell asleep, the Guardian watched over his close friend, whom he lovingly kissed on his forehead. Moving him into a deeper sleep for his protection until the final event.

The Guardian spoke to him as he slept, "I could not save you then, but you will have eternal life. I have another mission. As for the one who watched us die, I can't help but wish her ashes to be spread across the lower dungeon, stepped on repeatedly. Until Semperian sees fit for her to repeat human existence, if she is open to learning about life beyond the many moons. On the solstice, your life will continue, my friend. My place will be with her until it is safe for our return."

The Guardian opened the bedside window and pushed itself out into the elements, the only light shining in the city. It flew through the Village, circled the tombstones, over the fields and shallow hills, up to the frozen lake where it all began. It stood at the mouth of the cave, no longer afraid. The Guardian was emboldened, ready for the final countdown.

The transitioning moon rotated and blinked on and off, setting the stage for the finale. The remaining white lilacs rose, freed from the dark forest guarded by evil lilac trees.

They waited outside the invisible entry for his royal return.

Chapter 42

The One Who Came Before

Day 21 December 1634
Emperor Njinga Resurrected

The ocean floor was dark, much like it was when we crashed at sea in 1634, attacked by unfriendly fire.

I, Emperor Abiola Njinga II, prepared for that moment, knowing it was coming, although my beloved King would lose hope after this. Semperian allowed me to move in and out of Earth and carry the Janssen name and all that came with it. As for my loyal men, they remained ghosts chained to the deep for now, for it is by design.

After the ship sank, my spirit was pulled into Baldwin when the Towners were dying of the yellow plague. I smelled death all around me, especially my people. I wandered about, looking for my son, who had been hung and buried in an unmarked grave up the hill, looking down on that evil city. That's where she saw me.

The woman was beautiful. She had caramel skin, ruby-colored cheeks, and wooly brownish-blonde hair dropping down below her thighs. She was modestly dressed in a blue blouse tucked inside her long brown skirt, a red shawl thrown around her neck, and black knee-high ankle boots.

"Emperor Njinga, I've been waiting for you," she said.

"You can see me?" I answered, quite surprised.

She nodded, "Your soul has not ascended, so yes."

"I do not understand why I came here to this place. I want to find my son who no longer lives."

She walked over to me and stood close. I can smell her sweet scent. She says to me, "His soul lives."

I look at her closely now. Her Emerald eyes are the rainforest in Mali.

"I'm afraid his soul lingers between this world and the next. By nightfall, he will be bound to the third hell, along with his supporters who helped him against the Headmaster Thonis Baldwin, my brother-in-law."

"Please tell me what you mean. How may I bring my son home to rest?"

"You cannot," she said, "For the process has already begun to bring Baldwin back from the ashes."

"Tell me where I will stop them."

She smiled and said, "You cannot. You are a soul without power, which must come from your King. She has passed on to Semperian and awaits instruction for her return."

I dropped to my knees, my body shaken after hearing my King had died. And cry for my men left beneath the seas, as I promised to deliver them from their hell.

"You must be the one to enter the blood covenant with Thonis Baldwin when time."

What she said stopped my sorrow, and I stood up. "Blood covenant? Madness."

"I was sent here to prepare you," she said. "And I don't have much time, for I am being carried off to a place in the mountains and will be unable to assist.

"Why should I trust you will help me?"

"I am here to avenge my son's death, Prince Ndanga's heir, your grandson."

Seeing that she had startled me, she grabbed my hands, "You, the King, and your son have a great mission. This is all happening by design, sanctioned by the Semperian."

To think I have a grandson also murdered by these heathens. I am angered. My fleshless body tremors, but I resoundingly challenge her about speaking about Semperian.

"What do you know of Semperian? It reveals itself only to Africans. We are its infinite wisdom split into countless particles across the universe, sent to Earth as humans. Life is born from us as the original human."

"I do know all about this," she said. "My name on Earth is Kate. I am of the realm governed by the Wiccan order of light magic. I have also been granted the source of natural disasters, for I am the original Goddess of Calamity."

I think of her as quite bold for a woman, as she reached up to wipe the sweat from my brow.

"Your role will be the master of the Janssen family, carrying the name Emanuel Janssen. For decades, you will conduct the covenant as written, and every seventeen years. In 1908, this all changed because of the birth of the Semperian Daughter. Emanuella will be the one to free Prince Njinga when it is time and free the enslaved from bondage. Resetting the Semperian rule on this planet by Africans as it should be and as it was prophesized."

I looked up toward the sky, hearing a soft voice whisper to me from the realm, telling me what I must do.

"I will go with you to prepare," I said to her.

Kate passed her hand across my face, her hand on my heart, "The power invested in me by Semperian, I give you the power of shapeshifting."

I was now Emanuel Janssen and would soon take on another role as Mayor Lazarus Shipley, cousin to Thonis Baldwin, as a legacy master who would oversee the covenant. Grateful, the souls of the emperor's men would be released to the learning realm.

"Now," said Kate. "You are ready."

Blood Moon of 1651

A blood moon looked down on me as seventeen-year-old Emanuel Janssen, believed to be the reincarnation of Prince Njinga's newborn boy, killed to garner blood for the covenant's foundation. I stood before the hanging tree with seventeen-year-old Thonis Baldwin, the reincarnation of his mother's newborn. We, men, stood beside two women, both of Dutch heritage, we were to marry.

The one to marry Thonis carried the spirit of his mother, Juelle, brought back from the ashes by his father. Both were intertwined with the immortal soul of Thonis Baldwin of 1630.

I, as Emanuel, was made to wed a Dutch woman with lineage to the slave trade.

Both women would carry the immortal blood with the ability to reincarnate at each seventeen-year interval. The number seventeen was the sign of Apollyon. Reciting the ceremony through Rights of Passage beneath the blood moon every seventeen years, promised immortality, enormous power, and wealth on Earth for Towners.

Outside of the Baldwins and Janssens, Towners would be given immortality but not the Africans for their blood was needed to sustain Towner's immortality.

Thonis Baldwin chanted, calling upon Apollyon Diabolus, a name Luna gave him. She was the witch who roamed the cave as overseer and guarded the entrance to his hell. Where African children lost their lives to feed the demons who lived there. Demons and higher demonic authorities like Luna and Thonis consumed the blood of African children through a white lilac potion created from the Apollyon energy.

I, as Emanuel, stood there as instructed, as my role was part of the Semperian Trinity. We would lead the battle against the third lower realm.

As the ceremony closed, the energy of the blood moon passed to the legacy holders, Thonis, and me. Called the gift, it would be transferred every seventeen years to the next holders, the reincarnation of Thonis and me.

Kate and me knew of the prophecy. In 1908, Semperian would send its Daughter as the firstborn girl to help end it, Apollyon Diabolus. Followers of Apollyon would interpret the prophecy to be about a demon spawn being created to end it, Semperian.

In days, the brides of Thonis and Emanuel were impregnated with the next gift holders, and Baldwin was reborn.

The first blood covenant under the Hanging Tree began the reincarnation of Towners. Where Thonis and Emanuel stood, with their wives standing behind, swearing allegiance to the dark lord, Apollyon Diabolus, Fallen 17. Luna performed the first Rites of Passage.

In her astral body, Luna said to the brothers of the covenant, "I pass the responsibility of life onto you, in his name. Glory be our true father as we prepare for his return in 1925."

Around them, headstones toppled, the hardened burial dirt broke, and the original inhabitants of Baldwin Town pushed up from pine boxes. Men, women, and children shook off their contaminated flesh, eaten by smallpox. They were dressed in clean garments; girls and their mothers wore tight bonnets with linen and muslin dresses of pink and white, and yellow prints beneath their shawls. The boys and papas wore simple suits of browns, blues, and grays with Ascot caps on boys and wide-brimmed hats on fathers.

Immortality came with a transitioning ceremony. Towners would have to consume the blood of deceased Africans to transition from death back to life. Dr. Wolstein would provide them with the blood substance retrieved from bodies during embalming. They were also given an option to reincarnate into dissimilar roles. They would pass that way repeatedly as Towners. In his town, Baldwin Town. Never to succumb to disease, only to enjoy happiness and enormous wealth.

The stage was set to reveal in the coming years, one of Semperian, the other a demon, their destinies to collide at the Hanging Tree on December 21, 1925.

Chapter 43

The One Who Came Before

Day 21 December 1925
Solstice Day of Reckoning

Luna

The early morning darkness and fading lilac brought a modicum of hope as I walked with Thonis out to the perimeter. The Knight Lilac Trees were barely there, and white lilacs on the ground were all gone, reminding me that my life and that of my husband, Apollyon, would have ended tonight if the re-creation of the 1908 birth of the Janssen twins had failed. But it worked.

"Ye, Semperian energy is weakening."

"How can you be so sure?"

"The re-creation can only be sanctioned by Semperian. The words used are only known by a few, like Lepta. Using that spell should have killed me. But here I stand, and inside is our new Mirabella."

I responded, "You took a chance, old lady, your death would have ended this."

"Ta, ta. You should be applauding me, not spitting out anger. You are no stranger to testing boundaries."

Thonis remembered being admonished for mixing dark magic with the blood of the Semperian Prince, and it killed him. Although warned, he kept a vile in case of emergencies. He refused to entrust his entire immortality to Luna.

"What of Emanuel Janssen, ye. As humans would say, the ball's in your yard."

"You mean the ball's in your court, and those words we do not use. Emanuel will be at the ceremony and is committed to carrying out the terms of the blood covenant or being banished to the Apollyon Lake of Fire. That is not in my future."

"Well then, I look forward to tonight's festivities one last time."

I retraced my steps back to the cottage. It was time to reawaken the new Mirabella.

"Awaken, my daughter, and stand before me."

Our daughter stood in her fullness and adulthood like the original. Both were the same, made in his likeness.

"I have your dress ready for tonight's event. Thonis had his Mrs. create a new one for you. It is a replica of the original one you wore but without the stains and tears of the past."

The new Mirabella admired the dress before her. The full-length blood-red, satin gown with embroidery around the cuffs and low-cut neckline, outlining her cleavage.

"So beautiful, Mummy," she giggled.

"Yes indeed," I grinned at the reference used for Delilah. "This Mummy is so proud of who you are and will stand with you tonight as you take your crown. Together, we will await our lord."

The house trembled, acknowledging the coming of Apollyon there on Earth and in all the universe.

"How will we bring Father to us?"

"Bringing your father here will be a delicate process, but I have worked on this spell for centuries, and believe I have perfected it. It is a blending spell that will combine the energies of Prince Ndanga and Apollyon Diabolus. Semperian chose Prince Ndanga-Njinga to serve as his highest operative to rule all universal Guardians after his short stint on Earth. We've held him for centuries so I could pull bits of his Semperian energy through the portal in the cave, using wisdom from the light realms.

Tonight, in front of the Hanging Tree with the blood moon at its peak, I will direct Apollyon's energy from the portal through to you. Your body was made to carry his powerful evil into this world. At the same time, I will bring forth the remainder of Prince Ndanga's energy from the third lower realm through to the virgin at the time your father leaves your body and enters hers. My spell will combine both energies while inside the virgin. As one, they will be released across the universe and have the power to enter Semperian."

Mirabella giggled, "Mother Luna, I can't wait. It sounds like so much fun."

As I listened to her, I hoped that the new Miabella's thoughts would reach maturity in time for the ceremony. If not, her immaturity could be a problem, for it would not withstand Apollyon's ancient evil. It would take our full concentration.

"Daughter, I need to adjust your thoughts, so I am putting you into a temporary state of consciousness. In it, you will understand the seriousness of your role. You must not fail."

"Okay, Mummy."

As promised, the Goddess of Calamity rested, and the mystical storm retreated, and Semperian lifted the veil of protection around the Village.

Semperian anointed three thousand Africans—men, women, and children—as Semperian soldiers. They dressed in royal white garbs and moved into the streets, spreading across the Village on into Baldwin Town. They remained invisible until Semperian sounded the trumpet for them to end it.

The Village burial site jolted alive, and from the graves came African spirits dressed in the same clothing, ready for battle. Semperian began reconditioning, filling their minds with the truth of Semperian as pure energy and love, superior to evil and ruler of the universe.

I walked about a half mile down the long, dusty road before my feet started hurting and my eyes watered from the dust. Stepping into the grass, I hoped late-night critters ignored me and wild dogs left their dog doo elsewhere.

A river glistening on the other side of the tall grassy knoll hummed away the smoky twilight. No more shadows lurked between the river and Baldwin-Janssen Square.

Ahead, I looked for the Hiding Tree. It would be uphill from the main square. It came into view after passing clusters of Spanish Moss and coffee trees. Their leaves rustled from the howling of the wind as the stars melted into the sky, leaving only a blood moon in the blackened sky.

Clop, clop, clop. The sound of a buggy from behind. I wanted to look over my shoulder but was afraid. A Village girl out alone at night was dangerous. I tensed up, ready to run, when I heard a familiar voice, "Hello, young lady."

I looked over at the man in the buggy pulling up beside me. "Uh, hello, sir."

He reached over and helped me up to sit beside him on the buggy seat. Together, we rode to the square to lead the battle.

Once at the Tree, Mr. Emanuel helped me down, "I shall send someone to fetch you when the ceremony is ready to begin. Now move along, young lady."

"I will be ready." I ran over to the Hiding Tree and sat in the Victorian chair.

He grabbed the tip of his hat and nodded. Snapped the horse's straps, "Geddup." The horse jolted forward and pulled the buggy down the dusty road toward the event.

At the Hanging Tree, townsmen stood guard. They were dressed in all-black suits, white shirts with black bow ties, and black top hats. Their graying sideburns slid down the side of their face, connected to beards that hung two inches below the chin.

The red carpet sectioned off the aisles, totaling two thousand chairs.

"Please make your way to your seats. The ceremony will begin shortly," an usher shouted through a bullhorn.

The guards helped attendees to their seats. Girls and mothers wore all white gowns, and boys and papas in white suits.

In the left front row, Trevor Baldwin sat with his family.

Thonis moved to the stage with Emanuel Janssen. Trevor looked oblivious to his surroundings, yet Suanne and Sara Baldwin both had smiles on their faces. Sara looked over at the hiding tree and nodded.

A Semperian operative disguised as Delilah Janssen intercepted Sweet Tea, whom Luna had assigned to pose as the late Mrs. Janssen. She arrived with Mirabella separately from Mr. Emanuel. They sat in their assigned seats across the aisle from the Baldwin family. Mrs. Janssen looked over and nodded at Suanne, who acknowledged her.

Thonis was anxious to begin and stepped up to the podium, his cane in one hand but not for balancing. He spoke into the mic.

"Heller, my fine friends and family," He tipped his hat. "Thank you for gathering here today on this wonderful solstice evening in front of the Hanging Tree. We are blessed by the blood moon above, which has transitioned fully to seal our fates for eternity." He looked up and pointed to the moon with his finger.

"Emanuel Janssen and I, as founders of the blood covenant in 1651, are here to bear witness to the final Rites-of-Passage, which will join the union of Mirabella Janssen and Trevor Baldwin." He nodded to both sitting in the front row.

"We bestow upon you the knowledge of our town. What makes us who we are and why God himself has seen fit to give us life." Thonis paused, then continued.

"Baldwin Town will have eternal life, and its residents will have immortality without a seventeen-year disruption from the Semperian blood we captured in 1630. Whose restless spirit and his loyal soldiers are in hell. After tonight, they will no longer be a threat to us."

Thonis held out his hand to Mirabella and Trevor, "Will the two of you stand together here?"

They stood in front of the stage.

Emanuel and Thonis left the podium, headed down, stopping on the last step, and faced Mirabella and Trevor.

Emanuel spoke, "Ye, Thonis, since this will be our last audience for the covenant, I say we invite our families to join us here, especially our two wives, like in 1651."

Thonis raised his brow curiously but nodded, agreeing to Emanuel's request.

Mrs. Janssen walked up and stood on Emanuel's left, Suanne, and Sara to the left of Thonis.

Watching Sara stand beside Suanne made Thonis uneasy. He quickly glanced around at the audience. All seemed in good order, so he asked families to lock hands, and Mirabella and Trevor.

"We must have complete silence," Thonis affirmed. He raised the tip of his cane above Trevor's head, tapped once, then Mirabella's, tapped once. Motioned for Emanuel to be ready to transfer his legacy to Mirabella.

"It's time for the covenant prayer," said Thonis.

He closed his eyes, as did the Towners, Trevor, and Mirabella.

Thonis began the prayer.

Semperian Daughter

Inside the Hiding Tree.

"It is time," said Samuel. "As prophesized, you are the firstborn, the Semperian envoy sent to free Prince Ndanga-Njinga and stop Apollyon Diabolus."

I nodded, "And you will join me."

"Yes," said the Guardian. "I have made peace and accept my fate. He will ascend to the light realm as promised, and I, as his replacement, will guard you until we are reassigned."

We stepped out from inside the Hiding Tree arm-in-arm, dressed in Semperian energy of sun gold. Glowed while absorbing the energy from the pulsating halo surrounding their bodies. Our presence was felt throughout the darkest realm, where they would end the battle.

The smoldering, dimly lit space smelled of demonic human souls, and screams were heard from those burning in the lake of fire for not submitting once there.

It was a fishing sport for Apollyon to watch Earth and

entice humans to commit egregious acts. Taking the bait meant relinquishing their soul upon death to the masterful fisherman, Luna. She would capture their unsuspecting souls and pass them into Apollyon's hell.

Lucifer and Satana rarely sent human souls there, but Semperian permitted them to do so. Humans demonically infected over lifetimes with no hope of evolving out of that karmic cycle would ultimately be removed from reincarnation and eternal life. Sent to the third lower realm with Apollyon and souls sentenced there, they would be banished in the reckoning.

Apollyon Diabolus Fallen 17, cowered inside the cave set next to the lake. He enjoyed agony and pain. It invigorated his spirit but had weakened because today was Solstice, the day he would be removed permanently from the universal life cycle.

His movements and brash voice were heard throughout the realm, unnerving his followers. Romping around the rocky terrain, shouting at the virgin who had refused him since her capture there. Highly agitated, Apollyon had to will her to him. Her sacrifice would help Luna and his minions above to bring him to the surface. Lizi's soul was promised unwillingly by her mother, Cheeky, for this very day. The Earth virgin would be his queen, but right now, she was protected by Cece's power.

"I command you, virgin, join me now."

"No." It was Cece who responded on Lizi's behalf. "We are not at your mercy and will not submit."

"Curse you, I rule here. She will comply or else."

"Or else what?" Cece taunted.

She and Lizi were tucked inside one of the smaller caverns behind Apollyon's, where he held the prince.

Dr. Brown cast a sleeping spell on Cece and Lizi before taking them into the cave. Luna pushed them into the portal. Prince Ndanga-Njinga's energy, which Luna had attempted to steal little by little, intercepted their entry. His power was

Arthur Brown was twenty-eight when he fell in love with Nyna Levin, nicknamed Cheeky but had never told her. He rushed to the SugaShack to stop her from joining the dark forces after hearing Luna finalizing the deal with Apollyon. His father would do away with Cheeky once Lizi was ready to be his bride. A position Cheeky thought promised to her, as second wife next to Luna, his first.

But it was too late. Dr. Brown watched outside Cheeky's window as the spirit of Apollyon Diabolus entered her, his force attacking her flesh while the apparition of Luna chanted beside them. When done, Cheeky lay torn and bloody, her spirit broken. Consoling her would do nothing, for she had given her soul.

When Art Brown saw Luna later, she tormented him for days for defying Apollyon.

Arthur Jr. stood before Luna Diabolus to await his fate for defying his father. It would mean death.

She glared at the good-hearted doctor who was once the little boy who found his way to her.

"I cannot believe you have not learned your lesson. For my Apollyon to have such a weak seed is an embarrassment," she said, walking toward him, her hands raised. "Arthur Brown, I banish you to the cave to await Apollyon's return. When he does, he will deal with you."

Art Brown

Inside the cave, I was not alone.

The dim light allowed me to see the spirits lingering near the cave wall.

"Hello, son," two of the voices chimed.

"My boy," said the other.

I was confused by what I heard. Tears flooded my eyes,

But I quickly blinked them away.

"Did Luna send you? Are you illusions to lure me to hell?"

One apparition moved forward with outstretched arms, "No, my son, we are here to forgive you before we move on. Help you make amends for what you have been asked to do in his name."

I recognized the crinkle of her nose, my birth mother. Moving up beside her was the spirit of my Earth father. He said, "Regardless of who you were meant to be, you grew to have a heart. I saw that in you and prayed to Semperian to cleanse you."

The last apparition was an elder African man with the whitest hair, the same as he looked when he passed at the ripe old age of ninety.

He said, "I was that prayer, which is why you were drawn to doctoring. I came from the highest realm to walk with you through this existence to this place and time."

"Why are you here? He will come into the world here."

Dr. Matthews chuckled, "We are not afraid; he has no power over us."

"I now see the truth," said Lucille. "Like me, Semperian is giving you a chance."

"If you deny the help of Semperian, we must leave you to face hellfire for eternity," said Brown Sr.

"Semperian will permanently remove you from the cycle of life," said Dr. Matthews.

I reflected on my childhood and becoming a man. Fights with Mother Lucille seemed moot even as they pertained to my wife and children.

"Your wife and children will be spared," said Dr. Matthews. "Your children are of the Semperian; your wife resides on the light realm of learning set for reincarnation."

I grinned, "My children have an energy unlike any I have experienced. Often made me afraid."

"That, my son, was the light in your heart, which grew more when you were around your family," said Brown Sr. "They taught you to love. With them in your heart, you can complete the task in favor of Semperian."

"What might that be?"

"You must accompany Semperian Daughter and the Guardian on their descent into the third lower realm."

I had only met my father through Luna, and now I was being asked to face him on the side of Semperian. That unnerved me more than being sent to the cave for admonishment. Being near Apollyon could seal my allegiance to him.

"I will do what must be done."

"We suspected you would be amenable," said Dr. Matthews. "Do not worry about your weakness and the possibility that you may betray us. Semperian created Apollyon and will end it."

I smiled, "Of course."

Dr. Matthews tilted his ear toward heaven and said, "The Semperian trumpet has sounded to begin the battle."

Outside the cave, twenty million African souls lined the lake and embankment on both sides.

At the mouth of the cave were the spirits of children swallowed by the lake over centuries.

My children, little Lucille and Art, dressed in Semperian gold, would join them. But first, they stretched out their hands to me. I stood and held their hands. Together, we walked into the light.

Chapter 44

The One Who Came Before

Solstice Day

Day 21 December 1925
The Final Battle

Rocks fell to the ground, crashed, and split. Satan's beasts howled, and Lucifer's fallen shouted at Apollyon's minions, who begged for mercy while their leader raged on with futile demands and threats.

The underworld's angry thunder plowed through Baldwin, Baldwin-Janssen Square, and the African Village.

Additional Africans dressed as soldiers spread out up and down the path through the woods, where innocents once traveled to a mystical lake. They connected to the African souls crowded there. Some returned for the battle, others transitioned to the light realm.

Semperian energy contained the demon's thunder and redirected it beyond the cave to the hidden cabin. It struck the lilac trees; they fell and burned atop the empty ground. It stopped in front of the door and set it on fire. Semperian distinguished the thunder and hovered inside the cabin.

"Well, well," said Luna, dressed in purple and black armor. "I see you are in your glory, Lepta. This must mean you have returned from descending into the lower realms. How are Lucifer and Satan?"

Towners awakened from their trance and shrieked at what they saw. Standing beside Thonis and Emanuel were two women, each holding a newborn baby.

The town founder opened his eyes, as did the couple.

Trevor stood unfazed, but Mirabella looked on in shock. No Mother Luna came for her.

Thonis stared at the women with the newborns. The one on his side was his Suanne, dressed as the Juelle in 1634 before Thonis Baldwin resurrected her. Beside Emanuel was Kate, her sister. Their newborns were murdered to begin the first blood covenant in 1651.

The mortal Thonis worked with Luna to resurrect an immortal Thonis and a thought-to-be descendant of the great Prince Njinga, Emanuel Janssen. He was, in fact, the spirit of Prince Njinga's father, Emperor Njinga of the Songhai-Mali Partnership.

After the capture of Prince Ndanga-Njinga in 1630, Thonis Baldwin received news from Luna that Emperor Njinga was on his way to Baldwin to retrieve his son. Baldwin passed on the information to his partners, the Dutch, Portuguese, and Spaniards. But lied and said that Emperor Njinga, with two of his ships and five thousand Songhai-Mali soldiers, planned a secret attack on Portugal as revenge for giving refuge to Prince Ndanga III and the Royal Mother. And had the Songhai-Mali partnership planned to attack the Netherlands and Spain, stopping the slave trade.

Dutch, Portuguese, and Spanish were pressuring Emperor Njinga and his wife, King Ndanga-Njinga, to hand over thousands of Africans to serve as free labor in exchange for the return of their son.

A total of six ships from Portugal and the Netherlands attacked and slaughtered the soldiers and set fire to Njinga's ships. No one survived.

Years later, Kate, the mother of Prince Ndanga-Njinga's son, collaborated with her sister to get revenge. Through soul travel, Kate found Emperor Njinga's spirit wandering where Africans were buried outside Baldwin.

Kate and the Emperor hatched a plan that would bring them to this time in history, ready to battle the third hell.

Towners dropped: Men, women, and children turned to ashes. Fire consumed those who had witnessed the prince's hanging. As they burned, they cursed and pumped their fists.

Dr. Wolstein, holding onto his Kitty, looked up at Thonis as they ignited into flames.

Sara stepped in front of her father, smiling gleefully, "The tables are turned on you, father. The resurrection spell, huh, little did you know your wife was helping carry that out with the help of Semperian."

Mortified, Thonis glared at Suanne and then Emanuel. They were looking toward the hill, watching the deities float down toward the staging area.

Mirabella tried to run, "Mummy Luna, Father Apollyon, help."

Trevor vanished into the light realm of reincarnation.

"Now you know why I insisted on the name Trevor and not yours," said Suanne. "Trevor was the spirit of Timothy, the boy Luna murdered at the lake. Your evil deeds have not gone unnoticed."

Thonis pulled from his pocket a bottle he kept with him. He hadn't used it since it killed him the first time. He opened it and held it to his mouth as the laughter of African children filled the air.

Their spirits circled him and pushed him to the Hanging Tree. The bottle vanished from his hand before a hangman's noose dropped around his neck and tightened. The rope pulled him up to the top of the tree and held him there, choking, and his feet dangling. His soul was immortal, so he could not die. Yet.

As the full embodiment of Semperian Daughter, I walked over to Mirabella, "Ahh, you must be my newborn sister."

Mirabella looked confused and afraid.

"You were created to be his vessel. I must take you home to face your end."

The demon daughter shook her head, not understanding.

I joined my left hand to the Guardian's right and reached to the sky, "As it is above, it will be below."

They acknowledged Emanuel, Kate, Suanne, Sara, and Semperian Mother. Suanne and Sara will be with Kate in the upper-light realm for additional training in light magic.

Semperian Mother walked over and bowed, "As it is above, it is below. Be well, Daughter and Guardian. You will return home once the lower realms are back in balance and the darkest realm is brought up to Semperian."

The Daughter and Guardian nodded.

Guardian Samuel floated over to the hanging Thonis and held the rope.

I reached for Mirabella, "It's time to go, my sister."

The four of us vanished, descending into the third lower realm.

Once there, I first spoke to Lucifer and Satana.

"You are free to resume your worlds as promised."

"Thank you," said Lucifer. "We will continue as before until Semperian sees otherwise."

"Agreed," said Satana. "We have ordered its minions to the lake to await their removal." She nodded her head toward Apollyon, who was shouting at no one. "We will be grateful to be rid of it. It has created a stench that will take some time to clear."

"That will be our role," said the Guardian. "All will be in order as before."

"A big job only the highest can oversee," said Lucifer. "So shall it be."

He grabbed Satana's hand; they bowed, then vanished along with their fallen and beasts.

As Semperian Mother permitted, Cece, Lizi, and the newborn child reincarnated in Emanuella's earlier image would grow up as a normal child.

I stepped to my Earth sister, "You have done your part and successfully passed the test. You will pass this way again but as a lightworker. I will always love and remember you, although you will not."

I hugged her and Lizi.

Tears flowed down Cece's face as the Guardian released them to the Semperian realm of reincarnation. John Crumley took Zeke and Gabe there to be reborn.

Apollyon was losing strength but toyed with the prince, "I have owned you for centuries; it is not over."

Snap — the chain broke and dropped from the prince's neck and body.

"No, curses," he stomped.

The Guardian used its fingers to magically bind captives, Mirabella, and Thonis, in the chains once used for the prince and latched them to Apollyon's ankles, one on each side. They will join him along with the loyal soldier on her way.

"Prince Hereto Abiola Ndanga-Njinga, your stay here is complete. You are ready and worthy of the highest ascension to Semperian," I said.

The Guardian raised his hands, bringing a downpour of pure water dousing the prince, wiping away the filth from his body and hair, his face clean-shaven. The transformed prince glowed, dressed in Semperian gold, covering his entire body. On his head, a golden crown embedded with emeralds, rubies, and diamonds.

Prince Abiola Hereto Ndanga-Njinga reached out his hands, calling to his side the remaining children and his loyalists. Semperian water showered them, and their garments changed.

"Semperian Daughter, it has been a pleasure to be of service," said the prince. He hugged her.

"Guardian, your wit has always inspired me. I have never blamed you for our loss, for it was by design," he said, reaching over and embracing him. "My brother, always."

"Boli, Boli, Boli, we no longer have to run, no longer part of the karmic cycle of reincarnation," said Samuel, showing his face briefly as General Senegal Nirobi in 1630.

The Guardian released the prince to reclaim his crown at the helm of Semperian and rule the Semperian universe as it should.

A stream of light dropped down around the prince now of Semperian, his children, and followers; they faded with the light joining the battle above.

"Nooooooo," growled Apollyon, stomping his feet. "I am the gardener who gave Semperian its beauty. I deserve to be part of its consciousness. It would not have beauty without me."

Thonis remained silent, ready to face the hell he sentenced the prince to centuries ago. Holding his head down, the noose now turned to a chain around his neck, hell called for his soul if he did not complete the passage of the final blood covenant on that solstice day of December 21, 1925.

Mirabella entered hell with her eyes closed. Compared to Apollyon, she was tiny, her head below his thick knee. She looked up at her true father, who was nearly twenty feet tall. Seeing him for the first time, she screamed in disgust, "Get away from me, you ogre."

Apollyon yanked the ankle she was chained to, "Stop. You were created from my sperm. You shall not fear me."

Cunning Mirabella wanted no part of hell and a father of whom she had only heard. She imagined him to be handsome, sharing her and Luna's beauty, not hideous.

The new Mirabella had just started to reap the benefits of the Earth world and loved it. The sexual pleasures introduced by her Pet.

"Where is my Pet? Pet, come to me."

Her Pet was destroyed upon her entry there.

Mirabella looked at me and smiled as dust quickly soiled the creamy skin her mother, Delilah, cherished.

"Please allow me to join Lucifer's realm. I will be whatever you wish."

I held up my hand, "You will meet your intended fate with your father. Your Earth mother, Delilah, is already being processed for removal from the life cycle."

"Please spare me," the demon daughter begged. "I am your sister."

"Enough," said the Guardian. "You infuriate me."

He swooped toward Apollyon and whipped his arm around him, creating a cyclone that bundled the three of them into chains. Sent them screeching into the lake of fire, burning as they sank below the bubbling broil.

Semperian Daughter and Guardian waved their hands across the lake, covered it with invincible stone, and vanquished it.

Luna buckled as she heard Mirabella and Apollyon's cry of defeat. "This can't be. I've worked for centuries to ensure Apollyon's return. He was to be here with me."

"We know all this," said Lepta. "To think it could be of Semperian. And you. You were forbidden from using the sacred words. The arrogance."

"I know better than you," argued Luna. "I am more deserving, for you are weak."

"No more. You must meet your consequence," said Lepta. "Umaya, umaya, umaya." She whipped a Semperian chain around Luna.

Luna struggled, refusing without having her final say, "Oh, but sister, I have one last gift for all of you, whether I am here or not. I will live on."

Lepta laughed, "We know about the Onyx Stone you stole from Planet Nine, where you've hidden it, and that it did not pass to the new Mirabella. Foolishly, you do not know its true power and what it will take to activate it. That is where your blending spell failed."

"Ugh, curses! Umaya, umaya, u.." Before she finished, her body stiffened as Lepta dragged her from the cottage with the blood moon on the door. Set to perish along with the cave and lake.

Lepta pulled Luna through the air to the lake, where all the Semperian envoys stood, along with Arthur Brown and his children, waiting for her arrival.

Semperian Mother, Goddess of Calamity, and Emperor Njinga, who was once Emanuel Janssen, shifted into Mayor Lazarus and back, teasing Luna. She realized that they were steps ahead of her and Apollyon but hoped the true nature of the Onyx Stone would come to fruition. Within the old Mirabella, memories of her true mother surely existed.

Lepta dropped the witch atop the lake, shouting at Art Brown, "You will always be your father's son."

The Trinity, Lepta, Semperian soldiers, and souls of dead African children brought up from the lake chanted, "Umaya, umaya, umaya, we banish you in the name of Semperian. To the lake of fire, you go."

They forced the centuries-old evil, once of the light realm, down into the lake. As she sank, what was left of her stark white hair fell away. Her eyeballs dropped from their sockets, witnessing the final punishment and the painful cracking, cracking of her bones. No longer of power, she screamed in agony.

Apollyon's sea reptiles roared, busting up from the river down by the dock, thrashing and clawing at the air, attempting to escape their final hell, and Satan refusing their entry into her hell. Instead, they were destroyed by her beast as they battled the eight giant reptilians, dragging them into the third realm. Satan also sent its five-hundred-pound black bear to capture the clondike. Gave the bear permission to rip it to shreds before pulling the remains into the darkest realm. The enraged bear savagely tore apart the clondike. In its haste to gather its remains for disposal in the third lower realm, a piece of clondike flesh landed near the sleeping human hidden in one of the caverns.

Once all there, the Guardian quickly vanquished Apollyon's beasts, zap zap.

The seven-headed red beast was the last to appear. It rose from the lake bottom, lingering behind Luna. Its long necks swaying, gator heads with chattering shark teeth. One head clamped down on Luna's and snapped it from her body. Blood exploded into the air, the witch still shouting, "No, it is our time, Apollyon Diabolus. Uma.."

"Umaya, umaya, umaya," Semperian envoys chanted as the red beast, and Luna caught fire; the lake water turned into a boil, sinking, sinking, entering the underside of the sealed lake of fire. Luna vanished along with the red beast, joining Apollyon, Mirabella, and Thonis. Semperian would end it.

The air cleared, and the stench of evil dissipated, allowing the appearance of additional souls for a reunion.

The Trinity raised their arms and joined the tips of their fingers into a steeple, "Umaya, umaya, umaya."

Descending from the sky, Elder Emperor Njinga and his Queen, the Elder King Ndanga, and his Queen Shandake Aminatusa, and their first son, Prince Ndanga II.

Next came the son of Prince Abiola Hereto Ndanga-Njinga and Kate, Goddess of Calamity. Gliding in on a giant eagle, the little boy of five, dressed in gold, was set down between his father, Semperian Lord Ndanga-Njinga, and Kalinga, the prince's first love and wife. She would be the spiritual mother to the young prince.

Kate smiled brightly, allowing her human heart to linger as her soul faded. Ascending to the upper light realm, as promised. There, she would serve as second in command. Lepta would return as first, saying goodbye to her role as Josephine Crumley on Earth.

Elder King Ndanga shone brightly after enjoying rest in the light realm. He hugged his family, then snapped his fingers, bringing forth the Royal Mother and Prince Ndanga III, who ruled the kingdoms of Songhai-Mali with iron fists until its demise in the 1700s.

Their souls never passed from the Earth but haunted the current Africa, causing havoc across the land. Together, the Ndanga and Njinga families banished them into the boiling lake, screaming, following Luna to hell for permanent removal from the universal life cycle.

The souls of the African children held up their hands for the final takedown. The cave that once lured them to their deaths with the promise of pearls rumbled as they chanted loudly, "Umaya, umaya, umaya, we reclaim our souls for Semperian." The cave rattled, shook, and crumbled. No longer the entrance to the portal, leading into the third darkest realm, and no longer holding the Apollyon energy.

Baldwin Town, built on the blood of a prince, toppled and was wiped away along with the remaining Towners by the water between it and Mobile, leaving the Village on the hill awaiting its new mission.

As it is above, it is below.

The Guardian and I heard from Semperian Mother that Arthur Brown was released to the realm of learning along with his Earth family. No longer needed in the third darkest realm, for we defeated it.

We swooped our hands over the realm and crushed all but one cave, turning it into a Village of clay like the Songhai-Mali fortress.

Inside, we created light, and a stream backdropped by a waterfall like the one in Kate's cavern. The steamed water was of rose milk and sea salts, and a fresh garden filled with fruits and vegetables, the stone floors into wool and fluffy ostrich pallets.

The Guardian and I sat together in the middle of the rug. The Guardian snapped his fingers, releasing into the air the enjoyable aroma he brought from the mountain cave. Inhaled, held, and exhaled.

I giggled like the Emanuella I once was, "I hope you have enough. We may be here for a while.

The Guardian smiled, "I have that in common with a friend on the first lower realm."

"I hope that is all you have in common," I teased.

We settled into meditation, remaining until morning for breaking fast and Semperian baths. And until Semperian called our souls, releasing us as overseers of the darkest realm, no longer owned by the Fallen Guard 17's energy, once of name, but no more. Sent back to nothingness, never to be reborn.

Semperian won the battle and succeeded in rinsing away the stain from across the universe. It left behind on Earth tales of blood moons as lunar eclipses, and triads.

It was as it should be, Source Consciousness in action, that will be tested again on a new Earth.

I was born into this world to die, to free the enslaved Africans damned to his hell because of the blood covenant that brought about the rebirth of Baldwin Town. I have not failed, the heavens will not fall, and the darkest realm will not rise to live life immortal for all eternity.

—Knowledge of Semperian
Final Chapter Revealed

Epilogue

Beware of false prophets, those determined to change the course of history. They are remnants of the darkest evil but are of less power and mobility, so please do not fear. For, for I am Semperian, who created and devoured darkness. It lives in balance but not to destroy. Such arrogance to think they can rise to Semperian touch the heart of Source Consciousness. They cannot because they are impure. Operatives are permitted to cleanse the disorder, but vengeance will be mine without mercy.

—*Knowledge of Semperian*
New Beginning

Day 1 January 2016
Africa Town, Baldwin County, Alabama

Baldwin Town was no more except for the mystical Village Africa on the outskirts of town, where residents were light-workers but mortal in that existence: Cece as a schoolteacher, Lizi with her newborn baby, and Timothy as her husband.

Zeke and Gabriel's next incarnation would be best friends in 2027 and lead Earth's rebirth as Generation Alpha. Their mission extended beyond Alabama's shores, for there was a new threat. Persons of African descent and lightworkers were being targeted in the United States of America, so Semperian envoys were dispatched to right the wrong.

A stench like lilac rot grew vigorously. Hate and deep-rooted racism were designed to stop Africans from resisting and wiping their voices from Earth's history. Murders, mass killings, and modern-day lynchings continued and accelerated during 2016. Evil was permitted to reignite its cause, electing a leader intent on ruling in darkness, absent Semperian light.

Village Africa formed a partnership with Prince Nirobi, ruler of the new West Africa. He was connected to the greatest Semperian Guard, who ruled the universe with five hundred million Guards and Operatives. It included the Goddess of Calamity, Lepta, and Spiritual Mother Kalinga of Mali.

The partnership would serve as a pathway for African Americans to reconnect to their true spiritual roots and become empowered. Other lost Africans around the globe would also have an entry point.

As the Alliance took shape on Earth, thousands of people of African descent joined, appearing to those ready to hear the word of Semperian and prepared for a new battle for freedom.

The lilac rot faltered in and out of existence, not realizing the circumstances that brought it there over a century ago. Laid to rest in the mountain cave in the Netherlands, it grew alongside the offspring of that which feasted on hikers and campers. Both were being nurtured by a practitioner of the arts who learned from a powerful teacher. The practitioner was allowed to repeat the cycle of birth and death, desiring to move beyond attachment to the lingering evil within her. The two remaining entities would be her final opportunity.

"I've added a taste of sugar to our tea," she said to her companions. "I'm told this elixir may help us reach light beyond our entrapment here."

Semperian instructed the leader of the Semperian Lord to watch curiously until it was time to end it.

"We have spoken with the one once known as Sweet Tea. Her assistance in 1925 was invaluable. We have great hopes that she will succeed. The Onyx must be returned to its home planet before it harms Earth."

As I spoke those words to Semperian, the time would come to deploy our most powerful operatives to handle the task without triggering the Onyx.

We must proceed with caution.

About Amanishakhete

Atlanta Author Amanishakhete (Uh-ma-nee-shakeet), who renamed herself after the ancient Nubian Warrior Queen Amanishakheto, a Kandake of Kush, reigning from 10 BC to 1 AD, conjures up an imagination full of colorful characters, capturing readers from 16-60.

Like with her breakout series, LaTonya Trilogy, sold on Amazon and a host of online retailers, early readers rave about Wrong Daughter.

Filled with supernatural and magical realism, the story is based on the Mali and Songhai dynasties of the 1600s and extends beyond the heavens and below into the third darkest realm. Amanishakhete wrote Wrong Daughter with characters that come to life on every page, breathing life into her motto: Bringing fresh voices to the experience.

Amanishakhete has also dabbled in what she refers to as Word-Soul, spoken word lyrics underscored by original music composed by Portland hip-hop artist and producer, Anuff. She plays herself in the LaTonya Trilogy, and fans can purchase her music on CD Baby and iTunes.

Born in Osaka, Japan, to an Air Force family but raised in the States, Amanishakhete holds an Associate of Science and Bachelor of Science degrees in Business and Communications, Business and International Relations graduate studies in London, England, and a Master of Fine Arts in fiction writing.

Ashakhete@gmail.com
www.Amanishakhete.com